Discovering Me

VR Tennent

Spending the summer on the Spanish coast with ladies similar to myself seemed the best way to lick my wounds after my husband of twenty years left me for the woman four doors down.

The past year had been hard, almost unbearable. The woman I had become was not the person I wanted to be. Under the sun I hoped to find myself again. I wanted to learn to have fun and be free once more. A summer of decadent drinks, lively conversation and unplanned experiences would hopefully be the remedy to my perceived rock bottom.

I never expected to gain the attention of a man twelve years my junior. Our relationship was fun and unexpected. He made me feel alive once more. Perhaps life was only just beginning. But my head told me, a woman my age should not be fooling around with a man like him. My heart had other ideas forcing difficult decisions to be made.

Would I be able to leave my summer fumble behind when it was time to go home?

Author note: This book was previously partially published as Healing Under The Sun: A reverse age gap novella

Chapter One

Linda

My daughter swings open our living room door; it crashes off the wall. I wince, knowing there will be another blasted dent in the plaster. "Mum," she shrieks. "Mum, where are you?" Hastily, I minimise the window on the screen – she can't know about my plans yet. It's not going to go down well. I swing around in my office chair. Our small computer desk is crammed into the corner of our already-packed living room.

"I'm here," I say with a sigh. "Marina, what are you screeching about?"

"Ziggy asked me to travel with him this summer," she sings, and my heart sinks. *Ziggy, I assume that's not his real name, but I haven't been told an alternative.* "We're going to backpack around South America." She's bobbing from foot to foot with excitement. When I look at her, I see a younger version of myself, all bouncy brown curls and hazel eyes. "We leave on the fifth of June."

"Have you booked your tickets?" I ask, trying to stay calm and failing miserably. Hopefully this relationship will last until the end of their trip. I don't fancy the thought of having to track down her broken-hearted self in the middle of the Amazon Rainforest. It was bad enough having to travel to Rome last year and bring her home after she dumped Carl—or whatever his name was. On the flight out, I'd been terrified of what I might find when I got there. Coming home, I'd had a sobbing mess to direct through an airport and keep under control on the plane. It had been hell.

Marina is twenty-three with no intention of growing up, spending her time living pay cheque to pay cheque. Her father is constantly telling her to take control of her life and have a plan. A career. It makes me smile. When I was her age, I was married with a baby in my arms. It is the last thing I want for my daughter. She needs to enjoy her freedom, while it's hers to experience. Although, I wish she would be a bit more careful when planning and not bulldoze her way into new arrangements with no thought of what happens if it all turns to shit.

Her current boyfriend is an aspiring content creator. He spends his days setting up crazy pranks and videoing them with the hopes of going viral. They met at a music festival in the pouring rain whilst wearing wellies and hula skirts. It's been a matter of weeks since the romance started, and here we are charging on, as usual, jumping in with both feet. I may have to place my summer plans on hold until I see how this pans out.

"Do you want a cup of tea?" she asks. I blink at her, stunned momentarily. My daughter never offers to help with anything normally. She must be in a good mood.

"Please, darling, that would be lovely," I reply.

"What do you take again?" I roll my eyes at her, and she giggles. She should bloody know what I take in my tea.

"Just milk," I mumble. She skips off in the direction of the kitchen, slamming the door behind her. It rattles in its frame. No doubt the neighbour will start banging on the wall soon, screaming for us to keep the noise down.

For all her faults, ever since her father walked out on me last year, Marina's been like a mother hen, flapping around me, checking that I'm eating properly and seeing my friends. It's infuriating but heart-warming. When he left, the devastation was all-consuming, especially because it was for the local whore that lived four doors down the street. Twelve months later, I'm starting to rebuild my life. This trip is the new beginning I need.

I turn back to my computer and reopen the hidden website.

An escape designed for solo female travellers. Come to the Spanish coast and enjoy the company of women like you. The advert popped up on my newsfeed today, catching my eye. The school where I work as a support assistant will be closed for the summer holidays, and I have eight weeks of alone time to fill. Since it's going to be my first summer being single in over twenty years, the last thing I want to do is spend it at home being miserable. This seems like the perfect solution.

Decisiones De Vida is a small boutique hotel near the coastal town of El Faro in southern Spain. The name translates to *life choices*, which feels one hundred percent relevant at this point in my life. As I scan the website, I read all about the local markets, restaurants, and bustling nightlife. There are daily activities at the hotel for both residents and those from the local area. The only men on site are the ones who work at the hotel and apart from that, it is a ladies-only establishment. I like the idea of being surrounded by women and looking at the reviews, it is women of a similar age to me and older. Before Marina reappears, I quickly fill in my details on the contact page and hit send, immediately shutting the computer down to avoid being caught out.

She bursts back into the living room the way she left, this time carrying two steaming hot mugs of tea. "Come on, Mum," she says, "sit with me and tell me about your day." I rise then wander over to the sofas, sitting on the opposite one to her.

"Nothing exciting to report. Work was like it normally is," I tell her, sipping my drink. "Oh, and the lawyer called." Her eyebrows shoot up, her interest peaked. "The divorce should be finalised by the end of the month. That will be a relief. Have you spoken to your father?" She shakes her head. "Marina, we've talked about this. He's still your dad. I don't want you cutting all ties with him."

"But Mum," she whines, "he gives me such a hard time about work and life goals. He just doesn't understand me. Speaking to him is no fun." I chuckle. "He's such a bore. How he ever managed to cheat on you with anyone is a mystery to me."

"Marina, your father and I..."

"Yes, Mum. I know. You got together too young and grew apart. You were more friends than lovers," she mimics the words I've repeated to her over and over. "That doesn't excuse what he did to you. He was sleeping with her for months. Fuck knows how long it would have gone on if you hadn't caught them at it." A familiar pain shoots across my chest as I recollect catching him in the act. Even though our marriage wasn't perfect, his cheating on me was a bolt out of the blue.

"It happened Marina. We both need to move on from it. Please call him, or at least think about it." She mutters something incoherently. "What was that?"

"I'm not meeting him if that whore is there," she says defiantly, sticking out her chin to emphasise her point. I smile at my stubborn headstrong daughter. "But I'll think about it."

"That's all I'm asking," I reply. "Anyway, tell me all about this trip you and Ziggy have planned."

***

The following day, I'm sitting in the staff room at work chewing on a cheese sandwich whilst playing a random game on my phone. It's one of those games where you have to match three items of the same colour to make things explode. An email pops into my inbox, and I flick it open.

Good morning Linda,

Thank you so much for your interest in coming to stay with us this summer at Decisiones De Vida. We would be delighted if you came here for the eight weeks of your summer break. The rates on offer include your breakfast and evening meals. Drink packages are available on request.

We have an onsite spa with trained therapists both male and female. You have unrestricted use of all the facilities including the sauna, jacuzzi and pool. Every day there is a full range of activities including yoga and meditation.

We are a ladies-only establishment; however, we do understand that male company is sometimes required. So, please rest assured if the opportunity arises, you're welcome to have guests stay overnight.

At present, I have two rooms available for your requested dates. The deposit required is fifty percent on booking and the remainder on check-in. Please let me know if I can be of any further assistance.

Kind Regards,

Susan

I stare at the words on the screen. Male company. I almost choked on a bite of my sandwich when I read that. Chance would be a fine thing. Sadly, I'm on the wrong side of forty galloping towards fifty with ever-increasing wrinkles and rock-bottom self-esteem. Looking for or getting with another man hasn't crossed my mind since the devious bastard left. It's taken me a year to glue what was left of my heart back together. The last thing I need is another asshole to tear it to shreds.

Throwing caution to the wind, I decide to live for once, to stop conforming to what I think I should be doing and act on impulse. Before I can change my mind, I reply confirming my booking and ask Susan to forward the hotel bank details so I can pay the deposit. Within minutes, she responds with an invoice and a short message saying she can't wait to meet in person. I let out the breath I've been holding, and a smile spreads across my face. Excitement bubbles in my belly. I feel naughty booking this without telling anyone. Completely off my own back, I've decided to do something radical – it's so unlike me.

My colleague Rhian struts into the room. She's a similar age to me but oozes confidence. Tall and blonde with a killer figure, she knows how to flaunt her body whilst remaining classy. "Hi, Linda," she says then stops, giving me a curious look. "You look like the cat that got the cream. Go on, tell me what's making you smile like you've got Chris Hemsworth between your legs." I laugh out loud. "Nice vision, eh?"

"You're a filthy hoe," I say with a smirk.

"I'd be a wench, hoe, hoe bag, whore, slut or whatever else he fucking wanted if he went down on me," she replies. "Oh, I'll be thinking about him tonight when I meet up with Barry."

"Who's Barry?" I ask. Rhian has a constant stream of admirers and friends with benefits. None last more than a few weeks. She gets bored. *Why have one dick when there are thousands out there? All shapes and sizes waiting to be explored.* That's her motto, and my god, she sticks to it.

"Barry," she says with a dirty smile, "oh he's not a person. He's my toy." My jaw drops and she sniggers. "He's blue, ten inches long and has a girth like this." She holds her hands up making a circle with her fingers the size of a cucumber. I swallow at the thought. "He can last for hours, never comes before you, and do you know the best thing about Barry..." I shake my head, almost speechless. "You can switch him off."

"It sounds as if you have an exciting night ahead of you then," I say, slightly shell-shocked but intrigued at the same time. I've never owned a sex toy; maybe it's something I should consider. I make a mental note to investigate the possibility later.

"Oh, my dates with Barry are the best," she says, flashing me a cheeky smile. "Anyway, what were you smiling about?"

"I've just done something completely out of character," I whisper, glancing around the room as if I expect someone to appear from behind a curtain with a tape recorder. "I've booked a holiday."

"A holiday?" she responds, a confused expression on her face. "And that's radical?"

"Well, not just a holiday. An escape, completely on my own. Eight weeks in the Spanish sunshine over summer break. I've never travelled anywhere by myself, never mind to another country."

She walks over to me and places her hands on my shoulders. Her bright blue eyes bore into mine. "That's fantastic, Linda. Go and enjoy yourself. Give yourself permission to be free and have fun. You deserve it." She kisses my cheek then walks from the room.

Chapter Two

Max

"I'm sorry, Max, but there will never be anything more between us but friendship. I just don't see you in that way." My heart freefalls, again. "We've had this conversation multiple times. Why do you insist on putting me in this position?"

I look at the girl I've been mad about for years. One of my oldest friends. She's beautiful with long platinum hair and stunning brown eyes. "I thought maybe this time..." I trail off, unable to push any more words past my lips. "We get on so well. We have everything that you need for a good relationship."

"Except I don't fancy you," Bex says. Fuck, that hurts. "You're a good-looking guy, Max, but you're like a brother to me."

"A brother," I stammer. "This isn't to do with me. This is about him. He's not yours and he never will be. He's married for Christ's sake."

"Leave Ben out of this," she snarls. "It's none of your business."

"You're right. It isn't. But don't come crying to me heartbroken again. All I'm asking for is a chance. I'd treat you right. I adore you." She sighs softly and a single tear rolls down her cheek.

"I'm sorry," she whispers, then leaves my apartment. I sit looking at the closed door. Thank fuck school closes next week and the summer holidays start. We work in the same school but luckily not in the same department. I should be able to avoid her until we finish for the holidays. This is the third time in the past five years she's rejected me. Will I never learn? Bex is permanently living her own tragic love story; I doubt she'll ever shake free of it. She is the ultimate Juliet.

My aunt's email is still sitting in my inbox. I pull my phone from my pocket and open it again. *Are you coming over for the summer?* Every year since my late teens I've spent my summers at my aunt's ladies-only hotel on the coast of Southern Spain. The residents enjoy having a man around the place who is chatty but not overbearing. A bit of eye candy, my aunt says. Now, more than ten years on, I still spend my time there. I've undertaken courses in massage therapy and worked in all areas of hospitality, making my role diverse, which means it's even more enjoyable.

This year will be slightly different as I am unsure what I want to do with my life. My career as a secondary school geography teacher is progressing, but it is unfulfilling. It doesn't help that the love of my life is madly in love with a married man. It's broken my heart. So, this year, it is not only the ladies in residence who are trying to find themselves at *Decisiones De Vida,* I will be, too.

***

Schools are closed and my case is packed. Over the past few weeks, I've been out to El Faro at weekends to help my aunt set up for the summer season ahead. Thank goodness for cheap flights. It's been nice to have a focus, something else to concentrate on whilst letting my heart stitch itself back together. I even sent a message to Lacy, an old friend whom I have extra benefits with. We've been on and off for years. We've never been serious, so it could be just what I need this summer. Uncommitted fun with a pretty girl. She lives out there permanently and DJs in various hotels in the area. We've spent many hours in backstreet bars or snuggled under duvets. Her response was pretty much instantaneous – we are meeting up tomorrow. I start to look forward to my time away.

***

Lacy sits at the counter perched on a high stool. We're in a typical Spanish bar with red plastic chairs, terracotta floor tiles and plain cream walls. Groups of locals sit around sipping beers and chatting, the atmosphere relaxed. Lacy waves animatedly as I enter the bar. She's tall and blonde with a megawatt smile. A similar age to me, she's always been outgoing and fun to be around. She jumps down from her stool and skips across the room, throwing her arms around my neck in greeting. "It's so good to see you," she says, pulling back and holding me at arm's length. Her gaze drops to my feet then comes back to my eyes. "You're looking gorgeous as always."

"Not so bad yourself," I reply. "Will we get a drink? You grab a table." She saunters off to a table in the corner, plopping herself down then running a hand through her blonde hair. It's messy and shoots off in every direction possible. She has this naturally ruffled look. Her nipples are obvious through her thin white vest top which is teamed with the shortest shorts I've ever seen. On her feet, she wears her trusty white trainers. Yes, perhaps we could have another summer of uncomplicated fun. Tonight, the idea is appealing.

I place the two bottles of beer on the table and sit down beside her. She cocks her head to one side and smiles at me, shy almost. A redness creeps up from the base of her throat and her cheeks flush. "I've missed you, Max," she says in a whisper. "I was hoping you'd decide to visit this summer." Her voice is quiet, her gaze fixed on me. It makes me uncomfortable.

"Is everything all right?" I ask, taking a sip of my beer.

"I don't know," she says. "It depends on what happens in the next ten minutes." My skin crawls, uneasy at the direction this conversation is taking. I've only just sat down, and I have a feeling I won't be staying long. "What were you hoping for this summer?"

"What do you mean?" I say, confused. She narrows her eyes at me.

"You know damn fine what I mean. When you texted me last week, what were you hoping for?"

"To see you, of course. I was letting you know I'd decided to come after all. When we spoke before, I was unsure." She tilts her head to the opposite side, surveying me. It does nothing to settle my nerves.

"And what did you see happening between us?" Her words are direct and sharp. The bubbly Lacy I know has disappeared; this woman wants answers.

"Um..." I stammer.

"Are you back here looking for a fuck buddy? Or are you looking for something more?" she snaps.

I stare at her, stunned. Never in a million years did I expect to be having this conversation with her. Our times together have always been light-hearted and entertaining. "I'm confused and unsure what you want me to say." She blinks at me. Her silence stretches out forcing me to fill the void with words of some description. "I thought we were on the same page."

"And what page would that be?"

"The friends with benefits page." She glares at me, unhappy with the suggestion.

"You're a fucking idiot. In the past, that arrangement was alright but not anymore." My mouth drops open. "You and me, we have history. A lot of history. How many summers have we spent together?" She gestures at me for an answer, widening her eyes.

"I don't know, six or seven maybe."

"Nine, Max. Nine," she spits. "Nine bloody summers we've fucked around." I gawk at her. Jeez, I didn't realise that. "But we've never been together properly, just the odd night here and there."

"I thought you were happy with that arrangement?" I look at her for guidance. Her eyes are dark, angry. Tonight has not turned out as I hoped.

"I was," she mumbles, "but I'm not getting any younger, and I spend every summer waiting for you. I want more."

"More?" I repeat back to her.

"Yes, more. I want us to have a proper relationship. Be exclusive." My heart sinks as my guilt rises. "I don't just want to be the woman you sleep with sometimes."

"I'm sorry. I never realised you felt this way." She sighs softly. "But I'm not looking for a serious relationship, Lacy. I came here to get away. To find a bit of direction." My neck spasms, and I rub at it to relieve the tension. "I really am sorry. I can't offer you that. I'm not in the right head space." She hisses through her teeth in disgust.

"Well," she says, rising from her chair. "I'm not sleeping with you tonight. Let me go and lick my wounds. You really can be a stupid bastard," she mutters. I nod at her, not able to form a coherent sentence. "Maybe later in summer, we can meet up for old times' sake."

I watch her walk off across the room then climb the stairs out of the bar. Sitting on the old worn chair, I sip my beer, completely confused by how the night is turning out. She wants more. That's a curveball I didn't see coming.

Chapter Three

Linda

Beads of sweat trickle down my brow, and my teeth chatter with nerves. This has officially been the worst flight ever. The plane bounced its way from London to Malaga, throwing us all over the place in the process. I take another swig of wine. It does nothing to settle my heart rate. I set the plastic glass down on the tray table, but the tray vibrates violently before the cup tips over, splashing ruby-red liquid all over my lap.

"Shit!" I hiss, swiping frantically at the blood-like substance seeping into my crisp white linen dress. The material turns a fetching shade of pink along with my cheeks. I'm going to look a sight walking into the airport. What a start to the summer of finding myself under the Spanish sunshine.

Finally, the wheels touch down on the tarmac, and we taxi into our parking spot. A cheer goes up in the cabin as relief emanates from everyone, turning to excitement instantly. The plane is filled with stag and hen parties heading off for weekends of drunken fun. A group of women in their forties, like me, is dressed in clingy black dresses that show off every bump with bright-pink tutus marking their waistlines.

Each has a pair of oversized glasses that flash with the word *HEN DO* across the top. Years ago, I would have looked down my nose at them. Now, I crave their freedom of expression.

Standing on my toes, I reach to extract my holdall from the overhead locker. This simple pink bag has everything I have brought with me. Deciding a total overhaul of myself was required, all my subdued clothes are left hanging in my house in the city. The Linda of Spain is not the same woman of London. This Linda will be pushing herself out of her comfort zone. This Linda will be exciting and fun. This Linda will be colourful.

Throwing the holdall over my shoulder, I file out of the plane in the cram of passengers. Everyone jostles for position. A race ensues as we hit the terminal; men stride along the corridors, pulling their cases behind them, terrified to be left at the back of the queue. I saunter along behind them, smiling to myself, not in a rush to be anywhere.

I stalk past my fellow passengers swarming around the conveyor belt waiting for their precious bags to appear. A group of men stand to one side, one of them sitting on a suitcase that has been turned on its side. His friends are rubbing his shoulders in sympathy while the man grasps his head in his hands. "Awe mate, perhaps that third round of tequila was a bad idea," one of them says.

"No, he's just a fucking lightweight," another man responds and they all belly laugh. "That bloody woman of his has him painting every weekend instead of being out on the piss. You're losing your touch, Duke. All those years of training that liver of yours has gone to waste. We'll need to start again this weekend." The man on the suitcase groans at the thought of more drink. I chuckle to myself. As I'm exiting through the sliding doors, there is an uproar of angered male voices.

"Gadz, you're a dirty bastard!" They cry in unison. I turn around and see Duke has deposited his tequila and anything else he consumed on the floor of the baggage collection zone. I baulk, disgusted at the stupid man. Has he never heard of pacing himself? Individually, men can be idiots, but in groups, they're fucking reckless. Flicking my hair over my shoulder, I stride off in search of a taxi for me and my little holdall.

My hotel sits in a row of Spanish terrace houses, each one painted a bright colour, creating a jolly scene. It's late in the evening, and the summer heat hangs in the air. Looking up, I see the sky is dark and stars are glimmering above me. The night is so clear. The sound of waves lapping on the beach is calming. I can't wait to sink my toes into the warm sand tomorrow.

As I wander past the other buildings on the street, it's hard to tell if they are empty or lived in. Each one has shutters pulled firmly down over the windows and doors. I assume they must be lived in as people sit outside on chairs, playing cards and sipping beer. Children run around the almost deserted street, laughing and joking with each other. Each one smiles as I pass and wishes me a *buenas noches*. I think that means good night, but I'm not sure. Perhaps learning the basics of the language would have been a good idea before I came, but it's too late now.

Pushing open the front door of the hotel, my heart lifts as I enter the beautiful space. It feels more like walking into someone's home than a commercial property. The reception area is bright and airy. There is a large blue velvet sofa and a console table holding a stack of leaflets about attractions in the local area. Above is a skylight displaying the night sky. A desk sits at the back of the room, and a small woman with greying dark hair sits behind it, tapping away at her computer. Her skin is creased from years of exposure to the sun. Her eyes lift to mine, and she gives me a huge beaming smile in greeting. Rising from her seat, she steps out from behind the desk to welcome me.

"Good evening. You must be Ms Butterby. I'm your host, Susan," she says. Her voice is warm and welcoming. She takes my hand between hers then envelops me in a hug and kisses my cheek. "Come, let me show you to your room."

"Please call me Linda. Do you not need me to sign something?" I ask, surprised. I pull my passport from my bag. She waves it away.

"No, no. We can sort all that out in the morning. First things first, a welcome drink." She walks over to a small fridge in the corner, opens the door, and extracts a bottle of pink liquid. She pours it into a waiting wine glass with a flourish, repeating the process with a second glass, handing me one and taking the other herself. She raises her glass to mine. "To an eventful trip," she toasts and winks.

My room is located on the second floor with a balcony that overlooks the water. Tonight, I can hear and smell the ocean but not see it. Every surface of the room—the walls, the floor, and the furniture—is white. Huge paintings of the marine landscape are hanging on the walls. The bed is draped in blue and white linen. Exhausted, I strip from my wine-stained dress and fall onto the heap of pillows, immediately drifting off into a dreamless sleep.

The sun pouring in through the window wakes me. Salt fills my nostrils, and I smile idiotically at the ceiling above. After swinging my feet out of bed, they connect with the cool floor tiles; I flex my toes at the sensation. The old-fashioned analogue bedside clock reads nine a.m. The hands tick merrily around the old, battered face, counting every second, minute, and hour. My stomach growls hungrily. I need breakfast.

As I reach for my phone precariously perched on the side table, I see a message is blinking on the screen. Marina. She hadn't been thrilled when I told her about my trip. I didn't tell her until she skipped off to South America with Ziggy. I saw no point in creating a standoff argument before she left.

"You have never travelled alone before, Mum. It's not safe for a woman like you on your own," she said. Insulted by her audacity, I'd slammed the phone down and glared at it. We haven't spoken since. I read her message.

Mum, I'm sorry for what I said. Please let me know if you arrived all right. I'm worried about you.

My heart thaws slightly. She may be a pain in the ass and have no filter, but she's still mine and her heart is in the right place. She can wait for a response, however.

The only other outfit in my minuscule holdall was a tattered pair of denim shorts and a simple black vest. Today, I need to find a market and update my wardrobe with garments suitable for a solo lady soaking up the Spanish culture. I pull on my sole outfit and stare at myself in the mirror. I only brought a white bra which sits in glaring contrast to the dark straps of my tank top. I remove it then look at my reflection again – God, that's worse. The offensive garment is hoisted back into place, white straps and all. The shorts I've had for centuries; they finish at my knees and sit wide on my hips. What shape I do have disappears under the fabric. Sighing in defeat, I run a comb through my hair and steel myself to be seen in public looking like a prepubescent teen.

After leaving my room, I wander down the stairs to the reception area. Susan is in position behind her desk. Did she sleep at all? She still looks identical to when I last saw her, not a hair out of place. Her fingers are furiously tapping the keys on her keyboard. She smiles at me warmly, and my lips automatically respond with an answering grin. "Good morning, Linda. Did you sleep well?" she asks. "Are you able to complete the paperwork now? I will show you to the breakfast room afterwards."

"Of course," I respond, pulling my passport from my pocket. "What do you need?"

"Only your passport, a credit card and if you could just sign here." She taps at a line on the sheet of paper in front of me. There is no missing where she needs my name as it's highlighted in orange and a huge black cross marks the line. With the necessary documents completed and deposits paid, she shows me to the breakfast room, which doubles as a bar in the evenings.

"This is our social room in the hotel. All our guests are solo ladies like yourself. We have ten rooms in total, so the groups tend to be intimate but diverse. Breakfast is served between seven and ten each morning. At six a.m. every day, there is yoga in the garden. The on-site spa is available to use." She passes me a leaflet outlining the spa packages available. "If you want to book a treatment, please do let me know."

Susan continues to talk as my eyes scan the room. It's not a big area. There is a small wooden bar in the corner stocked with every imaginable alcoholic drink. Seating is arranged in groups of two and four, some sofas are set around coffee tables, and other areas have dining tables and chairs. The décor is simple white with accents of blue, the same as every part of the hotel I've seen so far. The ceiling has been painted with beach scenes in an attempt to bring the outside in.

"The bar is open from one in the afternoon until our last patron goes to bed. We have a small number of staff who take on a variety of duties. Don't be surprised if you see the same faces in various roles. We're all friends here at *Decisiones De Vida*."

"Susan?" I ask, stopping her monologue. If I don't, she may continue talking until it is time to go back to bed. "Is there a market on in town today? I need a few things to wear."

"Yes," she says. "The local market is only a ten-minute walk from here. I will give you the directions. But first, you must eat."

Chapter Four

Linda

Stalls, selling everything from clothes to tableware to rugs, line the narrow streets. People are crammed between them, stretching over each other, vying to get the stallholder's attention. The conversation is loud and unintelligible as they chatter at rapid speed. Having no history of Spanish at all means I understand nothing. It's only day one of my adventure, and I'm already feeling overwhelmed. Perhaps this wasn't such a good idea.

A young girl is weaving through the crowd determinedly. Her pace increases until she is running at full speed, dodging around the public. A whistle sounds from behind her; a police officer is giving chase. As I glance back to the runaway, I see she is heading straight in my direction. She connects with my body, and I stumble back, stunned. Whatever she barks at me is in Spanish, but I don't need to know the language to understand the curse. Stepping backwards to balance myself, I don't see the small ledge. My foot hits the air, and I fall onto a waiting table of shoes. An almighty crash sounds as I land on the stock of a local merchant, who looks less than happy.

"I'm sorry. I'm sorry," I splutter, trying to scramble to my feet. Glancing up, my eyes meet the deep-green eyes of a young man, possibly in his twenties. He is tall and dark, with a strong jaw and smattering of stubble. His muscles are clear beneath his fitted white T-shirt. His concerned face looks down at me, and he holds out his hand in assistance.

"Are you all right?" he asks. "Pickpockets are an absolute nuisance. I could see it happening, but I couldn't get to you in time to help." He gives me a lopsided smile.

"Thank you," I mumble, embarrassed. My cheeks burn as I look at him. His eyes remain on my face for a moment then drop down my body before returning to meet my gaze. "What a start to my holiday." He chuckles.

"Have you just arrived?" he asks, and I nod, unable to speak. Words are lodged in my throat as I stare at him. Fuck, he's gorgeous. And young. I don't remember men looking like that when I was in my twenties. "Well as long as you're all right," he says then saunters off in the direction he came from.

On my return to the hotel, I'm laden with bags; my shopping trip was a successful one. Once I had recovered from my incident, I drowned my embarrassment in purchases. Now, my wardrobe is packed full of summer dresses, sandals, and bikinis. As I scan the leaflet for the spa, my skin prickles at the thought of a massage. I've never had one before. Perhaps it is something the new me would enjoy.

I look at the array of swimwear I purchased today and choose a black bikini edged in sparkles with a matching cover-up. I stroll downstairs to speak to Susan about the options available. She is sitting at her desk, still tapping away merrily at her computer. "Excuse me, Susan?" She looks up from the screen with the same cheerful smile. "Could you explain the spa packages to me, please?" Embarrassed, I admit, "I've never had a spa day before."

Raising her eyebrows in surprise, she nods. "Never had a spa day? Well, I am glad you came here. I will make it my personal responsibility to convert you to a spa enthusiast." She gestures to me to pass her the leaflet clasped between my fingers. She opens it and spreads it on the counter, stabbing her finger at a package named *Sensual*. "This is where you need to begin. Access to the sauna, steam room, and therapy pools. Then, you'll need a full body massage to finish it off."

"Full body massage?" I squeak. "Like everywhere?"

She laughs and shakes her head. "Everywhere within reason. Don't worry, they won't slip their fingers in the till." My eyes pop open, shocked by her crudeness, and she laughs openly. "Unless you want them to." She winks and flashes me a wide grin "Right, I have work to do. Head down to the spa after lunch. I'll book you in now." Obviously, I'm having a spa whether I want to or not. She never even asked me if I wanted to book in or told me what the price was.

The hotel spa is located at the bottom of the quaint garden area in a small log cabin. A fountain bubbles merrily amongst the paving and palm trees. Surrounding the cabin are various therapy pools and a Jacuzzi to be enjoyed, and inside is a sauna and steam room, plus a private treatment room off to the right-hand side of the door. The smell of vanilla hits me on entry, and soft melodic music hangs in the air. No one is to be seen, but a bell chimes as the door swings open.

I sit down on the plush plum sofa to wait as my fingers trail over the magazines on the side table. They are all women's magazines promoting healthy eating and beauty products. It was issues like these that I used to form the basis of my lifestyle change this past year. Gone are the weekly takeaways, instead replaced by healthy home-cooked meals. Nights on the sofa with popcorn are now spent in the gym or on a long walk. The result is a three-stone weight loss and a body I don't know. My few female acquaintances say it's a kick in the teeth to my ex-husband, that I've shown him what he's missing out on. In all honesty, I just didn't want to be alone at home without a focus.

After a few minutes, the door to the treatment area slides open, and my rescuer from the market steps into view. I gawk at him in surprise. He smiles kindly as his eyes meet mine. "We meet again," he says, lifting an eyebrow. "Hopefully no one will knock you into next week this time." He holds out his hand. "I'm Max."

My blood boils, causing my cheeks to heat. I take his hand and shake it rapidly, pulling it away as if given an electric shock. "Max," I stammer, suddenly feeling extremely self-conscious in my limited attire. "I have a booking for a spa package this afternoon." My palms are slick with perspiration as I twist them together. "A sensual package," I add.

"Sensual Packages are my speciality," he replies, deadpan. Lost for words, my nipples harden against the skimpy material of my bikini top. Jeez, this man is fucking sex on legs.

And possibly young enough to be my son.

"You're the therapist?" I question.

"Well, I wouldn't wear all white out of choice, and walking around without shoes tends to be a hassle when out of the spa."

My gaze runs over him. He's clearly the therapist, wearing white knee-length shorts and a sleeveless top with the word SPA on the front. His feet are bare, and his strong calf muscles on display are decorated with a swirl of tattoos. Guiltily, I raise my eyes back to his, a knowing look on his face.

"The Sensual Package?" he prompts, and I nod, still unable to say anything intelligible. "This way."

I follow him through another door at the back of the reception area. It opens into a small changing room. "Just pop your stuff in the lockers. You have free use of the pools and saunas until your massage in an hour. I have another client in ten minutes. See you later." With that, he leaves, and I watch his taut backside amble away, my heart hammering in my chest. *You dirty old woman*, I scold myself.

One side of the room is filled with a huge mirror. I stare at myself. My dark hair is piled high on my head out of the way, apart from a few stray curls that refuse to stay put. With no makeup, crow's feet and age sadly mark my face. My breasts are large, but they hang lower than they did in the past. Gone are my perky boobs of yesteryear. The weight loss has meant my body has a few extra stretch marks and sags, even though my figure is better than it's been since my early twenties. It makes me self-conscious. For forty-five years old, I look all right, but I certainly haven't aged as well as I hoped.

The door swings open again, breaking my chain of thought. A small woman, dressed in a white dressing gown with a craze of red hair, waddles into the room. "Hi," she says, giving me a wide toothy grin.

"Are you new here? Not seen you around." She proceeds to let her gown drop to the floor and rummages in her locker, naked. My jaw drops. "My name is Crystal."

"Hi, Crystal," I say, not knowing where to look. As she moves around the room, her huge breasts swing from side to side, almost hitting her waistline. She is completely oblivious to the show I'm being subjected to. "Yes, I'm Linda. I arrived yesterday."

"Oh, you will love it here. Everyone is family." She smiles. "Right, off for my session with Maxy Boy. Have you seen him? Isn't he delish? What I would give for those hands to be pleasuring me out of choice." She cackles. "See you in the bar tonight, maybe?" I nod, and she scuttles off out the door in nothing but her birthday suit.

As I lie back in the Jacuzzi, the bubbles pop around me. Utter bliss. My eyes are closed behind my shades as the sun beats down on my face. Lord knows how long I've been out here; a time check will be needed soon. A deep voice penetrates my thoughts. "Do you want this massage or not?" it says sharply.

Blinking my eyes open, Max is standing at my head, looking down at me. The Jacuzzi is on a raised platform. As he leans over, his nose is within inches of mine. Startled, I sit up in a hurry, slipping from the seat and dropping into the centre of the tub. My head drops below the water level, and I flail around, trying to balance myself. Finally, I emerge from the water with dripping wet hair and a bright-red face. He watches my every move, biting his lip to hide a smile.

"Not fucking funny," I snap. "I could have drowned."

"Well, Milady, I like to finish work on time. Your appointment was twenty minutes ago. Some of us have places to be." He gives me a dark look as if daring me to challenge him.

"Sorry," I mumble. "Lost track of time."

He sighs, shaking his head. "Come on," he mutters. I climb out of the tub then follow him up the path back towards the treatment room, forgetting my towel abandoned on a chair. When we enter the building, he passes me a huge white bath sheet, and I wrap myself in it. It's soft and comforting. He pushes open the door of the treatment room, and I file in behind him.

Inside, there is a single massage bed covered in crisp clean towels. A unit to one side holds an array of oils. Burning candles are scattered around the room and sheer blinds are pulled across the windows giving the space a soft glow. "Take off your clothes and lie on the bed face down," he says, abruptly. My eyes widen at the directness of his words. He starts to move around the room, preparing oil and moving piles of towels around. "Don't worry. You don't have anything I ain't seen before." My stomach flips with nerves.

The only man who has seen me naked in the past twenty years is my ex-husband. The thought of this young hot guy surveying my aged bedraggled body is horrifying. As I undress, he keeps his eyes firmly fixed on his task with his back to me. I clamber onto the bed and fit my face into the hole. My ass is on full display. Was I meant to put a towel over myself? Being a massage virgin is a complicated experience. I've no fucking idea what I'm doing.

"You ready?" he asks.

"As I'll ever be," I respond, and he chuckles under his breath.

"What kind of pressure do you like?" He wanders around the bed, folding a cover and placing it over my body. Yep, I should have covered it up. He then stands at my feet with his hands on my calves. "Firm or light?"

"Um, I don't know. This is my first time."

"First time?" he asks.

"Yes, my first massage. It's not something I've ever considered getting before."

"Well, I'm honoured you chose me as the person to give you your first time. To pop your massage cherry as it were. I hope it's a memorable experience for you." His voice is strong and silky, every word laced with sexual innuendo. My mind starts imagining him running his hands over my body. The thought makes my stomach somersault, again. "I'll start off light and let you get used to the sensation. Then, we can see if you want more."

More? What the hell does that mean? The cover begins to move down my back, exposing my naked body. He folds it across my ass then walks to my head and stands in front of me. I see his feet beneath me; even they are sexy. Liquid squirts from a bottle, and I hear the rubbing of skin on skin. He places his hands on my shoulders and strokes down my back. Down, round, and up. They slide over my now oiled skin. I groan in pleasure.

"This pressure okay?" he asks. I mumble in assent, and he sniggers.

Nothing else is said. He moves down my body, caressing each part between his strong fingers. As his hands reach my lower back, he kneads the base of my spine to release years of built-up tension. Moving over my backside, he massages the back of my thighs, and my stomach tightens.

Shit, this is turning me on.

Unnerved, I try not to think of the young hot man currently running his oil-soaked hands over me. I'm in both torture and ecstasy for over an hour. My breathing picks up each time his fingers disconnect then reconnect with my flesh. Not being able to see, my imagination creates and throws inappropriate pictures around my mind. Lost in my thoughts, I'm surprised when he speaks.

"That's you," he says as he lays the cover over me completely once more. Without another word, he leaves the room.

Chapter Five

Max

"I'm telling you, Jace. I'm giving this old bird a massage, and I get a raging boner. So fucking embarrassing." My old friend laughs down the line. "It's never happened before. Why the fuck now?"

"You need a shag, pal," Jace advises. "How long has it been since that poor cock of yours has been within sniffing distance of a pussy?"

"None of your fucking business," I snap.

"That translates to months not weeks," he says with a snigger. "You must be desperate to get the hots for one of your aunt's clients." I roll my eyes at the phone. "Was she fuckable? Would she tame the beast as it were? At least where you are, you have plenty of desperate women on tap."

"Older women are not my type." I snort, then concede, "but as clients go, she's one of the best to look at. She obviously looks after herself, and her tits are still perky." What the hell am I saying. I mentally chastise myself for even thinking about it. "I'm not fucking going there." Jace chuckles.

"Maybe, you should snap a picture of her at her next massage then you can wank off to the image of her ass."

"I covered her ass up," I say annoyed. Why did I tell him about her lying on the bed butt naked? I'd turned around, and she had been face down waiting for me to touch her. Her pale clear skin shimmering in the soft light. It was the most arousing position I'd been in for months. My wayward cock sprung to attention. She looked incredible and completely at my mercy. This had started the hour of professional hell I had to endure. Touching her but not touching her the way I wanted to.

When I met her in the market this morning, there was an attraction, but I dismissed it, thinking I would never see her again. Imagine my surprise when she walked into the spa this afternoon. Now having spent an hour caressing her body, I can say with certainty that she is bloody smoking. I was dying to get snuggled between her butt cheeks. While working on her, I hardened further with each stroke. To avoid her noticing, I twisted my hips to the side to hide the offending object then scurried from the room as quickly as possible once it was over.

Jace's voice interrupts my errant thoughts. "Do you know how long she is staying at the hotel?"

"No, but no doubt our paths will cross again."

"Enjoy grabbing a granny, pal," he chuckles and disconnects the call.

My aunt, Susan, opened the hotel for female solo travellers after my uncle disappeared with his accountant. He emptied their bank account and fled the United Kingdom with everything he could. It turned out the couple had been cheating on both their spouses and the tax service for years. Left with nothing, my aunt had packed up and moved to sunny Spain. At first, she rented the hotel, but as the years passed, she was able to purchase it. Her aim was to provide somewhere safe for women to holiday on their own while they were recovering from whatever life trauma had affected them.

Five nights per week, I man the hotel bar. A lot of the residents return year after year, and I know them well. Many stay for a month or longer. They are like old friends rather than clients. It's not only the ladies staying in the hotel who frequent the bar; many come from the local area as well. No men allowed. Except me. My aunt has created a safe space for them to meet friends and express themselves. We host everything from bingo to book clubs and singers to salsa classes. The place is always filled with love and laughter.

After dressing in my denim cut-offs and fitted black T-shirt, I mess up my dark hair in the mirror. I need a shave, but time is not on my side. Tonight, I'm going with, what I hope, is designer stubble. I grab my keys and head towards the bar. My room is on the top floor of the hotel with direct access to the roof terrace. After everyone else is in bed, my happy place is there, listening to the waves lap the beach and filling my nostrils with salty sea air.

As I wander towards the bar, the chatter of excited voices fills my ears. There are already twenty ladies scattered around the place. A cheer erupts at my entrance. "Finally! Where have you been?" my Aunt Susan shrieks. "This lot is on fire tonight, Max, and I want to join in." She grins at me. "Over to you. I'm officially off duty."

Crystal waddles her way to the bar as I slip behind it. My gaze runs over the room of women watching me get prepared for what I know will be an eventful evening. This place is always full of hilarity and cheeky comments. "Are you going to take it easy on me tonight, ladies? Or do I need backup?" I shout, and they all cheer.

"When do we ever take it easy on you, Maxy?" Crystal whispers conspiratorially. "You're our plaything." I roll my eyes at her, and she giggles.

"You're lucky I don't take offence to all these sexist comments you subject me to Crystal." Raising my eyebrows, I say, blankly, "I'm not just a piece of meat."

"Did I ever say you were?" She pouts. "Be a good boy and pour me a vino."

The room is already filled with women cutting shapes on the tiny dancefloor in front of the soul singer entertaining this evening. They stand in circles with handbags piled in the centre, bobbing from foot to foot. The ladies here range from their mid-forties well into their eighties. They come from every part of the world and from all walks of life. Over the years, I've met lawyers, accountants, retired models and even a dolphin trainer. I've a lot of fond memories of being told life stories, many of them captivating. And their tellers are just happy to have someone willing to listen, smile and laugh at the appropriate moments.

My shift goes quickly, the drinks flowing. Most of the usual suspects are here, making inappropriate comments and touching my hand for a moment too long; I don't mind. Most of these ladies are lonely. Many have been left at a later stage in life, and they are navigating the world on their own for the first time in decades. If my smile or kind words can improve their day, it seems like a small sacrifice.

The music has finished, and people are leaving for their rooms. It's then I see her in the corner, propped on the sofa, covered in a blanket. Her head on the armrest with her dark curls spilling over the edge, and her legs pulled up beneath her. Crystal sees the direction of my glance.

"Think she maybe had one too many," she giggles. "Could you make sure she gets back to her room?"

"Sure," I say. It won't be the first time I've carried a resident to bed due to intoxication, but I've never had to carry one who gave me a boner before. Figuring that another thirty minutes on the sofa won't hurt, I finish clearing the glasses and tidying up. My body's reaction to her this afternoon makes me nervous to touch her. I wonder if she noticed. Hopefully, as I approach her, she will wake up, and it will just be a case of directing her to her room. The room key is clutched in her hand, and the number is on the fob. At least I know where she is meant to be.

"Linda," I whisper, but she doesn't respond. "Linda," I say louder. Nothing.

"She's out of it." My aunt's voice surprises me from behind. "Had a few too many shots. Another one struggling to come to terms with a broken marriage, judging by what she said tonight. You will probably be best to carry her."

It's then I notice her mascara has run down her cheeks with her tears. Dropping to my knees beside her, I run my thumb over her skin, trying to clear away the smudge. Up close, she is beautiful. Raw and real. Her eyelids flutter open, and I hear my aunt's footsteps recede from the room.

"Max?" she asks sleepily. "Where is everyone?"

I chuckle under my breath. "Bed. Exactly where you should be. Come on, let's get you settled."

With that, I stand and take her hand then lead her to her room.

Chapter Six

Linda

"Your aunt said I would find you up here," I say. Max is sprawled across a lounger on the roof terrace under the setting sun. "Is this your secret hiding place?"

He gives me a soft smile. "Something like that," he replies. "How's your head?"

Flush creeps up my neck and throat to my cheeks, while my skin heats with embarrassment. Since waking at one this afternoon, dread has filled me. Last night was the drunkest night in my memory, even compared to my teenage shenanigans. "I think the man drilling on my skull is giving it a rest. For now, anyway." He snickers under his breath.

Wearing only denim knee-length shorts, his bronze torso glints in the evening sunlight. Dark aviator shades hide his eyes, which feel fixed on me as I stand above him. "I just wanted to thank you," I say, "for helping me to my room last night. Please accept my apology for my errant behaviour; a drunk middle-aged woman is not something you should be dealing with in the workplace."

Leaning up on one elbow towards me, he props his sunglasses on top of his head. Emerald-green eyes run over my face then drop down my body before returning to my eyes. A wicked smile plays on his lips, and an eternity passes before he speaks. Silently, I will him to say something. Anything.

"Don't worry about it. I've seen worse." Expecting him to end the sentence with *Milady* it surprises me that he doesn't. His demeanour is different today, less gritty, more relaxed. "You were entertaining."

The comment is said lightly, but it feels like a blow. Snatching my eyes from his, I walk towards the balustrade, needing some distance. A rustling signals him standing, and his bare feet pad towards me.

"I'm sorry," he says. "That was insensitive. I was only teasing."

A sigh escapes my lips as my shoulders drop. "It's okay. I'm sure I was very entertaining, as you say."

He stands behind me, not quite touching me but invading my space. His hands move to my shoulders in comfort, and the blood rushes to the surface of my skin.

"Linda, please don't be uncomfortable. I'm sorry," he repeats. "What happened with you last night has happened with many of the women who visit. You are not the first and will not be the last resident I need to help to their room." He pauses to collect his thoughts. "Ladies come here to escape, to find themselves, and, sometimes, there are bumps in the road. It was nothing I hadn't seen or supported before." His words are soft with genuine care behind each one.

Turning to face him, my eyes lift to his. He's tall, and I squint into the disappearing sun behind him. Words hang unspoken in the air between us. "Okay," is the only one that comes to my lips.

With a small smile, he drops his lips to my forehead. I close my eyes, enjoying the moment. The gesture is simple but intimate. And far too comfortable for people who barely know each other. I clear my throat, the sound breaking the spell. Max steps back, the air surrounding me suddenly empty. The void is unpleasant.

"Anyway," he says, "I'd best go and start getting ready for work."

"Do you ever get a day off?" I ask.

"One day a week. Normally a Monday. Why? Are you going to ask me out on a date?" He raises his eyebrow, and my eyes widen in surprise.

"A date?" I squeak.

"Yes, a date. You know like dinner, drinks, maybe a walk down the beach? We would sit and chat. Have a basic conversation to find out more about each other."

"I know what a date is," I huff.

"Oh, that's good, then. I was concerned for a moment there." His lips move into a wide grin, exposing bright-white teeth. Against his tanned skin, he looks like he is posing for a modelling shoot. "Do you fancy doing something on my next day off then?"

"U-Um," I stammer. "Why on earth would you want to go on a date with me?"

"Why not?" he asks, looking genuinely surprised by my question.

"Well, how old are you?" I question. His brows draw together, his expression changing from relaxed to annoyed in a split second. "And do you normally date hotel residents?"

"I'm thirty-three." His hands move to his hips in displeasure. "And, no, I have never dated a lady staying in the hotel before. Linda, I asked if you wanted to go for dinner, not if you wanted to go to bed." My mouth drops open in shock. "I like you and just wondered if you wanted to spend some time together. But..." His voice trails off. He doesn't finish his sentence.

"But what?" I prompt. He gives me a blank look. "Max, I'm forty-five, and I have come here to escape my mundane life. What on earth about me could interest you? I'm a sad middle-aged woman with more wrinkles than a Shar-Pei dog. I'm sure there are plenty of young hot things running around the beach who would be far more your type."

Saying nothing, he steps forward and lifts his palm to my cheek. My face immediately moves towards his skin, and his fingers drum behind my ear, sending electric shocks through my body. "But," he whispers, "hot young beach bikinis aren't who I am hoping will ask me out." My heart crashes from my chest, before bursting back through my ribs. "Think about it."

I watch him walk off in the direction of the stairs. My heart rate returns to normal, and a huge smile spreads across my face. That gorgeous youthful specimen just asked me out on a date. Kind of. As far as evenings go, this is a great one.

As I stand in front of the full-length mirror in my room, I stare at my reflection for the thousandth time. My hair is down in soft curls around my face. My soft-ribbed black dress clings to my curves, accentuating my waist and finishing just above my knee. The neckline is high, and my breasts are pushed up with the best bra I could find in this sleepy town. Black strappy wedges increase my height by a good few inches while, *hopefully*, elongating my legs.

Applying another coat of foundation to my face in an attempt to hide the lines, my heart sinks. Age doesn't come on its own, and here I am trying to impress a guy twelve years my junior. Perhaps this is my rock bottom. This is me as a desperate woman. Did I imagine him flirting with me? Was it all a figment of my imagination?

After deciding not to hide in my room any longer, I muster my courage and head out. The walk to the bar feels never-ending, and the corridors are deserted. It's eleven o'clock on a Sunday night, and the party is underway. Most people will already be three sheets to the wind. Dance music fills my ears the closer I get to the bar. Having hidden in my room all day, only emerging to find Max, I haven't seen anyone. Last night is a blur to me; the events disappeared from my mind. How much I made a fool of myself, I do not know. It makes me nervous.

"Linda!" Crystal shouts from behind me as I reach the door. "I was just coming to find you. You can't miss it tonight. DJ Divine is amazing. She knows how to get a room going." She links her arm through mine. "Let's get our dancing shoes on."

The small space is packed from wall to wall. Lights are flying in all directions, and excitement fills the air. There is a sea of colour and sequins in front of me as I enter. Ladies of all ages are dressed in their finest. Faces turn to me as Crystal guides me through the crowd towards the bar, and each one gives me a smile in welcome. No one is laughing or pointing. No one is making cruel comments about the night before. I feel myself relax a little.

Susan is standing behind the bar as we come to a stop. Crystal taps me on my shoulder and rises to her toes to shout in my ear over the music, "What do you want to drink?"

"Just water," I reply.

"Water! *Pfft!*" She shakes her head and turns to Susan. "Two Sex on the Beach, please, Suzie." I frown at her. "Water is for wimps," she tells me with a look as if I'm an idiot. "If we can't have the real Sex on the Beach experience, we may as well have the cocktail."

I chuckle at her as my eyes scan the room, then I see him. He is behind the DJ decks talking to a tall blonde woman. She is casually dressed in shorts and a strappy vest top. With little makeup, she looks youthful and vibrant compared to every other female here. The average age of the rest of us must be sixty. Max is chatting animatedly with her. She smiles shyly at him as he speaks. Every so often, her fingers rise to his shoulder, dusting off invisible flecks.

After dropping my eyes to the floor, I chastise myself for being so stupid. Of course I imagined the flirting. I've turned into a needy middle-aged woman who lusts after young men. I've become everything I used to ridicule. Turning back to the bar, my drink is sitting waiting for me.

Susan smiles. "Enjoy," she says.

Lifting the glass to my lips, the sweet juice is explosive on my tongue. The chatter around me is happy and lively. This is what I came to Spain for – to enjoy the company of other ladies and decadent drinks, not chase after young men. Internally, I give myself a swift talking-to, and I decide to enjoy the night ahead.

***

Max

Lacy bats her baby blues in my direction again. DJ Divine, what a name. This is the first time I've seen her since our discussion at the bar a week or so ago. We haven't spoken at all. I was nervous about seeing her tonight, but we've been friends for years, and things seem to have returned to normal of a sort. Maybe I just never noticed the flirting before. I'm not sure.

After having my heart broken before summer, I promised myself that I wouldn't be looking for a relationship. This was a summer of fun and freedom. Lacy had factored in my thoughts, but my assumption was that things would be like they had been in the past. How wrong I was.

"Max," she prompts, "have you listened to a word I've said?"

"Sorry, miles away," I shout over the music. "What did you say?"

"When is your night off? Will we go grab some dinner? For old times' sake." She lifts her hand, places it on my shoulder, then runs it up and down my arm. "Twelve months apart gives us a lot to catch up on, whether you want to try the *more* thing or not."

"Perhaps," I mumble. "I'll need to check my days off." It's a poor excuse. I always know my schedule. She will know that; she has known me long enough. Her face twists in displeasure, and my skin prickles. Guilt bubbles in my stomach. I don't want to go back there again. It's not fair for either of us. I feel like a complete asshole for leading her on.

"Well, you can let me know." She pouts and turns back to her decks. Taking the gesture as my dismissal, I retreat to the safety of the bar. My aunt gives me a soft smile. We are close, and I'd confided in her when Lacy asked me to consider a relationship.

"Everything okay?" she asks. My shoulders lift and fall. "Ah, is she not taking the hint? Holiday romances rarely work, even if they take place over several years."

"We were never a couple," I remind her, and she lifts her eyebrows in challenge. Her lips pursed in open disapproval. "Not officially, anyway. Don't look at me like that. Don't you think I feel bad enough already?" She chuckles then returns to washing glasses under the tap.

The bar is heaving tonight. DJ nights always pull a big crowd, for us, anyway. The clients love the fact Lacy plays a wide range of music. She bends to the will of the people no matter what they ask for. All inhibitions are left at the door. It is perfectly normal to see a seventy-year-old break dancing in the centre of the room, while her companion directs a slosh rendition in the corner.

"Hey, Maxy." Crystal's shrill voice carries over the music. She is glugging down a red drink, which I assume is Sex on the Beach. My aunt always adds too much cranberry juice. "The pretty little thing behind the decks, what's her name again?"

"Lacy," I respond without looking up. She knows her bloody name. This is a fishing expedition.

"You and her, you have history," she states without question.

"Define 'history'," I say, impassive, and I raise my eyes, surprised as they meet Linda's hazel-brown ones. "Hello," I mumble, and she gives me a nod with a soft smile.

Crystal's voice cuts in. "Oh, you know. You've fucked. I'm pretty sure it is an annual event. I suspect she has it written on her calendar. The girl has been asking for weeks when you were due to arrive."

"Crystal, not that it is any of your business." I give her a dark look. "Lacy and I are friends. We have been for years. But, no, we're not fucking. Not that I would tell you if we were."

Without missing a beat, she gives me a wide toothy grin. "You don't need to, Maxy. I always know when a girl is in your room." My eyebrows shoot up. "You don't close your windows, and their moans fill the street." She nudges Linda then adds, "My room is below his. The headboard makes a hell of a racket, too."

"Fuck off, Crystal." It takes a lot for me to get angry. Normally, I'm the calming influence in the hotel, but today, Crystal is boiling my piss. Glancing in the mirror behind me, my cheeks are red with embarrassment. How did my sex life become a topic of conversation in front of the woman I attempted to flirt with only hours ago? Crystal turns with her glass held high and waddles off into the crowd. Linda is still standing on the other side of the bar, eyes fixed on me. She moves to sit on the high stool and crosses her legs. She's wearing a skin-tight black dress that highlights her womanly curves. Her lips are plump and painted in pillar box red. She looks incredible.

"Can I get you something?" I ask, unable to meet her eye.

"Possibly," she purrs, and the hair stands on the back of my neck. "Is it true? What Crystal said?"

Confused, I stare at her and shrug my shoulders. "Knowing Crystal, she could have told you anything. You're going to have to be more specific. If it's about Lacy, then yes and no. We have..." She holds her hand up to silence me.

"No, Max. I wasn't talking about who you had slept with." She takes a deep breath; her breasts rise and fall. My cock hardens. "I was wondering if your women's moans really do fill the street." She smiles sexily. "And if that headboard really is as noisy as she said it is."

Taken aback by her directness, my jaw drops. Panic flits across her face as her confidence wavers. Collecting my thoughts, I'm unsure if she is joking or not. Then, I laugh—it bursts from me—and she smiles. The air between us buzzes for a moment, and I put my hand over hers on the bar. She glances around nervously, wondering if anyone is watching.

"So, have you considered my proposition from earlier about a date? I have my day off tomorrow. I could show you around the local area," I suggest. She holds my gaze; I can almost see the cogs in her brain turning, considering her options. A sexy smile appears on her lips.

"That sounds lovely," she says, flicking a stray curl out of her line of vision. "I'll look forward to it."

Chapter Seven

Linda

The cocktails must have gone to my head and boosted my confidence in the process. Never in my life have I been so openly promiscuous, not even with my ex-husband. Two hours ago, I asked a man about his sex life and have flirted obscenely all evening since. Max has kept me entertained with light-hearted conversation, and my glass has been filled to the brim. He's charming and witty, complimenting me and singing along to whatever music is playing. Crystal has been dipping in and out of the conversation. No one seems to notice the open flirt-fest taking place at the bar.

"I've worked here since my teens," he tells me. "I enjoy it. I love Aunt Susan. She is like another mother to me." He talks with pride as he explains how she built the hotel up from nothing and has created this retreat for women to holiday solo. "The ladies here keep me entertained while giving me a hard time in the process."

The DJ announces the final song, and Crystal grabs my arm, dragging me up to dance. I roll my eyes at Max, and he laughs. Ricky Martin blares from the speakers, and ladies gyrate around me, carefree and loving life. No one cares what they look like or who is watching. A huge smile spreads across my face. Raising my hands in the air, I swing my hips in time with the music. As I close my eyes, I allow myself to be lost in the beat and let my body move freely for once. The music ends, and my eyes blink open. The lights come up as the crowd groans in annoyance. A bell sounds at the bar, and I look across. Max has climbed up on the surface. A hush falls over the ladies in the room.

"Right, ladies," he shouts. "Next round's on me. Who wants a shot? Tequila all round." He lifts his arms in the air and his t-shirt rises exposing tanned abs below.

A cheer fills the room, and he jumps off the bar. The shot glasses are already lined up in preparation. This must be a regular occurrence. The blonde DJ sidles up beside him, and he glances at her. She gives him a sexy smile and places her hand on his arm. He quickly moves it away, and she frowns in irritation. Taking a shot in each hand, she sinks one then the other, grimacing at the bitter taste before returning to pack up her equipment.

Thirty minutes later, many of the ladies are retiring for the night. Most are wobbling from side to side while singing at the top of their lungs as they leave. Crystal and I are sitting on a sofa, sipping the last of our drinks and chatting about nothing in particular. Max has been clearing glasses, not engaging in conversation with anyone. Lacy's eyes follow his every move.

"She's crazy about him," Crystal says, seeing the direction of my gaze. "He's all she ever talks about." I feign disinterest with a shrug. "I was talking to her before he arrived. They've been on and off for years, but she was hoping this year would be different."

"When did he get here?" I ask.

"Only a week or so before you. As soon as the schools closed. He's a teacher, but he was out for a few weekends beforehand," she explains. "Susan told Lacy that his heart had been broken by a friend he hoped would be more. He is taking the summer to consider his options. Lacy was going to make a play for him, but, seemingly, he shot her down at her first attempt."

"You really are a fountain of knowledge, Crystal." She laughs at my description. "Or a gossip. I haven't decided which yet."

Without a word, she kisses my cheek and rises to leave. I sit and sip my drink, enjoying the peace after a hectic night. Only a few residents are left in the bar. Max is helping Lacy carry cases of equipment from the room. They don't speak, but they work silently together as they have probably done one hundred times before.

Finishing my drink, I place it on the low coffee table in front of me and lay my head back on the sofa. Tiredness is overwhelming me. Five minutes relaxing here won't do any harm before I head to my room. The sofa sags beside me as someone sits down.

"Don't tell me I'm going to have to escort you to your room again tonight," he whispers.

"No, I have retained my faculties tonight, you will be pleased to know," I say turning to look at him.

"Shame," he says. "I quite enjoyed the task last night." My heart beats harder in my chest at his words laden with promise. "Is there anything, in particular, you want to see tomorrow?"

"To be honest, I did no research on the area before coming. Just show me the beach and what you think is important." He nods. His eyes scan my face, and his tongue runs over his bottom lip. It's sexy as hell. Visions of his mouth on mine flood my brain, and my nipples harden. *Control yourself, woman.*

"The tequila trick works a treat every time," he says. My eyes widen at the change of subject, and I wave my hand signalling for him to explain. "If I give everyone free shots, then I get to bed earlier." He chuckles. "There is nothing worse than being stuck behind the bar until four in the morning because two folks won't go to bed." He smiles broadly. "If I ply them with drink, they go to bed quicker."

I laugh.

"Plus," he says, "I have a very important day tomorrow, and I need my beauty sleep."

"You do?" I ask with a smirk.

His eyes fix on mine, and my blood rushes to the surface of my skin. Suddenly, my whole body is waiting on his next words.

"Yes, I have a lady to impress with my tour-guiding skills."

My phone ringing wakes me from my slumber. I stretch my hands above my head, and a giant yawn escapes my lips. The noise stops then restarts immediately. I blink my eyes open, accepting the phone won't stop until it's answered. It must be Marina; she is the only person who doesn't stop calling until she gets a response. Lifting the phone, I hit the green button and the loudspeaker.

"Morning, Mum," she trills down the line. "Hey, pick up your phone. This is a video call. I can only see the ceiling."

"Marina, you woke me up." I roll my eyes before plucking the phone from the pillow and turning the camera to face me. My daughter—a younger version of myself—blinks back at me. Her dark hair is pulled into a high ponytail, and her hazel-brown eyes are filled with fun. "How are you, darling?" I ask.

"Things are fantastic! Brazil is amazing. We are having an incredible time."

She rattles on for ten minutes, telling me about everything she and her current man have been getting up to. Marina has no filter; quite often, she divulges far too much information – far more than a mother wants to know.

"So, Mum, how are you enjoying your first solo excursion?" she asks. Her eyes dance with interest. "Met anyone interesting?" A small smile plays on my lips as I think of Max. If only she knew. "Oh, you have! You dirty minx!"

Rearranging my face to control my wayward features, I say, "No, Marina. I haven't met anyone. You just made me chuckle with your question. No one is going to be interested in an old woman like me." She scowls. "The ladies here are lovely, though, and we're having a lot of fun."

"Mum!" she snaps. "You're beautiful, and you're not old!" Her face is stern. "You deserve to have some action. If a nice man offers you a good time, you take the chance. Do you hear me?" I salute the camera, and she huffs.

"Right, darling," I say, not wanting to continue the conversation. "I have plans with a friend today. I need to get ready. Have fun and be safe. Love you." She blows a kiss into the phone and disconnects the call.

A soft knock at my door distracts me from my skincare routine. Padding over, I swing it open without checking who it is, assuming it must be the housekeeping staff. Max stands on the other side, dressed in black shorts and a bright-red T-shirt with the words *Tour Guide* written across his chest. I gape at him, and he gives me a sexy smile in return.

"Ready to go?" he asks.

"Do I look ready?" My hair is still in rat tails from bed. My skimpy nightie barely covers my ass, and my nipples poke through the soft fabric. His eyes drop to my toes then slowly rise over my body, pausing on my lips before coming back to my eyes.

"You look good to me," he says with a smirk. My skin flushes at his words, redness creeping up my neck.

Collecting my thoughts, I tell him, "Go downstairs. I'll meet you in reception in twenty minutes." He lifts an eyebrow at my tone, which should have been authoritative but sounded petulant instead.

"Please," he scolds me. "Let's save any awkward questions. There's a small coffee shop called Margo's down the street. They make the best coffee and tostadas. I'll meet you there in fifteen." He leans forward and places a soft kiss on my cheek. "I'm really looking forward to today." He turns and walks off down the corridor. Shocked by his open affection, all I can do is watch him. It's not something I'm used to; my ex-husband kept our intimacy behind closed doors and, even then, there wasn't a great deal of it. I was often left feeling more of a cook and housekeeper rather than a much-loved wife.

Margo's Coffee Shop sits on the end of the row of buildings that incorporates the hotel. There are four tables outside under a red-and-white striped awning, and each sits four. Max is sitting at the furthest table, already sipping a huge mug of steaming liquid and chatting to the person sitting opposite him. As I approach, I realise to my horror that it is Crystal. He glances at me and smiles.

"Here she is," he says, and Crystal turns in her seat. Her eyes pop open when she sees me. She quickly rearranges her face from shocked to friendly.

"Morning, Linda. Beautiful day, isn't it? I've just been to my morning yoga session at the beach. It really gets the blood flowing. Perhaps you would like to join me one time?" She speaks rapidly, her excitement evident.

"Perhaps," I mumble, wanting the earth to open up and swallow me whole.

She rises from her chair and waddles off in the direction of the hotel, calling over her shoulder, "Well, you two enjoy your day."

Max's focus stays glued to my face. "Coffee?" he asks.

"Yes, please," I say, dropping into the seat Crystal just vacated. "What did you tell her?"

He taps a finger to his lips as if trying to remember. "Just that we were fucking."

"What?" I snap, and he belly laughs. "You didn't!"

An older woman with dyed blonde hair places a cup of steaming coffee in front of me. I never noticed him order it. "Thanks, Margo," Max says, and she touches his shoulder in thanks. He picks up a packet of sugar, pours it into his cup, then lifts his spoon to stir it.

"*Max*!" I whisper angrily.

He flashes me a sexy smile before shaking his head.

"Of course, I didn't. I told her I was meeting a friend for the day." He rolls his eyes. "She didn't believe me and said she was hanging around to find out who the lucky lady is. Her face was a picture when she saw you. Tongues will be wagging at the hotel all day now."

As I place my elbows on the table, my head drops to my hands. I'm going to get a reputation. I've not even been here a week, and I'm going to be known as a whore who chases young men and spends their days off with them. He flicks a stray curl from in front of my face then places a finger under my chin to raise my eyes to his.

"Don't worry about it. If they're talking about you, they're leaving someone else alone," he says and drains his mug before standing. "You ready to go?" His hand is thrust towards me, his palm open. I take it. What do I have to lose? My half-drunk coffee is left on the table as we leave.

We wander through the streets of the old town; it's beautiful. People of all ages sit on deck chairs, enjoying the early afternoon sunshine. I pull my large floppy hat down on my head to block out the rays. The temperature has risen quickly, and my soft-white beach dress is damp with perspiration. Underneath, I'm wearing a blush-pink bikini decorated with white daisies, the colour shimmering through the thin material. Max holds my hand as he directs me around the town, explaining the history of the area and telling me stories from years gone by. He is charismatic and easy to be around.

"Do you want to get some lunch?" he asks. "Then, we can spend a few hours at the beach. There is a lovely stretch a few minutes' walk from here."

"Sounds lovely," I tell him, and he leads me in the direction of a small restaurant on the promenade. We sit inside as temperatures have now hit thirty-five degrees. With large tables of ten or more sitting down to lunch, the place is buzzing. The waiter guides us to a table for two in the corner and places a fresh salad in front of us. It's filled with crisp lettuce, sweetcorn, strips of carrot, and plump cherry tomatoes.

"*Menu Del Día*," Max explains. "Menu of the day. You get a salad, bread, two courses, a dessert, and coffee. This restaurant mainly serves fish. I hope that's okay with you. I like to eat this way; quite often, I won't need anything to eat at night. Well, not food, anyway."

"Sounds delicious," I say, trying to ignore the sexual energy buzzing around us. "Yes, I won't need anything to eat later either. That's a lot of food for the middle of the day."

He chuckles. "When in Spain, do as the Spaniards do. Nights are for other activities, not eating." A dark smile is on his lips, and his eyes bore into mine. I swallow as nerves rise in my stomach. He is making his intentions clear. Sensing my nervousness, he changes the subject and passes me a menu. "What would you like for lunch?"

The afternoon passes in a haze of seafood and wine. We chat about his time in Spain and his job back in London as a geography teacher. He hasn't mentioned the girl who broke his heart, and I have refrained from discussions of my past life. It turns out we live a mere forty minutes from each other and know a lot of the same places in the city. It's nice to have someone to talk to who knows where I'm from but not my past. So many acquaintances look at me with pity; I'm the woman whose husband got bored and ran away.

"Will we head to the beach now?" Max asks, interrupting my thoughts.

"Sounds great," I reply.

He pays the bill, and we wander down the promenade away from town. The streets are busy but not mobbed. The beach is to our left and houses are on our right. The further we get from the centre, the quieter it becomes. He stops at a small path that leads down onto the white sand. There are only a few couples lying around sunbathing; one is playing classical music from a Bluetooth speaker, which gives the place a romantic feel. Taking my hand again, he guides me to the beach and picks a spot to lay out our towels under a huge palm tree for shade. I watch as he unpacks the beach bag he has carried all day for me. After placing the sun cream and bottles of water next to our towels, he kicks off his flip-flops and lifts his T-shirt over his head before wriggling out of his shorts. He's wearing only a small pair of blue trunks leaving his body on full display. The tattoos on his legs are mirrored across his back, and taut stomach muscles guide my eyes to the package between his legs.

"Like what you see?" he asks, and my eyes snap back to his. Shit, he caught me staring at his junk. How fucking embarrassing. Suddenly nervous, I want to stay beneath the safety of my dress. What will my body look like in comparison to his? Old and decrepit.

"Your turn," he prompts, and my heart sinks.

Chapter Eight

Max

Her big hazel-brown eyes peek at me from under her huge hat. Stray curls fall around her face like they have every time I've seen her. She looks nervous. The day has gone well, and we have enjoyed each other's company. During our time together, I've tried to make my intentions clear. She must know I find her attractive. She must know I want to be here with her. The comments she made about young bikini-clad women have circled in my mind since she said it. I wonder what she sees when she looks in the mirror.

"Are you going to take that off?" I prompt. "Or do I have to throw you in the water with it on?" I take a step towards her, and she moves back, her back connecting with the palm tree. Slowly, she lifts the white dress over her head, and her hat drops to the floor with it. She keeps her eyes firmly between her feet, not wanting to look up. Her cheeks pink, and she trails a toe through the sand. We stand not speaking for a few minutes, the atmosphere has changed from relaxed to charged.

"Say something," she whispers. The strong, confident woman of the past few hours disappears before my eyes. It saddens me that she can't see what I do. The swell of her breasts in her bikini, in contrast with her nipped waist, highlights the stunning woman she is. Her skin is pale and clear, yet to be tinged gold with the sun. Bright-pink nails on the end of her fingers and toes give her a playful edge. This woman looks after her body, and, as a man, I find that incredibly attractive. I love a woman who embraces herself.

"You look beautiful," I tell her. She shakes her head, still not meeting my eye. Stepping forward, I take her hands in mine. They are slick with perspiration. "Look at me," I say. She shakes her head again. "Linda, look at me." Slowly, her eyes rise to mine. "You are beautiful," I repeat, and I drop a kiss onto her lips.

"I'm not beautiful," she mumbles. "I'm old and worn, with more bumps and lines than I care to accept. This has been so unexpected, whatever this is."

My mouth moves to hers, stopping the self-hate spilling from her lips. Her eyes close, and her lips part, submitting to me, softly, gently, and intimately. My hands move to her hips, and I pull her towards me; the feel of her body on mine speaks directly to my cock. *Control yourself. Don't scare her off.*

"Let's sit," I suggest, and we drop to the towels beside each other. Sitting with my back against the tree, I signal for her to sit next to me, and I wrap my arm around her. She turns her head to face me. "If you think a few extra creases on your skin make you less attractive to me, you're mistaken. I like you, and, right now, keeping my hands off you is a difficult task. Trust me when I tell you, you are beautiful."

She doesn't respond, but she visibly relaxes beside me. We sit for a while just watching the water lap onto the beach. Up close, she smells incredible, a mixture of sea salt and vanilla.

"Shall we go for a dip?" I ask, and she murmurs assent. I stand then pull her to her feet, taking her hand and leading her to the water's edge. We paddle out into the sea up to our waists. The water is warm, heated by the constant summer sun.

Turning to speak to her, I'm met with a face full of water. She laughs and continues to splash water in my direction.

"Got you!" she shouts. Her crazy curls are damp hanging around her face, and a beaming smile is aimed at me. "If you're not fast, you're last!"

"This is war!" I growl, grabbing her around the waist to pull her into my arms. She squeals with delight, then I launch her into the water in front of us. Her thrilled face disappears below the surface, and I dive in after her. Wrapped around each other and giggling, we both stagger to our feet.

"I give as good as I get," I whisper in her ear. She stops laughing and swallows audibly.

"Do you promise?" she asks, a sexy smile on her lips. "Do you promise you're a giver?" Her arms are draped around my neck, and I lift her up so she can wrap her legs around my waist. Arousal shoots through me, and my cock hardens between her legs. Her eyes pop open in surprise.

"I told you I was having a hard time keeping my hands off you. Now you're in them, and I don't think I can let you go." She takes my mouth with hers, her tongue invading mine. It takes all my control not to slip her bottoms to the side and spear her here in the middle of the sea. "You're a fucking sexy woman. Remember that." I place her back onto her feet, and she pouts at me. "As tempting as you are, I don't fancy being lifted by the local police for indecent behaviour. Have you seen the Spanish police force? They're bloody scary."

We swim for a while then head back to the beach to lie down and dry off. She tells me about her daughter, Marina, and her job at a local school. Her ex-husband is never mentioned, and I don't ask. The only reason I know about him is she told my aunt her life story the night she got drunk. My aunt can never keep stories to herself, so she told me the whole sorry tale over breakfast the next morning. It was a story I had heard many times before. The husband gets bored and runs away with the woman down the street, leaving behind a shattered and confused partner of decades.

Lying back on my towel, she snuggles in under my arm, head on my chest. When I ran away from my broken heart, back here to Spain, the last thing I imagined getting was a holiday romance. Before it happened, I hadn't planned to come this summer at all, but I decided that some space was required. I assumed Lacy and I would resume our friends-with-benefits arrangement until she served up a curveball, too. Now, here I am, lying under the sun with a beautiful older woman in my arms.

"Linda," I whisper into her curls. She doesn't respond. Glancing down, her chest is rising and falling in a steady rhythm. A small snore escapes her lips. She looks so peaceful. Not wanting to disturb her, I lay back and enjoy the warmth of the afternoon that hangs in the air. Ten minutes pass, and my phone buzzes in the bag. Gently, I extricate myself from beneath her, placing her head on a folded towel for comfort. She moans but doesn't wake. After rummaging in the huge beach bag she insisted on bringing, I find my phone under the pile of crap it contains.

The name *Lacy* lights up the screen. Great. Right now, I really don't want to talk to her. I send the call to the answerphone. A message immediately pings into my inbox.

Crystal said you're on a date. With who?

Fucking Crystal sticking her nose in where it's not wanted. She's been playing matchmaker and gossip for years. Closing my eyes, I consider what response to use in reply; not that I can really justify my actions. This is not all Crystal's fault. Another message pops up before I can type a letter.

Max, you led me on. Rejected me. And now I find out you're dating! You're an asshole. For years, I've hung around waiting for you each summer. Never again. Go take a long walk off a short cliff.

Underneath the words is a barrage of angry emoji. Deciding her summary doesn't need a response just now, I throw the phone back in the bag. I will track her down later and apologise, not that she will accept it. Lacy likes to hold a grudge. This will be the first time I'm at the end of it.

Other beachgoers are starting to pack up as the sun begins its descent for the evening. Checking my watch, it is 8:30 p.m. I begin packing up our belongings, leaving Linda to sleep as long as she can.

Her eyes flutter open, and she gives me a shy smile. "Sorry, did I fall asleep?" she asks. "Too much excitement for one day."

"You did, but you were so peaceful, I didn't want to disturb you. Are you hungry? It's almost nine o'clock."

She shakes her head and pushes herself up to sit. Her bikini has moved while she rested, and one pert pink nipple pops from its casing. Her eyes follow the direction of my gaze, and she blushes crimson. I snigger.

Don't worry, beautiful, I plan to see a lot more than your nipples, I think cynically.

"Shall we go?" I ask, changing the subject.

Our walk back to the hotel is quiet. We wander along, our fingers intertwined. "Do you want to get a drink when we get back?" she asks. It surprises me, as she was nervous about people knowing we had spent the day together.

"Sure," I say. "Monday nights are normally quiet in the bar; everyone is recovering from the weekend. We shouldn't get asked too many awkward questions." Her lips twist into a sad smile. "What?"

"Nothing. As you said, if they are gossiping about us, someone else is being left alone." She sighs softly. "I've had a wonderful day, Max. Thank you." Stopping abruptly, she turns to me and takes my face in her hands. Then, she rises on her tiptoes and pecks me softly on the mouth.

The hotel is silent when we enter. As we get closer to the bar, the hum of chattering fills the air – perhaps two or three ladies, not many. Linda drops my hand as we step through the door; the action upsets me. The feeling of her hand in mine is comforting. All the talking stops as we enter. Crystal is sitting at the bar, talking to my aunt. They both look up and smile at us.

"Hello," my aunt calls. "That must have been some tour Max gave you, Linda." She raises her eyebrows in jest. "You've been gone for hours."

"Um," Linda mutters, stumbling over her words.

"Maxy boy," Crystal interrupts. "How do I book a private tour with you? And I want all the extras she's getting, too."

The pair of witches at the bar cackle at the crude joke. I glare at them as Linda flushes bright red. My aunt bursts out laughing. "Okay, the joke's over. What do you both want to drink?" she asks.

The four of us sit at a low table and sip our wine. Linda recalls the day to the girls, missing out on the intimate parts. I sit next to her, hanging off every word. She is well-spoken and smart. The way her eyes light up when she is telling a story makes her excitement evident. From what she has said to the others, I'm confident she has enjoyed the day. The clock signals midnight, and we all rise to leave for our rooms.

"Night!" Crystal shouts as she waddles off. "Don't you two be making too much noise tonight and move the bed away from the wall. Some of us need our beauty sleep."

I move to help my aunt finish clearing the bar, she waves me away. "It's your day off. Off you go," she orders.

Following Linda from the room, her hair, decorated with sand and stray bits of greenery, hangs in curls down her back. We reach her door, and my heart is drumming in my chest. She stops and pulls the key from her bag before turning to face me. Her eyes are directed at the floor. Eventually, they lift to mine. My cock is waking from its slumber, and I am not sure how to play the next few moments. Do I make a move? Or do I let her suggest the night is not over?

"Max," she says, her tone wary. "I've had a wonderful day. But..." She trails off, and my heart sinks. "I can't sleep with you. Not tonight. It's too quick. We've only just met and—"

My lips silence her. We kiss hungrily, and her hands move to my hair. I pull her into my body, the full length of her up against me feels incredible. It takes all my strength not to push her through the fucking door and beg her to fuck me. Visions of her bouncing up and down on top of me flood my mind. I need to keep my cool.

To break the moment, I step back and give her a smile in reassurance. "I understand," I tell her. "There's no rush. I've had a fantastic day." Lifting her hand to my lips, I kiss her knuckles. "Now, go inside. Good night, Beautiful."

She slides through the door and shuts it softly behind her. I rest my forehead on the closed door. My cock is rock-solid, and it is cursing me for being a gentleman. Accepting the night has not quite finished how I hoped, I saunter back to my room, pondering whether the Wi-Fi will be strong enough for *Pornhub* not to buffer.

Chapter Nine

Linda

I toss and turn under the covers. It's so bloody hot, and I'm not talking about the temperature. My phone tells me it's 1:15 a.m. It's been an hour since I sent Max back to his own room. Don't get me wrong, I was tempted. Gagging for it. The thought of him having his way with me is a dream and nightmare all in one go. Would I be able to keep up with him? Would I know the moves? Does my pussy look the same as the young women he is used to?

Only having been with the same man since my early twenties, my experience in the bedroom is limited. I'm not even sure I will remember what to do when the time comes. At the end of our marriage, our sex life was non-existent. When we did do the deed, laying back and zoning out tended to be my solution. Get it over with as quickly as possible. My ex-husband was only in the mood when he had a skin full, so there was never much foreplay, if any at all. It was wham, bam, thank you, ma'am, and that was if he could keep it up long enough to slide it in. Eventually, I discovered he was eating his cake elsewhere.

As I force my eyes closed for what feels like the thousandth time, I try to chase the thoughts of Max's toned abs from my mind. When he had stripped down to his trunks on the beach, I almost self-combusted with the heat flowing through my veins. Then, in the sea, with my legs wrapped around his trim waist and his nose in my neck, I allowed myself to enjoy the time with him, being flirty and fun, the way I promised myself I would live my life moving forward.

When we left the beach, I'd intended to bring him back to my room and ride him hard. I had visions of us bursting through the door and him throwing me on the bed. He would drop between my legs to prepare me for his onslaught before I straddled him and rode him like the stallion he is.

But on our return to the hotel, meeting Susan and Crystal in the bar made my resolve waver. The cheeky remarks were said in fun, but there was truth behind them. I was living the fantasy of a lot of older women like me. A young hot guy asks you out and treats you well under the sunshine. But very few of those fantasies have happy endings, and I will not be one of those broken-hearted middle-aged losers again. Living life to the fullest does not mean throwing all caution to the wind. I need to protect myself.

My phone has lain silently on my bedside table through the night. Perhaps all he was after was a quick fumble, and, when I rejected him, he lost interest. It doesn't feel like that, though. He was so sweet and charming, and he listened to my concerns, but I suppose all men do that when they want a shag.

Glancing at the clock, it now shows it's eleven in the morning. Good, he'll be at the spa now; he told me he was working today, a full day of those strong hands caressing the bodies of other women. Jealousy bubbles in my stomach.

Don't be so ridiculous. He's not yours to be jealous over. He can caress whomever he wants, privately or commercially.

My heart doesn't agree with my head, and it tightens slightly. It has only been a week since I arrived, and I've fallen for the massage boy. What a whore. I've missed breakfast, too. I'm too embarrassed to face him or anyone else who may know what I was up to yesterday. Not that there was anything X-rated about our day – that only happened in my mind.

On entering the reception, I see Susan is in her usual spot, typing frantically on her computer. I wonder if she has another job that requires so much computer work.

"Linda," she calls as I try to escape out the front door unnoticed. "Max left this for you." My heart explodes at his name. She walks towards me and hands me a white envelope, then turns and struts back to her desk. Inside is a small white card.

Thanks for a lovely day. I've booked a massage for you at 3 p.m. Enjoy x

I stare at the card dumbly before regaining my senses and leaving through the front door. Then, a dirty smile spreads across my face. I wanted a sign he wanted to see me again, and, hell, this is a clear one. Today will be spent enjoying the local area before I head off to be pleasured by a hunk of a man. Happy Tuesday to me.

Three o'clock rolls around fast, and I head in the direction of the spa. I'm wearing my sexiest bikini. It is dark blue with a plunging neckline and enough underwire to push my boobs to my eyes. Over the top is a sheer cover that ties with a single ribbon at the front. Soft feathers trim the collar. My wedge sandals give me a little height and elongate my legs. The look I'm going for is a Hollywood movie star on vacation.

As I push open the door to the treatment rooms, the similar smell of vanilla fills my nostrils. I stop dead when I'm greeted by a tall redheaded woman in a therapist uniform. She smiles at me kindly.

"Good afternoon," she says. "You must be Linda. I'm Jessica. I will be your therapist today."

My mouth drops open, and my eyes scan the room. "Um," I say. That is the only word I can muster. She signals for me to go through to the treatment area.

"Just undress but leave your bottoms on." I flush at the instruction, remembering my bare ass on full display for Max only days ago. He must have warned her. "Then lie on the bed face down. I'll only be a moment."

Calm acoustic music is playing quietly in the background, but it does nothing to steady my nerves. Where is he? Why plan me a massage and not do it himself? I climb up on the bed as instructed and wait. Minutes later, the door opens and closes.

"This is a full body massage with essential oils. Lavender is good for relaxing the body." Jessica continues to prattle on about massage techniques and pressure requirements. I'm not listening, too busy wondering why Max didn't come to relax me himself.

Her hands come to my shoulders, and I can see her feet through the hole in the bed. She is wearing a toe ring with a small pink stone, and her nails are painted a similar colour. I notice with disgust that her legs are *au naturel*; this is a woman who embraces her body hair.

After closing my eyes to relax into the treatment, my body submits to her firm fingers as she moves them across my skin. Aches and strains disappear with my worry.

The door opening and closing again distracts me momentarily, but Jessica continues her process. Familiar male feet appear below me. A snake tattoo twists from his ankle around his calf, disappearing into his shorts. He places his hands on my head, pulls my hair into a rough bun, and secures it with a band. His toes flex beneath me, and I am aware of him readjusting his shorts. The door closing once more signals Jessica's departure.

He says nothing. His fingers do the talking. Starting at the base of my back, his huge frame leans across me as he moves over my body. My breathing quickens as my arousal builds with each stroke. Wetness builds between my legs the closer his fingers get to my pussy. After touching every part of my body, he leans down to my ear and whispers, "Turn over." On cue, my nipples harden to their breaking points, and a gasp breaks from my lips. The room is dim, and I blink to clear my eyes.

"No looking," he scolds. Then, he places a mask across my eyes and a pillow beneath my head. Soft fabric is laid across my chest to maintain what little dignity I have left. This time, he starts at my feet, moving up my body insanely slow and skipping completely over the tops of my thighs. On reaching my head, he places a soft kiss on my lips. The fact I can't see him is completely erotic. My mind fills in the blanks.

"Linda," he whispers. "Do you want a special massage? An intimate one?" My brain misfires, and I giggle nervously. "But I warn you, once I start, there will be no stopping."

This is it. This is my chance to be the wild free Linda I want to be. The woman who lives life in the moment, not caring what others think. I don't know if it's the music, the vanilla, or the fucking sex god massaging my middle-aged body, but I say, "Yes. Fucking yes."

He laughs softly and removes the cover from my breasts. Taking a nipple between his fingers, he slowly rotates it between them, and, somehow, they firm further.

"Fucking beautiful," he mumbles and drops his lips to where his fingers once were, licking, sucking, and teasing each nipple in turn. My hands move to his hair, and I run my fingers through his locks, tightening my grip in rhythm with my sex. My pussy is slick, vibrations of excitement buzzing between my legs for what is to come.

His tongue runs down my stomach to my bikini bottoms. He nips at the waistband with his teeth. Then, using strong fingers, he unties each side of the briefs. They fall open, exposing me. All of me. He is breathing hard now as he leans over my body. I can feel his hard cock pressing against my skin.

"Do you want this?" he asks. I nod. "Tell me," he growls. "You need to tell me you want me to fuck you."

"Fuck me," I whisper. "Now."

"Good girl," he says, and my pussy contracts in excitement. "Now, I'm going to slide my fingers inside you. We'll take it slow. No rush. I want you to scream, Beautiful. Even if it takes all night, I'm going to break you in ecstasy."

There is the sound of oil being squeezed from a bottle before his hand is on my pubic bone. His fingers drum on my lips, finding my clit and massaging gently. He strokes all of me before sliding one then two fingers inside. I submit willingly and groan in pleasure, pulling my knees back towards my head.

"You like that?"

"Um, yep," I say with a giggle. "Having a hot sexy massage therapist certainly has its benefits."

"Having a sexy hot client with a wet pussy and tits I want to fuck is a benefit for the therapist, too," he responds. "Do you want me, Beautiful? Want me inside you?"

"Uh-huh," I mumble.

"Tell me properly," he growls and nips my neck. Then, he removes the mask from my eyes.

"Yes, Max. I want you inside me. Now." As soon as the words are past my lips, he strips from his clothes and climbs onto the bed above me. On his knees, between my legs, I have a full view of his cock, hard, engorged, and ready to take me. He rips open the silver packet between his fingers and slides the condom down onto his length.

Placing one hand on either side of my head, he covers my body with his. His cock nudges at my opening then slides in deep. Above me, he closes his eyes as he moves inside me. My body falls into rhythm with his, and I match him thrust for thrust. The sensation builds as we rock, my legs wrapping around his waist. He's breathing hard now.

"You're going to need to come, Beautiful," he mutters, and I squeeze. We explode together in a wave of ecstasy.

Max kept his promise. He's a giver.

Chapter Ten

Max

"Let's go to the beach later," I suggest. Linda and I are lying on my roof terrace enjoying the early morning sunshine. For the past week, we've spent every morning here, drinking coffee and chatting until I need to go to work. She's topless, wearing only a small white thong. Her confidence around me increases each day. Now, she seems completely comfortable in my presence clothed or otherwise. I've pushed our loungers up against each other to create something that resembles a double bed. I love the way she lays her head on my chest as we talk.

"Are you not working today?" she asks.

"Yes, but I'll be finished by twelve. I'm on the bar tonight." I glance at my watch. "I need to get going. Are you staying here, or will I meet you somewhere else after my shift?"

"I'll still be here when you get back. The beach sounds great for later," she mumbles, reclosing her eyes. I drop my lips to hers in farewell.

"See you later, Beautiful."

Crystal is sitting in the waiting area of the spa when I arrive. "Morning, Maxy," she chirps. "It's not like you to be late. Is Linda wearing you out?" She beams at me, and I roll my eyes to feign annoyance.

"No, Crystal. I'm on time. Your appointment isn't for another ten minutes. You're early." She watches me intently as I pull towels from the cupboard then take off my shoes.

"I never saw it coming, I have to admit."

"Saw what coming?" I say, glancing at her.

"You and Linda. They do say opposite attracts. How did Lacy take the rejection?"

"I think you know the answer to that question," I shoot back. "No doubt my aunt has filled you in on the irate messages that bombarded my phone."

"Poor girl," Crystal mutters, shaking her head, but a smile plays on her lips. "She was hopeful that this year would be the one where you woke up and smelt the coffee. I think she was hoping for an epic romantic gesture. She probably has a picture of you pinned on her headboard."

"Did everyone know the fucking situation except me?" I hiss and run my hand through my hair in frustration. "As far as I knew we were no more than friends who slept together on occasion." She gives me a look that tells me I'm an idiot. "Why the fuck am I even justifying myself to you?"

"Oh Maxy, when you look like you do, there are going to be some broken hearts along the way."

"It's normally my heart that's ripped to shreds," I say. She ignores me.

"So, what's it like bonking an older woman? Go on, tell your Auntie Crystal."

"Did you actually just ask me that? You're a reliable pain in the ass." She grins at me. "I'm telling you nothing. Do you want a massage or not?"

"Of course I do, Maxy. I'm just pissed off I have to pay for your attention and Linda is getting more than me for free," she says, then wobbles past me into the treatment room.

***

Linda

Max appears back at his room bang on twelve o'clock. I'm ready with my beach bag and cooler box filled with beer and goodies. He walks in, striding across to where I am standing looking out the window. His arms wrap around me, pulling me close. He kisses my forehead softly; it reminds me of our initial moment on the roof terrace. The moment that started this hair-brained romance I'm currently part of. "I've missed you," he whispers into my hair.

"You've been gone the whole of three hours," I tell him.

"And they were the longest three hours of my life. If I have to listen to Crystal rabbiting on about anything again soon, I may not be able to date you any longer."

"What could speaking to Crystal have to do with you dating me?" I ask, snuggling in against his chest.

"I may be locked up for life for drowning her in the jacuzzi," he says, unsmiling. "Bloody hell, nothing is sacred when it comes to her. I dread to think what she tells people about me. I'm pretty sure what she doesn't know, she makes up." I snort loudly, then snap my hand over my mouth and nose. "It's ok," he says with a smirk, "I've seen and touched the dirtiest parts of you. We're past the embarrassing stage. I want to hear every disgusting sound you can make." My breath catches in my throat. "Thinking about it...causing you to squeak could be a lot of fun." He stares at me, and his eyes darken. "The next time we're in bed, I want to see what tune I can play."

"Let's go," I whisper, breathless.

"Are you that keen to get to the beach?" he asks, running his fingers over my shoulder and down my arm.

"If we don't go now, I doubt we will." He laughs softly.

"I think you're right." He releases me and walks over to pick up the bag and cooler. "Come on then, let's go catch some rays."

Now, we're back at the same secluded beach as before. Once again, a few couples are scattered around except for one larger group down near the water's edge. They all look a similar age to Max. The boys are playing volleyball whilst the girls sit chatting, examining a magazine spread out in front of them. What looks like an old-fashioned child's karaoke machine is playing modern music beside them. They all look happy and relaxed.

"Is here all right?" Max asks, seeing the direction of my gaze.

"Of course," I reply with a smile. "Do you want a drink?" He nods, and I pull two beers from the box. We sit down on the towels he's meticulously spread out, and immediately sand pour over the edges. "Sand gets everywhere," I mutter.

"Don't worry. I'll help you get clean later." He drops a kiss on my shoulder causing butterflies to reappear in my belly. Whenever I'm around him, I'm either constantly aroused, excited or both. "Your room has a bigger bath than mine," he says, darkly. "I'm sure we will be able to put it to good use."

Unable to respond, I gaze at him. Fuck, he's beautiful as well as everything we're told a gentleman should be. What he's doing here sitting with me, I don't know. I open my mouth to answer him, and Spanish music suddenly cuts through the air. We turn in unison in its direction to see the larger group standing. The men hold out their hands to the woman beside them, then they start to dance. Four couples, all in swimwear, Latin dancing on the warm sand. A smile splits my face. It is possibly the most beautiful and romantic moment I've ever seen. Their hips all swing to the music, each person laughing, enjoying the fun.

I look up and Max is standing above me, his hand stretched out in front of him. "Do you want to dance?" he asks, and I gawk at him. "Come here, Beautiful. Instead of watching the fun, we should join in."

"Max, I don't..." I start to protest but he ignores me. Taking both my hands, he pulls me to my feet and walks me down to where the group are. They smile at us. I try to copy what is obviously a known routine. Max falls into step beside them; he knows the moves. I follow along the best I can. Every so often his arms snake around my waist and he pulls me to him, placing a kiss on my lips. As the song draws to a close, he holds me close, and his mouth takes mine. Hungry. Needy. "I can't wait until our bath later," he whispers.

Another song begins and the group moves again. We dance for what seems like hours with the warm sand between our toes. Finally, exhausted, we sit and chat with the strangers we danced with. It turns out they are four couples who live in the local area. They come here as this beach is unknown to most tourists. Most speak a small amount of English, but the majority of the conversation is in Spanish. I watch on as Max listens to what is being said and translates for me. "I didn't know you spoke fluently?" I say, bumping his shoulder with mine.

"I'm not exactly fluent," he replies, "but I know enough to get by. It's easier after a few of these." He holds up his beer and toasts the man across the circle. What an amazing afternoon, spent with the most incredible man. As the sun starts its decent, we wish everyone goodbye and begin to pack our things away. "Shit," he snaps, looking at his watch. "I'm meant to start work in ten minutes. I completely forgot." He turns to me, lifting me up and swinging me around. "You're one hell of a fucking distraction." We throw the last of our stuff in our bags and take off at a run towards the hotel.

Once there, Max takes the stairs two at a time in front of me. The beach bag over his shoulder, the cooler box dumped at the front door. I stand on the bottom step and watch his taut behind as he climbs. "Stop ogling me, Beautiful," he calls over his shoulder.

I snigger and shout back, "Don't be so cute then." I turn around and Crystal is standing behind me, an ear-to-ear smile on her face. She raises her eyebrows giving me a knowing look.

"Good day?" she asks.

"The best," I say. I know my face is lit up like a Christmas tree. I'm so fucking happy. Happier than I've been in years. And, it's all because I took a risk and came here, then I met him. He's the remedy I've been needing.

"Time for a drink?" she asks.

"Sure, I've nowhere to be."

"Or no one to be under," she replies, then cackles to herself. I scowl at her, and she waves me away. "Don't be such a prude. You're the one banging the pool boy." I blink at her, momentarily taken aback. "I would too if I was given the chance. Us ladies must take our kicks when we can. None of us are getting any younger." She wanders off in the direction of the bar. I follow behind, slightly deflated by her teasing.

Max appears ten minutes later, freshly showered and changed. He runs into the room then jumps over the countertop in one swift move. Susan glares at him, then looks at her watch. "You're late," she mutters, tapping at her wrist. "What's your excuse?"

"Too much fun in the sun with the best distraction on the planet," he replies, smoothly. They all turn to look at me, and I feel myself turning as red as a beetroot.

"Bloody *Romeo and Juliet*," she mumbles whilst walking around to the other side of the bar and clambering up on a stool. "I feel like we're living in a rom-com movie. All we need are bloody floating hearts surrounding the two of you."

"Don't be such an old goat," Max says with a cheeky smile. "You were young once Aunt Susan. Surely you remember that feeling. That first rush of love." *Love*. I gape at him slightly. This man takes my breath away with his honesty. He opens his mouth and whatever endearing comment he was thinking pops out. It's both heart-warming and slightly terrifying. Susan grunts but doesn't reply. He places a freshly poured glass of white wine in front of her, and I visibly see her spirits lift.

There isn't any planned entertainment in the bar tonight. Ladies start to appear, order their drinks then peel off in small groups to chat. Crystal and I move to a sofa in the corner. We sit talking about nothing in particular. She asks about my job and my daughter. She is mid-sentence when she stops speaking, her focus fixed on the entrance. Her mouth drops open fractionally, and I turn to see what she's looking at.

Lacy stands in the doorway, dressed to impress. She's wearing a short denim skirt, that if she bends over you most definitely will see what she's had for breakfast. It's paired with an almost see-through vest top and underneath is a bright red bra. I look from her to Max who is standing behind the counter serving drinks, completely oblivious to the vision that has just arrived. He is the only man here. There can only be one reason she came here dressed like that – him.

Placing one red high-heeled foot in front of the other, she struts across the floor directly to the bar, her eyes fixed on the prize. Max glances up and pauses when he sees her. I watch on, horrified but mesmerised. Without a word, she climbs up on a stool and crosses one sexy leg over the other then flashes him a megawatt smile. "I think you have competition," Crystal whispers in my ear. "Little chica has brought out the big guns."

"Shhh…" I hiss. We're close enough to hear what's being said if I concentrate. Max's focus moves to me, then returns to Lacy when she starts to speak.

"Hi," she purrs. "A small beer, please." He nods but doesn't respond, moving to get a bottle out of the fridge, popping the cap and handing it to her. "I'm sorry," she says, "about all the messages." Messages? He never said anything to me, but he has no reason to. I wonder what they were about. My confidence wavers as I listen on.

"It's all right. It's understandable you were pissed off. I'm sorry, Lacy. I feel terrible about everything."

She waves away his apology. "So, did you get a second date?" she asks. He looks momentarily taken aback. I see him pause to collect his thoughts.

"Yes, I've been seeing someone," he says, and her eyes narrow.

"Who?" she snaps.

"It's not really any of your concern."

"You told me you weren't looking for a relationship. What's so special about her? Why does she get to date you and I don't."

"Because it's different. It feels different, and I want to see where it goes." He reaches for her hand sitting on bar. She snaps it away. "I am sorry. I never wanted to hurt you."

"Well, you fucking have," she snarls. She lifts the bottle of beer to her lips, drains it then jumps off the stool and stomps out the room, calling over her shoulder, "She can bloody have you. You asshole."

Chapter Eleven

Linda

Four weeks of sleeping with Max. Four weeks of having him worship my body every night. And they have been the best four fucking weeks of my life. We never talk about the future or anything serious. We laugh, we love, and we adore each other every damn day.

It's Monday. I love Monday mornings. It's the start of his day off. For the past three, we haven't even left his room, stocking up on drinks and snacks the day before. We lazed around in our birthday suits, watched old movies, and kissed like teenagers.

He is snoring softly beside me, the covers pooling around his waist. The familiar snake tattoo wraps around his leg. I asked why he had a snake on his leg, and he told me it was a bet from a boy's holiday in his late teens. At that time, his girlfriend had the nickname Snake, and his mates dared him to have one tattooed on his body. The tattoo artist had convinced him a huge boa wrapping around his leg would be much cooler than a puny grass snake on his ankle. Upon his return from holiday, she dumped him. The sentimental tattoo became nothing more than a holiday dare. I laughed so hard at the story that my wine shot out of my nose.

Bright-green eyes blink open in the morning sunshine, and he gives me a sexy smile. "Morning, Beautiful," he murmurs.

Propped up on pillows, reading my book, I glance down at him.

"What do you want to do today?" he asks. "I wonder if I could convince you to spend a fourth consecutive Monday in bed." He reaches up and runs a finger over my jaw then places it on my lips. I kiss it gently before taking it in my mouth, sucking deeply. He groans. "God, I would like to put something else in there, but I'm starving," he says, then adds, "for food."

Sitting up, he kisses me, invading my mouth with his tongue. His tongue dances with mine, and he massages my breast with one hand, leaning against the wall with the other. His body pushes me back into the headboard. Suddenly, he releases me and leaps from the bed, grabbing clothes from the floor and pulling them on. I could sit here all day and watch that lythe, athletic body move around the room. Sometimes, I must pinch myself to know that this is real.

"What's the rush?" I purr. "Can you not eat me first?"

Dark eyes meet mine. He sniggers before resuming looking for his shoes. "Let's go eat. You're wearing me out, woman." I pout at him. "If you told me banging an old bird would be this much fun, I would have tried it years ago." The pillow connects with his head. He snorts then grabs the bed covers and pulls them from my body. He raises an eyebrow. "Love bites at your age, Linda? You'll be getting a reputation."

"Love bites?" I shout. Jumping from the bed and running to the bathroom, I stare in the bathroom mirror, and a huge purple welt on my neck glares back at me. "Max! You gave me a hickey. How the hell am I meant to cover that up? It's huge! I'm like a fucking errant schoolgirl."

He appears behind me and wraps his arms around my waist, placing his chin on my shoulder. "Sorry," he whispers in my ear as we both look at the offending mark. "I can't control myself around you. You turn me into a sex maniac. Did you get a lot of hickeys at school? I bet you were one of the dirty girls. Did you meet boys behind the bike shed?"

"Asshole," I mutter. "You owe me twenty orgasms in compensation." I try to maintain an air of annoyance but fail miserably. "Make it thirty orgasms and dinner. Plus, I won't suck your dick until I'm fully compensated."

"Deal," he says. "Now, get ready, Beautiful. We're going for food." He slaps me on the ass hard before turning and leaving the bathroom. I smile goofily in the mirror. How the hell is this my life? I bloody won the fuck buddy bingo when he landed in my bed.

After breakfast at Margo's and a wander through the old streets, we head back to the hotel. Holding his hand feels so natural now. It's hard to believe a few weeks ago I was nervous to be seen with him.

It had all been blown out in the open the night Lacy turned up at the bar. Max had finished his shift and we were leaving when she reappeared. Her eyes popped wide open when she clocked his arm around my shoulders. "Her," she stammered. "You chose that over me?" His eyes narrowed.

"Stop talking, Lacy," he warned.

"I was hurt," she growled, "but now I'm fucking offended. She's so old." She turned on her heel and stalked off out the hotel. Concerned eyes turned to me.

"I'm sorry you had to hear that," he said, quietly. "I..." He trailed off.

"She's right, you know," I told him. "This, what we're doing, people won't understand."

"They don't need to, Beautiful." He linked his fingers through mine. "Come on, I promised you a bath." He dragged me upstairs and we stopped outside my door. I opened it, and we walked in. "Get undressed," he said, "I'll run it." He disappeared into the bathroom, and I heard the taps turn on, the flow of running water cut through the silence.

I walked over to the mirror hanging on the wall, staring at my reflection. I looked so much older than him. He appeared in front of me, blocking my view. "Clothes off." His strong fingers moved to the hem of my dress. In one smooth move, he lifted it up over my head then slid my panties down my legs. He was already naked. "Bath, now. Stop thinking about what she said. It means nothing."

He climbed in first then signalled for me to sit in front of him between his legs. The water was warm and filled with sweet smelling bubbles. He took a sponge from the shelf dipping it in the water, then squeezed it over my chest. I sighed softly as the suds skimmed down my body. "This is my favourite task of the day, getting you clean," he whispered. Slowly, he ran the sponge over every part of me, first what he could reach wrapped around me then moving me forward to clean my back.

"My turn," I told him, picking up the sponge from between his fingers and turning on all fours to face him. I sat back on my knees and started to wipe his chest. He gave me a look that would melt my panties if I had any on. "Bloody hell, you're hot," I muttered. He took my hand and placed it on his cock, which was standing proud, the tip grazing the surface of the water.

"Ride me, Beautiful. Climb on top, sink me inside you and ride me," he said, darkly. I didn't need to be prompted twice. I straddled him, lining myself up and lowering down onto him. He slid in easily, filling me up. He lay back, a satisfied smile on his lips. "Now go," he mouthed, "I'm going to sit here and enjoy the show."

Crystal is sitting in the social room and calls us over, snapping me from my recollection. "Do you want to join me for a drink?" she asks. The ladies at the hotel, especially Crystal, like to chat about my relationship. I never need to say much. They make up all their own stories about what Max and I get up to. It makes me smile as they live vicariously through me.

"Sure," I reply. Max squeezes my hand, and I turn to him. He pops a kiss on my forehead.

"I'm going to head to the spa for an hour. I have a few things to do before tomorrow. You ladies enjoy a drink and a chat. Don't spend the whole time talking about me." He winks and saunters out of the room.

"You're all we fucking talk about, Maxy," Crystal calls behind him. She turns back to me. "I still can't believe you're banging him," she says. "Now that the others aren't here, I want all the gory details. Positions, timescales, and an in-depth description of his dick. I bet he's magnificent." I flush bright red, and she giggles. "Come on, Linda. It's not fair you're the one having all the fun. Make an old lady happy, will you?"

"My lips are sealed," I say as firmly as I can. She sticks out her lip then shrugs her shoulders.

"Well, you can buy the drinks," she mutters.

The following morning, a knock at my bedroom door wakes me from my slumber. Max is still sleeping, as usual. He never wakes before the alarm at 7:30 a.m. Thinking I must have imagined the noise; I cuddle down under the covers. The banging sounds again, this time louder. Swinging my legs out of bed, I stand and pull on my silk dressing gown before walking over to the door. Turning the key but not releasing the chain, I open it slowly until the chain stops it. Peeking out, my daughter is on the other side. Without thinking, I quickly release the door and open it wide.

She stands in the hall, her dark hair messy and unruly around her face. Tears are streaming down her cheeks. Her clothes are dirty and hang off her slight frame.

"Marina?" I ask. "What happened?" She runs into my arms and holds on tight. Huge sobs escape from her body. "Marina?" I ask again. "Are you hurt? Tell me, baby, what's going on?"

"He left me!" she shrieks. "In the middle of Rio De Janeiro! We were staying in a crappy hotel, and he fucked off. Took all our cash and my phone."

"Why didn't you call me? Could you not borrow someone's phone?" I ask, stunned. "I would have come for you." She shakes her head sadly.

"No, Mum, I didn't want you having to come and save me again. It's embarrassing."

"You listen to me, young lady," I scold, "I'm your mother, and whenever you need me, you bloody call me."

Her eyes lift and stare over my shoulder at something behind me. My heart sinks. Max. Turning around, I see he has woken up and climbed out of bed. The sheet is wrapped around his waist. Marina looks from him to me and back again.

"Marina," I say. "This is my friend, Max."

"Your friend?" she splutters, her jaw dropping open. "And do friends…" – she holds her fingers up to make speech marks – "…normally sleep with you in your bed naked? What the fuck is going on, Mum? He's young enough to be your son!"

"Marina, calm down," I whisper. "I know this is a shock."

"Not quite young enough to be her son," Max says. His voice is calm, and he smiles sweetly at my daughter who looks as if she's about to explode. "I think it would be best if I go back to my room." He walks across to me, still only covered by the sheet, kisses my cheek, and saunters out of the door.

"Mum!" Marina screeches again. "Is this hotel some kind of whore house? Is he being paid to sleep with you?"

"What?" I growl at her, my eyes wide with fury. "How bloody dare you! Why can't a good-looking young man be interested in me? I'm not quite ready to be burned to a crisp yet, Marina." Her eyebrows draw together, and she gives me a dirty look. "Max and I are having fun together. He makes me happy. It's not serious, and we enjoy each other's company. What's wrong with that?"

"Look at him!" she squeals. "He's fucking gorgeous! Men like that only sleep with older women for their money. He's probably after my inheritance." I see red and slap her hard across the face. Tears roll down my cheeks as I look at the younger version of myself having a temper tantrum in front of me.

"What happened to your earlier advice?" I bark. "Live life now, Mum. If a man offers you some action, enjoy it, Mum. Does that only stand if he's old bald and past it?"

"Of course not!" she snaps, "but he's…"

"He's what Marina? Too good looking for me?"

She sighs and moves to sit on the bed then jumps up quickly. "Urgh, you've been fucking on this bed." She screws her nose up, and I giggle. "I'll sleep on the sofa. The thought of you and him. It's gross."

Gee thanks.

"Marina, first, I used to sleep with your father in our bed, and you were happy to cuddle up on that," I say and she flinches. "Second, you're staying?"

"Yes, is that all right? Just for a few days until I decide what to do." I look at my clueless, wayless daughter, and my heart melts. She needs her mum, and here I am. Toyboys and sexy shenanigans will just have to fall into line below the needs of my child.

"Of course, darling," I tell her. Walking over and taking her in my arms again, I press my lips to her forehead. "Stay as long as you want. I will clear it with the management."

Chapter Twelve

Max

"Mate!" I bark. "Stop bloody laughing! It's not fucking funny!" My old friend's laughter echoes down the phone line. I can imagine him sitting on his chair, beer in hand, with tears streaming down his face. "Jace," I say, "please stop enjoying my misfortune. It's getting old." He takes a breath then chuckles, trying to control his outburst but struggling to.

"So, let me get this right..." he says. "You're in bed with your MILF."

I groan. Jace cannot get over me sleeping with a much older woman. He is fascinated and keeps asking for a photo. I've refused.

"Don't call her that," I mumble.

"Okay, okay. I will use her full title," he teases. "You're in bed with your *Mother I Would Like to Fuck*. MILF sounds sexier, by the way."

Telling him any of this was a mistake. I need to learn to keep my mouth shut.

Jace continues, "You're both just waking up after a hard night of banging. There is a knock at the door, and her daughter arrives."

"Yes," I say. He sniggers.

"The daughter is the spitting image of her mother but younger. Hotter?"

"I didn't say that." I glare at the phone. Now, he's putting fucking words in my mouth. He ignores my growl down the line and continues.

"In my imagination, she is," he says. "Did she look angry or mad that she was missing out?" He hisses through his teeth, his fantasy taking shape. "A mother and daughter sandwich. Think about it. What a story to tell the grandkids!"

"She was angry, mate, not gagging to join in." He's pissing me off now.

He chuckles. "She catches you both at it, is pissed off because you're a lot younger than mummy and has a hissy fit. You proceed to get up, bollock naked, wrap a sheet around yourself, then walk out of the room, but not before making a public display of affection to the old woman you're bonking."

Deciding not to argue with him, I say, "Sounds about right."

His voice softens. "Pal, I know Bex broke your heart but is this rebound relationship not a bit extreme?" Jace may be an asshole, but he knows me, probably better than I know myself. "Linda would never be someone you looked at before. And now, there is a daughter who is closer to your age on the scene. What happened to a summer away from it all? A summer of fun. Lacy? What happened to her?" he asks.

"It's not a relationship," I state, not even convincing myself. "We are just enjoying each other's company. Lacy is pissed off, but she'll get over it."

"You've spent multiple summers in Spain with Lacy, and you have never spoken about her in the way you do Linda." He pauses. "You're spending every night together. What happens in four weeks when you both go back to London? What then?"

Not knowing what to say, I say nothing. Going back to London is not something I'm looking forward to. Being without Linda isn't worth thinking about. Neither of us have mentioned what will happen once summer finishes, once the everyday routine returns to our lives. If she had lived hundreds of miles from me, a line could have been drawn as soon as we step on the plane home, but she only lives forty minutes away. Could our romance continue on home soil? My head says to be realistic. My heart hopes not to be.

"Got to go," I tell my friend. "Are you still planning on visiting?"

"Next week," he says. "Have you organised a few days off?"

"Sure have. Great, mate. Let me know when to expect you."

As I go to cut the call, he says, "Max, protect yourself, yeah? Don't put everything on the line for this woman. I don't want to see you hurt again, pal."

I hang up.

Tuesday evenings are always quiet in the bar. There is bingo on down the street at a café that offers a free wine with every playing card bought. Our ladies don't start rolling in until nearer to ten, high on alcohol and low on funds. Crouching down, I empty the under-counter fridges of all stock before cleaning the glass inside and out. The bell sounds from above me; someone is looking for service. Standing, I come face to face with the young version of Linda. She is on her own and gives me a shy smile.

"Hello," she says and holds her hand out. "I'm sorry about yesterday. It was a shock seeing you with my mum." She jumps up onto the barstool across the counter. "I'm completely embarrassed with my behaviour." She bats her eyelashes innocently.

"That's all right. It must have been strange for you." My eyes scan the room for her mother, but she's nowhere to be seen. "Is your mum with you?" She shakes her head. "Oh, okay," I mumble. "Can I get you something to drink?"

"A vodka with lime, please. Mum said she might pop down later. To be honest, I think she is a bit uncomfortable about yesterday." She giggles. "It's sweet, though." I frown at her. "Well, you're here keeping old women happy. Complimenting them. It's impressive the lengths you go to."

"I'm not sure I understand what you mean," I say, pouring the vodka over the ice cubes. "Sleeping with your mum isn't part of my job description." I slide the drink across to her, and she reaches for it, touching my hand in the process. It makes me uneasy.

"Why else would you?" she asks. My brain explodes, and I blink at her, stunned. "Let's be realistic, Max. It's not as if you can find her attractive."

"I can assure you; I find your mum very attractive. It's not a pity fuck," I snap before dropping back behind the counter to get on with my task. A few minutes later, the bell sounds again. As I rise, I pray she's left the room and someone else has materialised from thin air.

"Can I have another drink?" she purrs. "A cocktail. Surprise me." Her eyes sparkle with mischief. She's enjoying making me uncomfortable. After an hour of eyelashes being fluttered, she leaves to go back to her room. Linda is nowhere to be seen; I haven't heard from her since yesterday morning. After our interruption, I had gone back to my room and texted her. She didn't reply. I assumed she was busy with her daughter. More than twenty-four hours on, there's still radio silence.

It's pushing half past ten, and a gaggle of women, back from bingo, appear at the bar. I hear them before I see them. Hopefully, with some company, my night will pass a bit quicker. My phone has lain silent on the bar for hours. Crystal marches in with a trail of women behind her.

"Maxy!" she shouts. "Open the cava! We won!" Her smile reaches her ears. She's hyper from alcohol and success.

"Well done, ladies," I say, getting two bottles of pink fizz and lining up a row of champagne flutes. I flick the music to upbeat pop, turn up the volume, and they dance around the room to the beat as I pass over their celebratory drinks. Crystal's drink sploshes over the edges of her glass as she wobbles from foot to foot.

Linda appears at the bar from behind the crowd. She keeps her eyes fixed on the counter, only glancing up to speak. "Two white wines, please, Max," she says. Her demeanour is distant. I serve her the drinks, and she turns, walking from the bar without looking back. Watching her makes my heart tighten. She barely gave me a moment of her time.

The hours pass, and the ladies peel off to bed. Each one more pissed than the last. My mood lowered as the night progressed. Crystal wanders over, her face concerned. "Everything all right, Maxy?" I shrug my shoulders. "You and Linda had a fight?"

"Not that I'm aware of," I mutter. She tuts then scuttles off in the direction of her room. After deciding that going to bed alone again tonight for no apparent reason isn't something I want to do, I walk over to where Linda and Marina are sitting. They are on leather chairs, facing each other over a small table.

"Linda," I say, and she looks up. "Can I speak to you for a moment?"

"Not tonight, Max," she responds, firmly. "I'll talk to you tomorrow."

"Don't go out of your way," I snarl. "Whenever it suits you, tell me what the fucking issue is. I'll wait over there like a good boy."

She scowls as her lips tighten to a thin line. "I'll talk to you tomorrow," she repeats. She sounds like my mother. "Now, please let me speak to my daughter alone."

"Fine!" I snap. "The bar's closed."

After marching back to the bar, I finish tidying and leave the room without looking in her direction again. My mind is racing with possibilities of what has gone wrong. Yesterday morning was awkward but not a disaster. I thought we would laugh it off. As I climb the stairs to my room, my mood lowers further. Four weeks of fun ended, and I don't even know why.

When I push open my bedroom door, a beer bottle greets me on the other side. Jace is holding it towards me with a huge grin on his face. "Surprise!" he yells. "Freshen up, we're going out!" He grabs me into a hug, and beer splashes onto my T-shirt.

"Jace," I say, startled. "When did you arrive?"

"An hour ago." He smiles. "After talking to you today, I thought you needed a pick-me-up, so here I am."

I laugh. My old friend is always the life of the party. He's short and stocky with more hair on his chin than on his head. The shirt he's wearing is decorated with tropical flowers in garish colours teamed with pink board shorts. His stubby toes poke through leather sandals.

"Let me get changed, then we can head into town." Slipping out of my T-shirt, I find a fresh one in the wardrobe. I ruffle my hair, and I am ready to go. We wander down the stairs then out the front door, seeing no one. There is a bar a few doors down that has live music playing into the early hours. In the past, I've stumbled back to the hotel at five in the morning after being there.

The place is packed, and we find a table in the corner. Jace heads to the bar to order some beers. After a few jars down, we are chatting like old times. The distraction from Linda is welcome.

Lacy appears from nowhere and drops into the chair beside me. "Hey," she says, a sad smile on her lips. "How are you?"

"I'm okay," I answer, not inviting any further discussion.

Before she can speak again, Jace skips over and pulls her off the seat into a bear hug. She giggles at his antics.

"Hello, gorgeous," he says with a wink, then holds her at arm's length and runs his eyes over her body. "Looking incredible as always. What do you want to drink?"

She flushes pink. "A vodka and coke, please. When did *you* arrive? I didn't know you were coming to visit."

"Today!" he shouts over the music. "A lad's night out was required, so here I am." He holds his arms wide and turns three-hundred-and-sixty degrees, then walks back to the bar.

Lacy plonks herself back down beside me, placing her hand on my forearm. Her cautious eyes meet mine. "Max," she says, "I'm sorry for springing the relationship thing on you. I realise it must have been a shock, but now you and that woman are finished, perhaps we could..." She trails off when she sees my expression.

"Who told you that?" I whisper angrily. Her face drops at my tone.

"U-Um," she stutters. "Her daughter, Maria, is it?"

"Marina," I hiss, correcting her. "When the fuck did she tell you that?"

"This afternoon. I met her when I was picking up equipment at the hotel. She said her mum had come to her senses and realised you were far too young for her. According to Marina, her mum's a bit of a laughingstock with her family. Marina had been concerned and phoned her uncle to tell him about you and what her mum was getting up to over here. He called her mum and talked some sense into her. She was talking about bringing her flight home forward."

My mouth drops open, and Lacy smiles. "It's okay," she says. "I'm here." She places her hand on my arm again and rubs it slowly. She leans forward to kiss me, and I pull back.

"Lacy!" I snap. "I'm not interested." Standing abruptly, my chair falls to the floor. Jace appears back at the table as I'm leaving.

"What's up?" he asks.

"I need to go." He widens his eyes, signalling for more information. "There is shit going on at the hotel, and I need to sort it out. You stay with her," I say, gesturing at Lacy. She looks furious. Without looking back, I exit the bar to go and find out what the hell is going on.

Chapter Thirteen

Linda

My suitcase is lying open on my bed, nothing packed in it. Opening my wardrobe, I stare at the dresses and swimwear hanging up. Perhaps I should just leave it all here. The likelihood of me being abroad any time soon is slight. The last four weeks have been fun but ridiculous. Who was I to think I could have a relationship with someone like him? I must be a pathetic case for him to sleep with me out of pity.

"Mum!" Marina shouts from the bathroom. "Are you nearly packed? I can't believe you booked a flight for five in the morning. This hour doesn't suit me."

"It was the first flight I could get," I say. "You said you wanted out of here."

After speaking to my brother this morning, my confidence is at an all-time low. Marina has been reporting all my escapades to him.

"Linda," he said, "I know the last year has been rough. That bastard walking out on you for someone else must sting, but sleeping around isn't going to fix the pain. Is it true this guy is more than ten years younger than you?" I mumbled into the phone. He already knew how old Max was. He sighed, disappointed. "Sis, come home. We're worried about you."

"You don't have to be," I protested. "I'm fine. It was just a little fun in the sun."

"Linda, middle-aged divorcées get bad reputations by fooling around with young men. What would everyone think about you sucking the face off a toyboy?" Tears sprung to my eyes. "Come home, then we can get you back to normal. There is a flight in the morning."

Normal? What's normal? Being alone in my house. Exercising three times a day so I don't sit down to stew on my own thoughts. Going to work every morning, doing my job, and coming home again. Cooking a microwave meal for one. Walking out my front door and seeing my ex-husband with another woman. That's been my normal for the past year. It's been hell.

"Mum," Marina's voice interrupts my recollections. "You've nothing in your suitcase. We need to leave soon."

Making a snap decision, I say, "I'm not going." She stops dead in her tracks. "I want to stay until the end of summer."

"What?" she shrieks. "No, you're coming home. No arguments. I'm not leaving you here to make a fool of yourself. Stop being an idiot and get your case packed."

I look at my daughter, and my heart sinks. Even though I love her, right now, I don't like her. She's spoiled, opinionated, and demanding.

"Marina," I say, trying to stay calm. "This isn't your decision to make. I came to Spain to have some fun, to be a different person than I am at home. That's what I've been doing. It's important to me that I finish what I set out to do: eight weeks of freedom before I move on with my life as a single woman."

"He hit on me, you know?" she spits. She widens her eyes and nods her head to accentuate her point.

"Who?" I ask.

"Max, your plaything," she responds. "In the bar. I was having a few drinks while you went to bingo. He was trying it on, asking if I wanted to go out sometime."

The revelation hurts. Perhaps he is a player, hitting on various women over the summer. My resolve to stay wavers, but I stand my ground.

"No, I'm staying. Not for Max but for me." Lifting the suitcase off the bed, I close it and place it back in the wardrobe. Marina looks at me furiously then grabs her suitcase and storms from the room, slamming the door behind her.

Standing at the window, I see the taxi arrive, and she climbs in. It drives off down the road, and I watch it for as long as I can see the taillights. Once they're gone, I exhale in relief.

There is a subtle knock at the door. Someone must have come to check I am all right. Our argument wasn't quiet; the whole hotel probably heard the screaming. Walking over, I open the door to Max standing in the hall. He gives me a soft smile.

"Can we talk now?" he asks. I nod, opening the door further to let him in. He wanders around the room, not looking at me. "What happened? I don't understand."

I take a breath. "It's been a rough few days. Marina arriving unexpectedly was a shock. She struggled to accept that I was seeing someone, especially someone your age." My eyes drop between my feet. I wonder what he's doing here. With the way I treated him for the past twenty-four hours, he shouldn't want to speak to me. "I'm sorry. I've behaved poorly."

"Were you going to leave without telling me?" he asks sadly. "I only found out because of gossip. We haven't known each other long, but the past four weeks have been amazing for me. I thought they had been for you, too."

Standing in my room, he looks forlorn; all I want to do is take him in my arms and make him feel better, but Marina's words come back to me like a sledgehammer. He hit on her. Or did he? I need to know. My daughter can be dramatic to get her own way. Two summers, two road trips, and two boyfriends broken up with mid-vacation speaks volumes.

"Can I ask you something?" I ask, and he shrugs. "Last night, did you ask my daughter out?"

"What?" he splutters, his eyebrows drawn together. "No! Why on earth would I do that? Is that what she said?" He shakes his head and rubs his forehead in frustration. "I wouldn't do that. It's not my style. She was flirting with me."

I believe him. His hurt expression is clear.

"When do you leave?" he asks. My eyebrows shoot up, surprised by his question. I assumed he overheard the fight earlier.

"I'm not," I say. "I want to finish what I started. My plan was to stay for eight weeks, and I'm going to see it through."

My mind races. What will I do? Forget the past two days happened and try to pick up where we left off or spend the next four weeks with the other women and resign Max to my memories. I don't believe Marina's story. My gut is telling me it's a lie, and that saddens me. My daughter manipulated the situation to get her own way. Deciding that life is too short, I take the plunge. "Do you want to experience the next four weeks with me? Will we be each other's summer fumble?"

He smiles, and it's breathtaking. Then, his eyes darken as they hold mine. "I thought you would never ask," he says. Moments later, I'm in his arms, and he is lowering me down onto the bed, climbing up beside me. "Don't do that to me again. Don't ghost me. If there is a problem, speak to me. If this is only happening for summer, don't take a moment away from me."

"If?" I say, confused. "This can only be a holiday romance. You need a woman to have a life with, a young woman with her whole life ahead of her. Let's enjoy what we have now and not think about the future."

"Agreed," he whispers, closing his eyes and lowering his mouth to mine. We lie and kiss, slowly, taking our time to enjoy every part of each other. His hand goes to the tie on my red wrap-dress, he masterfully undoes the knot, and it falls open, exposing my breasts. He smiles against my mouth, snuggling closer, his cock hard against my hip bone. "Two days without you in my bed is too long, Beautiful. I need you."

My hands go to his face, and my thumbs stroke his cheeks as tears form in my eyes. Our tongues dance together, enjoying their reunion.

He plays with my nipples, twisting and teasing until they both stand to attention. Then, he trails his fingers down my stomach, stopping north of my pussy. She's throbbing with want. After an eternity, his hand moves lower, his fingers massaging the outside of my panties.

"Max," I moan. "Please." He lifts the edge of my underwear with one finger and runs it over my lips before sliding it inside.

"Wet," he murmurs in my ear. "Does my girl want some cock?"

I groan at his words. Sitting up, he lifts his T-shirt over his head before removing his shorts. His erection is straining against his boxers. Taking my hands, he pulls me up to sit before sliding my already open dress off my shoulders.

"Turn over on all fours," he orders. He leans over and lifts the silver packet he sat on the bedside table earlier. I place my hand on his, and he gives me a curious look.

"It's ok, we don't need that," I tell him. "My time has passed now. You can have me au natural." His eyes light up at the news.

"Au natural is my favourite flavour," he growls, "now do as I told you. On all fours." He slaps my backside, and I quickly change position.

I kneel in front of him in only a small black thong. He spreads my legs with his knee. As I balance on my hands and knees, my breasts hang loose and free. Max moves to kneel behind me, taking my hips in his hands and resting his hard length against my butt cheeks. He massages my behind then slides two fingers inside my pussy. Pumping slowly, my wetness intensifies.

He leans forward, drops a kiss on the back of my neck, then trails his tongue down my spine. I sense him removing his boxers, and, with one finger, he moves my underwear to the side. "Lean down, ass in the air," he instructs, and I do as I'm told.

The tip of his cock nudges my opening then slides in with no mercy, filling me up. He stills inside me before he starts to move, rocking his hips slowly and holding me hard against him. A hiss escapes from between his teeth as sensation builds between us. I spread my legs further, dropping my hips to increase the friction. He moves faster and grabs at my breasts with one hand, surrounding me in every way he can.

He's pumping hard now, lost in the moment. Knowing my peak is near, I clench, and my orgasm spirals from me. He shoots inside me as he climaxes. After we lie together in a tangle of sweaty limbs with dirty great smiles on our faces. He is twisting a strand of my hair between his fingers, lost in thought.

"What are you thinking about?" I ask him. He glances at me and smiles sexily. Then, he shakes his head. "Tell me," I prompt. "You're a million miles away."

"I was thinking what a shame it would have been if you had left during the night." He kisses my forehead. "What made you want to go?"

I swallow nervously. "My brother," I answer, honestly. "He called yesterday and lectured me on how I was embarrassing the family with my behaviour. Marina was reporting to him about what I had been up to. My brother is very conservative. Me being divorced is enough of a stain on the family, never mind running away to Spain and shagging you." I grin, and he laughs. "But I figured it would be much more fun bouncing on your dick than sitting at home in my living room alone."

Max wraps his arms around me. "It's hard when life doesn't turn out the way you expect it to," he says. "People let you down or don't feel the same as you, and you're expected to just suck it up."

"You're talking from experience."

He gives me a sad smile. "There is a girl. I've known her since school, but she doesn't feel the same way as me. She's one of my best friends, but she's in love with someone else. And he's married. He's broken her heart so many times. It kills me to see her shattered and unable to fix it. It sucks."

I nod in agreement. "My husband ran off with our neighbour. They live four doors down from me," I tell him. "Worst part of it is, she's got no teeth and wears leopard print daily, *everywhere*." We both laugh then fall quiet.

Less than four weeks together—that's what we have now—before we must go home and face our demons. No matter how magnetised our bodies are to each other, how they yearn for each other. We both know our relationship has no future. Hopefully, we will both be ready to move on from our pasts and each other once the plane leaves the Spanish tarmac.

Chapter Fourteen

Max

These are our final days together. In two days, Linda is jetting back to London. I'm staying on for another few days to help my aunt prepare for the partial winter shutdown. The hotel remains open all year round; there are always ladies looking to escape from their mundane lives. My aunt enjoys the company during the winter months, too. We are carrying out a stock take in the bar and deep cleaning.

"Are you looking forward to going home?" my aunt asks. Focused on my task of emptying the shelves, I grunt noncommittally. "Do you and Linda have plans to see each other? She doesn't live that far away."

I pause and turn to face her. She is sitting on a dining chair, folding napkins into a box. She doesn't look at me, her eyes staying fixed on the square of material in front of her.

"We haven't discussed it," I say. She nods and murmurs something under her breath. "What was that?" I ask.

"Nothing. It's none of my business."

"You're right about that," I mutter. "But you said something. What was it? I may as well know your opinion on my love life." She glances over, and I wave my hand at her, signalling for her to get on with it.

"I've never seen you so happy," she simply says. "Come and sit down." She pats the space on the table directly opposite her. "And bring two beers with you."

"It's ten in the morning," I protest.

"When in Spain, do as the Spaniards do," she says and winks. After retrieving two beers from the fridge, I plonk myself down next to her.

"You've been coming here a long time. In some ways, I see you as my son, not my nephew. There have been girls over the years here and back at home. You've had your heart broken by the girl who you thought was the one." I listen to her, hanging off each word. My aunt doesn't dole out advice unnecessarily. "Linda may not be the person you think you should be with, but she is the person who makes you smile. I watch you together, and I wish I had experienced a relationship as good."

"She told me in the beginning that this was only for the summer," I whisper. "I doubt she has changed her mind."

"Perhaps not. Perhaps you were a summer fling to get over her destructed life." She shrugs. "But the way she looks at you says otherwise. Risk-takers get the biggest rewards." She stands. "Let's take a break."

"We only started an hour ago."

"There are more important things to be doing. Go find her. Enjoy the last of your time together under the sun." She signals for me to leave and snatches the beer from between my fingers. "Now, go."

Linda is lying on my lounger on the roof terrace. Her white bikini is in stark contrast to her golden skin. Dark curls are piled on top of her head, secured by a bright-red band. She's lying face down with her earbuds in. Her toes wiggle in time to the music. I walk over and crouch down beside her, then run a finger over her shoulder. Sleepy eyes flutter open, and she smiles softly. "I thought you were working," she whispers, pushing herself up to sit. She blinks at me as I sit mutely, watching her. "Is everything all right?"

"I'm not sure," I say honestly. "It depends on what happens in the next forty-eight hours." She screws up her face, displeased with the conversation. "I know you don't want to talk about this."

She sighs. "You're right. I don't want to talk about this. There is no reason to. In two days, I will be stepping on that plane and flying back to grey skies. The thought of going back to my miserable existence is soul-destroying." Her eyes water as she wrinkles her nose. "The past eight weeks with you have been incredible. You have helped me love myself in ways you will never understand."

"Does this have to end here?" I ask. "We live in the same city. We could date. We could go to the theatre, out for dinner, anything." She takes my hands in hers and shakes her head. "Why? I don't understand. You told me I make you happy. You told me we are incredible together."

"Max," she whispers, her voice soft. "This was a summer fling. You and I would never work long term. I'm in my mid-forties and have had a family already. I couldn't give you all the things you should want in your future."

"Don't tell me what I want," I hiss, pulling my hands from hers. "So, you're going to be able to walk away? Not look back and wonder what would have happened if we tried? Is writing off our relationship so easy for you? Am I just a notch on your newly single bedpost?"

"You're not being fair!" she shouts, and her eyes blaze angrily. "This relationship, as you call it, wasn't even a relationship. It was a fling. No more, no less. We agreed on this. After a few weeks of fun, we would return to our normal lives. No strings. No feelings."

"No strings. No feelings," I repeat back to her. "You have no feelings for me? None?"

"I didn't mean it that way," she wails. Tears are streaming down her face now. "Don't twist my words, please." Her supposedly waterproof mascara is creating tram lines down her cheeks. Waterproof my arse. "Of course I care for you, but we both knew this wasn't more than it is."

"And what is that? Enlighten me, because when you decided to stay on a few weeks ago, part of me hoped I was a small part of your reasoning. That you wanted to stay with me for the person I am, not just to fuck my cock. Is that really all I have been to you? A holiday fuck?" I turn away, not wanting to look at her. I'm furious and devastated. As I walk over to the balustrade, I stare out over the ocean. Linda walks up behind me and places a hand on my shoulder.

"I'm sorry for giving you false hope. I never meant to hurt you. Thank you for everything. I will cherish this time with you, but this is goodbye."

"Goodbye for now or goodbye forever?" I can't look at her, but her eyes are boring into the back of my head, willing me to turn around. She sniffs away her tears. "Actually, don't answer that. I already know the answer," I snarl. My heart tightens, knowing this is goodbye forever. Deep down, I'd hoped she would give us a chance in the real world. I prayed she felt our relationship was worth trying for.

"Okay," she says, quietly. "I'll go." She places her lips on the back of my shoulder. "Thank you," she whispers again. "You will never know how much you have improved my life. I know, right now, it doesn't feel like it, but I care for you deeply. This is the right thing to do. I would be selfish to take things any further."

With that, she walks away. I don't turn around. A single tear falls and makes a trail down my cheek. It's over.

A week later, I land back on British soil. Tomorrow, I return to my job as a geography teacher. My summer of love, fun, and sex is done. Since she left, Linda hasn't made any contact with me. The day we had the conversation on the roof, she packed up and left. My aunt said she moved to a hotel near the airport for her final nights in Spain.

Even though I haven't spoken to her, she is with me constantly in my mind. All our moments together are etched there permanently – the feel of her fingers on my skin, the way her tongue caressed mine, the ecstasy she brought to me when we made love.

Fucked. I correct myself. We weren't serious; there was no lovemaking, only carnal fucking by two people who needed their release. Two people who needed to lose themselves in each other to forget their shitty pasts.

My heart protests, not agreeing with my summary. It strains in my chest, begging me to listen. It was more than fucking, so much more—for me, anyway—but it's over, and she's gone back to her normal life as a middle-aged divorcée, toeing the line about who or what is acceptable to have in her life. Sadness overwhelms me, not only for me, but for Linda, the woman I came to know so well under the sun. The beautiful, sexy woman who danced on the beach and made love with me on the roof terrace. When we sang in the streets and paddled in the ocean, that woman was joyful and colourful. She loved living her life. I hope it is that woman who has landed back in London, not the broken woman of the beginning of summer. I hope our relationship was for something. I hope it has given Linda the confidence to move forward with her life.

Jace is standing, waiting for me in arrivals at the airport. He waves dramatically as I walk through the sliding doors. He has a huge smile on his face that disappears when he sees me.

"You look like shit, pal," he says. "Was the flight rough?"

"No, it was fine," I reply, grumpily. "I'm just tired. The last few days have been busy; we've been finishing up for winter at the hotel."

He raises his eyebrows but says nothing. I follow him to the car silently, throwing my bag on the back seat before climbing into the passenger side.

"Drink?" he asks, and I nod. He pulls out of his parking spot, and we drive sedately, for him, to our local bar. "You grab that table in the corner," he orders. "I'll get the drinks. Fuck the beer, you look like you need tequila." Minutes later, he places a shot glass in front of me and sits down on the opposite seat. "Are you going to tell me what happened?"

"I told you everything on the phone," I say evasively.

"No, what you said was Linda left last week. That you've no plans to contact her." He taps his lips with his finger. "There's more to it. Well, your Aunt Susan thinks so, anyway."

"How the fuck would you know what she thinks?" I hiss.

"She phoned me," he says. "Phoned me to warn me that you are moping around like a broken-hearted schoolboy. So, what happened? I'm assuming the decision not to see each other again wasn't yours?"

I shrug. "No, it wasn't. She wasn't willing to see me here at home. She gave me a long spiel about how she wasn't what I needed, how she couldn't give me a family, and how our lives were at different stages. She left."

"That sucks," he says, nodding sympathetically.

I don't respond. There is nothing more to say. My summer ended the way it began – my heart shattered into pieces and wanting a woman who doesn't want me back. This was a summer where I fell in love, and, once again, it wasn't reciprocated.

Chapter Fifteen

Linda

London is as miserable as always. The skies are dark, and people scurry around the streets as fast as they can. No one smiles. Everyone rushes about their lives, barely pausing for breath. The light I experienced over summer is long gone and my mood with it. In the four weeks I've been back, every bit of gained confidence has slowly seeped away.

On my return, my brother invited me round to his house for Sunday lunch. He sat me down and lectured me on the importance of remembering what age I am and how I should behave. "People will talk," he said. "You can't prance around the city in skimpy dresses with boys hanging off your arm. What happened this summer needs to be archived, Linda. You need to get back to normal and start looking for an older dependable man to take care of you." He wagged his finger at me and added, "Bernie is still single."

"Bernie?" I spluttered. "Bernie as in your mechanic with the trousers that don't cover his arse crack? *That* Bernie?" He frowned at me, unimpressed with my reaction.

"Bernie is a good man," he argued. "He has a business and a house of his own. He works hard, and I like him."

"*You* fucking date him, then!" I spat.

"Now, Linda, don't be unreasonable. At your stage in life, you can't be fussy. There isn't a long line of millionaire models vying for your attention. I'll call him and set you up," he stated, ignoring the growl emanating from me.

"Don't you fucking dare!" I shrieked. "Listen to me. I have spent the last eight weeks wrapped in the arms of a gorgeous young man who worshipped me, and I told him we couldn't see each other because of your prejudices. This idiotic need of yours to keep our family name golden!"

I smile, remembering my brother's face as I lost my shit with him. He had never seen me that way. I would never have had the confidence to stand up for myself before. I stormed from the house and haven't spoken to him since.

My heart breaks again at the thought of Max; the pieces haven't permanently glued themselves back together yet. Our conversation on the roof terrace the last time I saw him was excruciating, walking away from him more so. But it was the right thing to do. He is a young man with his whole life ahead of him. I am not the woman for him.

"Mum," Marina calls from her bedroom, interrupting my pity party. I traipse up the stairs to see what she wants now. She has secured a job at the local call centre and is focused on determining a life plan. "Would I be able to borrow the car tomorrow, please?" she asks. I smile. She said please; that is an improvement.

"Sure. Have you any exciting plans?" She drops her eyes shyly and twists her fingers together. My heart sinks. Another boy. Even though

Marina is in her twenties, every man she dates seems to be an overgrown child, like her. "Do you have a date?" I prompt.

"No," she says. "I have an interview."

"An interview? For what? You just started working at the call centre. I thought it was all going well."

"It's not for a job," she says. "Well, it is, but it won't affect my proper job," she explains, but I'm none the wiser.

"You're going to have to explain it to me. I have no idea what on earth you're talking about," I tell her, and she giggles.

"I have an audition for a pole dancing club." She looks at me with her eyes wide and bites her lip. She's nervous telling me this. I knew she pole danced for fitness in the past, but never did I think she would want to work in the industry.

"It's all above board. Nothing dodgy goes on. It's something I've always wanted to do."

For a few minutes, I say nothing, trying to collect my thoughts into a coherent sentence. I doubt any mother would be delighted to find out their daughter dreams of being a pole dancer, but her life is not mine to live. This is not my choice to make.

"Thank you for telling me," I say. "If this is what you want, I'm one hundred percent behind you."

Her face relaxes into a smile, and she walks over to me, taking me in her arms. "I love you, Mum," she whispers. "Thank you for always being there."

Our relationship has been strained since my return four weeks ago. There was an awkward conversation when I arrived home about my plans moving forward. "Is your plaything coming to visit? Do I need to invest in some earplugs?" she snarled. I'd literally walked in and sat down, depositing my suitcase at the door on the way in.

"Marina, can you at least let me pause for a breath before attacking me with questions?" I pushed my curls out of my face, scowling at her. "I'm just home."

"Overtired?" She said, raising an eyebrow. "Too much extracurricular activity?"

"Marina!" I snapped, "It's none of your bloody business. I don't want to be having this conversation with you. We need to talk, but not about my relationship with Max."

"What else is there to talk about?" she spat. "You chose him over me."

"No, I chose my happiness over your demands. That's a completely different thing." I sighed softly, steeling myself because I knew my next statement would not go down well. "I know you lied to me." The words hang in the air between us. "I asked Max about what you said, him hitting on you." Her face fell. "He told me its wasn't true, and I believe him."

"Mum, I…"

"No matter what you say, you can't justify this behaviour. You can't always get your own way. Life doesn't work like that."

"I was worried about you," she whispered.

"No, you were worried about how me being with him would reflect on you. You were protecting your own reputation by trying to ruin my fun. I was never under any illusions that what Max and I had could continue after summer, but he was good for me. We enjoyed our time together." She blinked at me. I saw her struggling to process what I was saying. "I'll miss him," I added, quietly under my breath.

"I'm sorry," she mumbled, looking at me then snapping her eyes away. Her sincerity was dubious.

"Well, it happened. We're both here now. I want to draw a line and move on. We've both had good and bad experiences this summer. Are you all right with that? Let's try to get along." She nodded. Hopefully now, we can move forward and enjoy being mother and daughter.

***

My cheese sandwich sweats in its cellophane wrapper. I open the Tupperware box and stuff it back in. My stomach flips. The black water bottle I carry every day sits on the table, and my colleagues chatter around me. It's lunchtime in the school cafeteria, and the same scenario is playing out before my eyes. Nothing has changed.

Inwardly, I curse myself. *So much for a summer of finding yourself.*

"Spain must feel like a lifetime ago," Rhian, the head of the infant department at the school, says, breaking my self-loathing. "I hate that about holidays. You get back, and it feels like it never happened. What I would give to be able to bottle up some of the fun and bring it home."

I smile sadly at her. "Yes, it was an incredible summer," I mumble. "But it's over."

"Would you do it again?"

"Do what?" I ask, taken off guard. Nerves dance in my stomach. Does she know about me dating a younger man?

"Go away all summer?" she replies, her eyebrows drawn in confusion at my sharp tone. "What did you think I was talking about?" I shrug. "So, would you do it again?"

Images of Max and I play in my mind like I'm watching an old family film. "I would repeat every damn moment," I say, fiercely. "It's almost as if it never happened, and everything has gone back to how it was."

"Linda, I hope you don't mind me saying, but you seem to be even more down than before you left, and that's saying something. What happened over there?"

Not knowing what to say, I tell the truth. "I fell for someone I shouldn't have."

"A bloke?" she asks, and I chuckle.

"Yes, a bloke. A younger guy than me." Rhian and I are not close, but she's easy to talk to, and the words roll off my tongue. "We had eight weeks of bliss. Then, it ended when I came home."

"Oh," she says. "Long distance relationships are hard. I understand."

"It wasn't the distance, he lives in London," I admit. She stares at me as if I'm an idiot. "He's twelve years younger than me." My voice rises, trying to emphasise my point.

"So?"

"Well, there's no future in it. He should be looking for someone to settle down with and have a family."

"Did he say that? Or are you putting words in his mouth?" Her eyebrow raises in question, and I bristle at her tone.

"That's not the point," I mutter, annoyed at her interrogation. "It wouldn't work back here."

"What does he do?" she asks, changing the subject.

"He's a high school geography teacher."

"And he agreed to end your relationship on your return?"

"Not exactly, but I told him it was for the best."

She tuts audibly and shakes her head. "So, let me get this right. A young hot guy—I'm assuming he's hot?" I nod, and my cheeks flush. "I'll take that as a yes. This guy spends eight weeks with you. You have a great time together. He lives in the same city as you, and you break up with him. You're an idiot."

Before I can defend myself, she stands and leaves the table. I watch her walk away, my jaw almost on the floor. She's right; I am an idiot.

Sandbank High School is an inner-city school with low budgets and high enrolment rates. I've heard of it but never been here. It's not somewhere I would accept a job; it comes with a soiled reputation. I'd been surprised when Max told me he was moving here from the private school he worked at. The school sign is decorated with graffiti;

someone has turned the "L" in school into a penis. Litter edges the playground and pavements.

After stopping my car in a side street with a view of the car park, I sit and wait. Waves of teenagers dressed in black file out of the gates. The girls barely wear skirts, and the boys use their ties as headbands. After ten minutes, the children are gone, and teachers carrying stacks of paperwork appear in the car park. One by one, they negotiate the slimy steps, jump into their vehicles, and leave.

My eyes stay focused on the door to the school. I have no idea what I'm going to say to him. He will most likely tell me to fuck off after our last conversation. But life's short, and I must try. When I had almost given up hope, the door to the school opens again. He appears with an older man at his side. Max takes the books he is holding from him, and they chat for a minute before walking to their individual cars. Seeing my chance, I push open the car door and stride across the road towards the car park as fast as my heels will allow.

He is fumbling in his pocket for something, his keys, perhaps. His eyes are focused on his task. He doesn't see me approach him, only glancing up when he hears the click of my shoes. His eyes rise to mine, deep green and just as beautiful as I remember them. His shirt is undone at the collar, and his hair is tousled in a sexy rough way.

"Hello, Max," I say, softly. He looks at me as if I'm a figment of his imagination. "Can we talk?" My words sound pathetic out loud.

"About what?" he responds. His eyes are wary, unsure.

"About us."

"Us?" he says, scowling at me. "There isn't an us. You told me that yourself."

Chapter Sixteen

Max

Linda is standing opposite me in the school car park on a Friday afternoon. It's been eight weeks since she walked away from me on the roof terrace. I never expected to see her again, never mind appear unannounced at my place of work. She's wanting to talk, her words tumbling out between us. I stand silent, unnerved by her sudden appearance.

"I was wrong. I'm sorry. I was trying to do the right thing, but I hurt both of us instead," she says as I stare at her. "Hear me out, please. Then, if you never want to talk to me again, I'll walk away."

"You already did," I snap, and she winces. Tears fill her eyes, and she wipes them away with her sleeve. My heart strains – this woman broke me. I'm not sure why she's here or if I can trust her. Her eyes plead with me, wordlessly. One part of me wants to listen, but I also want to tell her to leave and not come back, hurt her like she hurt me.

We stand less than a metre apart but miles from each other. She takes a step forward reaching for me with one hand. I automatically withdraw. She pauses, panic flitting across her face like it has every time I've seen her confidence falter. The next few minutes pass and neither of us speaks. Our focus on each other never breaks, each of us willing the other to make a move, show their hand.

My curiousness defeats me. I want to know what she has to say. "Okay," I mumble, finally. "There is a café down the street called Margo's." She widens her eyes in surprise. *Ironic Beautiful, eh?* I chuckle at her expression. "It's true, there is." I point behind her to a blue awning that extends from a building in the distance. "Meet me there in ten minutes." She nods, turns away, then walks off in the direction of the café. I watch her until she crosses the street, she doesn't look back.

I climb into my car, wanting to take a moment to compose myself. My mind is whirling with possibilities of what she could want to talk to me about. What she could be proposing. She said the conversation on the roof terrace was a mistake, but she was so certain we wouldn't work on home soil. My fingers slip my key into the ignition; I consider turning it and driving off. As I rest my elbows on the steering wheel, I drop my head into my hands. My palms are slick against my brow. I sit for ten minutes, then take a breath, get out and walk towards the café.

Margo places two steaming cups of coffee on the table. We sit in silence, watching each other. "How are you?" Linda asks.

I groan. "Linda, I'm not being funny, but I doubt you appeared outside my work two months since I saw you for no reason or to ask me how I am. What do you want?" My tone is sharp, so unlike me.

"U-Um," she stammers. "I miss you." I give her a blank look. "I was wrong to not give us a chance. Walking away from you on that roof terrace was one of the worst decisions I've ever made." My brain misfires. I wasn't expecting that.

"You've still not told me what you want," I say, the edge evaporating from my voice.

"You," she replies simply. "I want you." Her eyes never leave mine as her words sit between us. "When I decided to have the summer in Spain, the only thing I planned to bring home was a tan and a few stories. But then I met you."

"And?" I prompt. I'm not going to make this easy for her. Even though right now all I want to do is take her in my arms and hold her. Tell her it doesn't matter, she's here now. But I've been hurt before, and I need to protect myself.

"And you showed me that life can be fun and colourful, that I can be spontaneous and live in the moment." She takes a deep breath, her gaze fixed on me. "Max, I fell in love with you, and it terrified me. That's why I ran, because, on paper, you are everything I shouldn't want." I close my eyes and rub my forehead with my hand. "Please think about giving us a chance to see where this relationship will take us."

I watch her. My mind is attempting to process what she said. She's lobbed the ball directly into my court. Offering me what I wanted eight weeks ago. A chance. A chance to show her we are possible.

"I don't know," I whisper, "this is all so sudden. You left me. No strings, no feelings, you said. Told me I was no more than a fling."

"I never said that," she says, her voice breaking. "I said what we had could never be more than a fling. But. It's so much more."

***

Linda

I've done it. Put it all out there in the open. Told him how I feel and what I want. My heart is strapped to the emotional trainline, waiting to be saved or smashed to smithereens. He swallows visibly while running one hand through his hair. There's something else I need to tell him, but I want to wait to see his reaction to me first. I want to see if I was enough for him to give us a chance. If what he said on that roof terrace holds true. To see if he wants me, for me.

He pushes his chair back, and it slides noisily against the tiles of the floor. He stands and walks around the table to me then takes both my hands in his before pulling me to my feet. I stand in front of him, my heart bursting from my chest. He cups my face as I lose myself in his eyes.

"I've missed you," he whispers, dropping a kiss onto my lips. It's soft and gentle, and my heart explodes on impact. "I can't go through this again. If you want me, be with me. Because I want you. But don't run away from me. Twice I've watched you bolt for the door."

"I'm here," I say, softly. Guilt bubbling in my belly for hurting him.

"You have to let go of the negative thoughts and comments. People will always have an opinion on how other people live. As long as we are together, what does it matter? They can't extinguish how we feel, no matter what they think."

I wrap my arms around his waist, snuggling against his broad chest. One of his arms snakes around me, the other strokes my curls. "I'm sorry," I say for what must be the millionth time. "I'm a silly old woman who couldn't see what she had until she didn't have it. Who wasn't confident enough in her own judgment to listen to her heart."

"You're here now," he says, quietly. "And that's what matters. We're here together now." His embrace on me tightens, and he rests his chin on the top of my head. I go to open my mouth, but he starts to speak again. "Do you know what I thought you came here to tell me?"

"What did you think I was going to tell you?" I wriggle out from under his chin and look up at him. He rolls his eyes, embarrassed. He's considering whether to tell me or not.

He gives me a lopsided smile, then says, "That you were carrying my child, but I know that's impossible." Our gazes hold as the comment bounces between us.

"And how would that make you feel?" I ask. He moves to nuzzle my neck with his nose, and my stomach flips.

"Terrified and excited," he replies. "And even more in love with you."

"Max," I whisper. "I am. You're going to be a daddy."

Chapter Seventeen

Max

Linda sits on the couch in my apartment, her floral long-sleeved dress skims her curves, the swell of her breasts evident through the soft material. Fuck, I've missed her. It's been three hours since she appeared outside my work, and I'm not sure I even believe it yet. These weeks without her have been hell and now she's back. I'm already terrified she'll leave again.

My relationship with the girl I was crazy about before had never progressed beyond the friend zone. There had been no romantic strolls on the beach, no making love in the ocean, and never had she felt like my partner. What I'd experienced with Linda had never happened to me before. With her, it was different, and that's why my heart shattered on the roof terrace in Spain during our final conversation.

Between our time together, my feelings towards her and my discussion with my aunt, I'd convinced myself she would give us a chance. When she said no, my world stopped, and pain ravaged my body and soul. Even though the reasons she gave for us not being together made sense logically, my heart didn't agree. Every excuse she gave frustrated me further. It made me question my ability to read people and understand their motives. Ultimately, it hurt. For a few weeks, I hated her for breaking my heart, for dismissing me when my usefulness was over. Then the sorrow hit hard, the loneliness and the fear that I would never find someone who made me feel the way she did.

"Do you need some help?" she asks, distracting me from my thoughts. I'm in my cupboard of a kitchen supposedly making two cups of tea. Really, I've only just flicked the kettle on. I needed a moment to myself. Her reappearance has been a shock, a good one, but a revelation, nonetheless. Never mind the fact she's pregnant with my child.

"No," I call back. "Almost ready."

"Good, I'm dying of thirst out here. I thought you'd gone to India to collect the tea leaves. It better be a bloody good cuppa," she replies, and I smirk. She's still as snarky as ever. I love her cheeky comments and playful attitude; she makes me smile. I'm relieved to see the Linda of Spain is still here and hasn't reclused away back to the woman she was when we met.

"Be polite or I'll pour your cup down the sink. Don't you know when you're a guest in someone's home you're meant to be courteous?" I shout back. She giggles, and it's the most beautiful sound. I've missed that. It's even better when we're in bed and I run my tongue over her body. Her skin is so sensitive that with each lap a murmur of some description normally leaves her lips. These sounds I came to know so well speak directly to my cock, and I harden within my jeans. Maybe I'll get to revisit these moments soon. *One step at a time. She's only just come back.* Can pregnant women even have sex? It's not something I've ever considered before. The thought of not being able to be inside her for months causes my excitement to waver.

"Ok, I'll be polite," she replies, her voice husky. "But tell me, sir, what would my punishment be if I'm not?" I imagine her sitting on my sofa, legs pulled up underneath her, biting her bottom lip the way she does when she's aroused, playing with me. Over the summer, we kept each other entertained with cheeky comments and remarks laden with sexual innuendo. I glance up and she's standing in the doorway watching me. "You're taking your time," she says. "Thought I would hurry you along a bit. I don't need tea."

My kitchen is so small that there is only enough space for one person to walk in, turn around and walk back out again. She's leaning against the doorframe with her head cocked to the side and biting that damn lip. We stare at each other. No words need to be spoken; we both know what we want and need. I put the single teaspoon I'm holding on to the counter and step towards her, taking both her hands in mine. She glances away and her cheeks flush; that's so her. She's brazen then shy immediately afterwards as her confidence fails. I run one hand through her dark curls then stroke her cheek with my thumb. "I've missed you," I tell her, again, "more than you can imagine."

"Will you show me how much?" Her eyes widen as she meets my gaze. "Can we go to bed? I need to be with you, wrapped around you. It's been too long."

"Are we all right to...you know...with the baby?" I stutter, signalling to her stomach with my eyes. She gives me a breath-taking smile.

"Are you asking if we can have sex while I'm pregnant?" she inquires with a smirk. I flush. This is a question I should know the answer to. She moves closer to me so her breasts graze against my shirt then rises on tiptoe to kiss my cheek.

"Yes," she whispers in my ear, "it's perfectly safe for us to have sex whilst I'm pregnant." I blow out a breath in relief, and she grins at me. "Did you think you were going to have to be a monk for the next six months?"

"Well, I've never been in this position," I justify. "I thought perhaps it wasn't the done thing. I was thinking about whether I needed to invest in top shelf magazines."

Her hand glides over my erection, and she drums her fingers on the denim. I harden further. "Oh, trust me, magazines won't be required. You'll have your own personal sex service. I certainly want you to do that thing to me, whether it's the done thing or not," she purrs. "Come on, show me how much you've missed me." She takes my hand. "Show me your bedroom."

Inside, I close the door softly behind us. She stands in front of me, looking around the room. "You're very much the bachelor," she says, almost to herself.

My bedroom is minimalist. It has everything I need: a double bed, a wardrobe, and a chest of drawers. The walls are plain white apart from a huge world map which hangs above my headboard. Each place I've travelled to is marked with a red dot. Dirty washing is piled in the corner. I keep forgetting to buy a washing basket. The bedcovers are grey with simple black lines and one pillow on each side of the bed. Stepping back, I try to see the room from her point of view, and I must admit it is very masculine.

"Only me here," I reply. "Perhaps it needs a feminine touch to soften the edges for me."

I stand behind her and place my hands on her hips. She sinks back into me, leaning her head against my chest. My cock is pressed against her back. I flex my hips and rub against her. My lips drop to her neck, travelling from her ear to her collarbone trailing kisses. She sighs deeply, relaxing further. My hands investigate her stomach rising to her breasts. I can feel them, soft and perky through the fabric, her nipples elongating beneath my fingers causing bumps in the material. "Arms up," I instruct and lift her dress from the hem cleanly over her head. Her brown curls lift with the dress then fall onto her shoulders. I turn her to face me and step back.

She stands in front of me wearing nothing but a small black lace thong and heels. She cocks her head to the side and smiles softly. I walk in a circle around her, my gaze never leaving her body. "You'll do," I whisper, and she slaps my shoulder in jest then grabs for my shirt buttons. I stop her hands holding them in mine on my chest.

"Not fair," she says, pouting at me. She goes to pull her fingers from my grip, and I squeeze them tighter.

"I want to enjoy you first," I tell her, releasing her fingers. "Go and lie on the bed." She saunters away, swinging her hips, the little black string nestled between her buttocks accentuating their roundness. She slides onto my bed, lying with her head on the pillow, and gives me a sexy smile.

"Come on then," she cajoles. "It's rude to keep a lady waiting." I raise an eyebrow at her, and she giggles.

"You are no lady," I say. "I've experienced what you're capable of doing with both your tongue and your teeth." She flushes at my words, the redness creeping up her neck as well as highlighting her cheekbones.

I slip off my shoes and walk over to the bed, standing beside her and looking down at the exquisite vision in front of me. Slowly, I unbutton my shirt, shrugging it off my shoulders before letting it drop to the floor. Her breathing hitches slightly. She reaches up and trails her fingers across my abs then down to the waistband of my jeans, hooking her fingers between the fabric and my skin. She pulls me gently towards her until I kneel above her on the bed.

Placing my hands on either side of her head, I lean down and pop a kiss on her lips. She responds by kissing me fiercely, her tongue invading my mouth and wrapping her arms around my neck, pulling me down onto her. Conscious of her precious cargo, I still. "The baby," I whisper.

"It's okay," she says. "He can't hear you."

"It's a boy?" I splutter, surprised, and she laughs, shaking her head.

"No silly, we don't know. But I think it's a boy. This time feels different to when I was pregnant with Marina. So, I'm assuming it's a him."

"Okay," I reply, grumpily. "And I didn't think he could hear us, but I don't want to hurt either of you."

"Max, I'm not made of glass. I won't break," she says, reaching up and grazing my cheek with her fingers. "Just make love to me like you have before. I need you." She smiles encouragingly. "You won't hurt me or our baby." Our baby. The simple phrase stops me in my tracks. I'm going to be a father with a woman I met only a matter of months ago. Since we reconciled outside the school, the hours have passed but the reality hasn't quite sunk in. "Max," she prompts, "you look like you've seen a ghost. Are you all right?"

"Yes," I mumble, sitting up on the edge of the bed and placing my feet on the floor. The enormity of the situation enveloping me. "Our baby. I'm going to be a dad." My words are quiet, almost like I'm speaking to myself. Linda sits up behind me and wraps her arms around me. She kisses my shoulder gently, then lays her forehead against it.

"Please tell me you're okay," she whispers.

"I'm okay," I reply, but I don't feel it. Within four hours, the woman who broke my heart two months ago returned unexpectedly, told me she was pregnant and is now in my bed. My life irreversibly changed in the blink of an eye. "Linda," I say, "I'm sorry. We have things to discuss before we move forward. I can't sleep with you until I know you won't disappear."

"I'm not going anywhere." She tenses her arms around me and presses her lips to my skin again. With my elbows on my knees, my head drops into my hands, my fingers messing up my hair. "Please" she pleads, "give us a chance."

"Of course, I will," I tell her. "This is all happening so fast that I need a moment to catch up." I turn to face her, tears wetting her cheeks. Leaning forward, I kiss her softly. She closes her eyes under my touch. "When you walked away from me before, it fucking destroyed me."

"Max," she interrupts.

"Please, let me speak. What we have is special. I love you. I can't lose you again. You or my child. We need to commit to being a family," I say, determinedly. "This must work from now on. I won't bring my child up in a broken home."

"I'm here because I want to be," she says. "I want to make you happy."

"I know, Beautiful. I know. Can we just slow things down for a moment, please? Let me get my head around the past few hours." I stand then grab a fresh t-shirt from my wardrobe, throwing it on. Her eyes follow me around the room. "I'm sorry."

"It's understandable," she mutters pulling the duvet up around her. "Could you pass me my dress please?" I collect the pool of fabric off the floor and pass it to her. She gives me a sad smile. "I'm sorry too," she says, "but you're right. We have a lot to discuss."

Chapter Eighteen

Linda

He rejected me. Our reconciliation at the school had gone too smoothly. Yes, he'd been reserved, not answered my questions swiftly and made me sweat for a few minutes, but ultimately, he had come around a lot quicker than I predicted. After I told him about the baby in the café, my emotions and hormones went into overdrive. We kissed and then walked hand in hand through the streets for an hour catching up on the weeks we missed out on. Our baby wasn't mentioned, and I assumed he was taking some time to process the information.

We are back in the living room after the awkward situation in the bedroom. Max is in the kitchen again finishing making the cups of tea he started an hour ago. His whole apartment screams that a single man lives here. Everything is a shade of white, black, or grey. It had been idiotic of me to try and take him to bed so soon. I've had weeks to process the information; he's had minutes. No wonder he's in shock.

"Do you want a biscuit?" he calls. I glance at my watch. He's stalling. It doesn't take this long to prepare two cups of tea. What happens if delayed panic sets in and he runs. But I'm in his house, so I can wait for him here I decide. What if he decides that it's too much of a change and he wants his single life back? Or he realises he's landed himself with a middle-aged woman who will look more like a granny than a mother in years to come. My heart falls. These are fears constantly swirling around my brain. If he rejects me permanently, I'm not sure what I'll do. "Biscuit?" he prompts, wandering back into the room holding a small plate piled with chocolate delights.

"Please," I say, staring up at him. He is beautiful. His dark hair is messy from our over-excitement cut short. Fitted jeans hug him in all the right places complimented by a t-shirt which has the same effect. His eyes soften slightly as they meet mine, and he smiles. After placing the plate on the coffee table, he sits down beside me. I've still not got my cup of tea. "I'm sorry," he says for what must be the tenth time. "It's not that I don't want you. I'm trying to protect both of us, the three of us." He leans forward and kisses my cheek. "I do love you, Beautiful. Don't ever doubt that." This man always knows how to quash my concerns with his words. It's like he can read my mind.

"Am I ever going to get that cuppa?" I jibe, and he widens his eyes as if he's forgotten. Then he rises and returns to the kitchen to retrieve the two cups.

We're settled beside each other, his arm around me, each sipping from the plain white mugs. I have the plate of chocolate biscuits balanced on my knee. Each time I take one, he signals to me with his eyes that he wants one too and I pop it between his lips. The conversation hasn't begun yet. We've just sat and enjoyed the proximity of each other. His hand has never left my body since we sat down.

"Have you told Marina about the baby?" he asks, and I shake my head. "Do you want me to be there when you do?" There he is. The man I love until my heart bursts. Max is always considerate of my feelings and how he can support me, as he has been since our first day together. I think back to being on the beach and removing my dress in front of him, how nervous I'd been. Then how his words and actions had taken those nerves away – he'd made me feel beautiful. From that point, I couldn't get enough of him; he was my personal drug to binge on. "When do you want to tell her?"

"I'm not quite twelve weeks yet," I say. "But I will need to tell her soon. She's already suspicious that I've cut out wine." He chuckles. "Sooner rather than later is probably best." I glance at him, his eyes fixed on me, listening intently.

"Whatever you need, Beautiful," he says. "I'm here."

Over the next two hours, we discuss how we are going to navigate our relationship and our soon-to-be new addition. We agree that even though our feelings for each other are strong, the fact our relationship and breakup only span four months, to take things steadily would be best. We will maintain our two homes so we each have our space, but I hope after this heart-to-heart he's going to take me to bed. I've missed him. Right now, all I want is to be wrapped in his arms. My phone rings in my pocket, and on retrieving the handset, my daughter's name lights up the screen. "Hello," I answer.

"Mum, where are you?" she says, her voice sharp. She's annoyed at the change of routine. Normally when Marina gets home from her back shift, I'm there with the dinner on the table. For all my daughter is behaving better, she's certainly not perfect. We've never discussed our issues fully, only papered over the cracks. "I got home and you're not here." *No shit, Sherlock.*

"No, darling. I'm at friends. I'm not sure when I'll be home," I tell her, and she huffs. Max squeezes my thigh. His gaze holds mine and he mouths, "*In the morning.*" I smile at him. "Actually darling, we're going to have a few drinks, so I'll see you tomorrow."

"Tomorrow?" she splutters. "Who are you with? This isn't like you."

"I told you," I respond. "I'm with a friend, and I'll see you tomorrow. Goodnight, Marina." Before she can protest, I cut the call and put the phone back in my pocket. It immediately starts to ring again, and I roll my eyes. As I reach for the irate device, Max stops me by placing his hand on mine.

"Leave it. Let it ring out. She'll get the message. You and I have far more important issues to talk about, then I want to take you to bed." My face breaks into a wide smile and he smirks. "Did you honestly think I would let you stay here and not have my wicked way with you?"

"I hoped not," I say, my voice husky.

"Can I ask you something?" he says, dropping his gaze to the floor. Suddenly shy. Nervous even.

"Anything."

"Before this happens, I need to know. Did you sleep with anyone else since we were together?" My skin prickles at the insinuation.

"No," I snap. "Why would you think I had?"

"I didn't say I thought you had. I asked if you had. We broke up, Linda. You left me."

"And you thought there must be someone else?" He sighs. "Thanks for the vote of confidence," I spit.

Rubbing his hand over his face, he considers his words before speaking. Right now, I'd quite happily reach down his throat and rip the words out for him. *Asshole.* "Linda," he says, his voice firm. "If you had slept with someone, you'd have been perfectly entitled to. But you're here carrying my baby. I need to know if another man's hands have been on your skin. If I don't ask you then it will eat away at me. I don't want any secrets between us. I want this to work." I soften immediately. He's trying to do the right thing; that's so like the Max I know and love.

"No," I say, "there's been no one else." He visibly relaxes in front of me and leans in, kissing the tip of my nose.

"Good." It's a single-word reply which speaks volumes. He pauses as if waiting for me to say more. I don't. I don't want to ask him the same question. I don't need to know.

After another hour of discussion about what will happen over the coming months, we've exhausted the subject of babies, living arrangements, and telling my spoilt daughter about her future sibling. "Will you come with me tomorrow? To tell her?" He nods and takes both my hands in his. It's two in the morning, and the clock on the wall chimes to tell us so.

"I think we've covered plenty today, do you not?" he says, rising to his feet and pulling me up with him. "We're both still here. Will we go to bed?"

"I thought you'd never ask."

Back in his bedroom, I feel like an errant schoolgirl who's been dismissed then allowed to join back in the extracurricular activities. His hands haven't left my body for hours; when one is removed, the other connects within moments. He led me through here, and I'd followed him like a lamb. Being with him makes me the happiest I've ever been in my adult life. I feel secure and safe.

Standing by his bed, he lifts my dress over my head. This time, he lets me remove his t-shirt and jeans. My fingers fumble with the buttons as his erection grows beneath them. His body is so familiar but again, foreign. Two months without touching him felt like an eternity. He guides me to the bed, and we lie down beside each other. I'm on my back, and he's propped up on one elbow, looking down at me. His fingers play with my curls, then his mouth takes mine. His kiss is gentle but fierce, claiming what is his. One hand remains in my hair. He twists it around his hand and pulls gently, causing a moan to escape my lips. The other hand roams over my body, squeezing my breasts and rotating my nipples. After they stand to attention, it continues its journey across my stomach, pausing over my abdomen where our baby lies, currently the size of a raspberry. His hand splays across my belly protectively, and his kiss becomes more passionate.

"I can't believe a part of you and a part of me is in there," he whispers. "It's incredible. You're incredible."

"As much as I'm enjoying all the lovey-dovey talk," I say, and he stills. "I really wish you would get to the good bit." He chuckles and his hand immediately moves between my legs. He hooks his finger into my thong and pulls, the material gives way with a satisfying snap.

"Oops," he mumbles. "I better get down there and see what the noise was." He moves between my legs, his tongue playing with my clit. My body buzzes greedily in response. I pull my knees up and widen my legs to give him better access. "I love this. I love you. And I can't wait to sink myself inside you," he says, darkly. A single finger nudges my entrance then slides in. He groans as he feels my slick sides around his finger. A second immediately enters with the first and rhythmic pumps join his tongue still focused on my clit. I ruffle his hair, and he glances up at me.

"Come here," I purr. "I'm ready for you." He grins then goes back to his task. "Max," I groan. "Please."

"You'll get fucked when I say you can," he says. "I'm in control tonight. Now, lift your legs." I pull my knees up, my hips rocking in time with his hand. Then it happens, the peak comes, and my body vibrates with the sensation. "Now I'll fuck you." He climbs over my body, holding his body weight above me. We stare at each other as he slides home, back exactly where he should be.

The following morning, we sit in the living room wrapped around each other. I'm so relieved I chose a Friday to visit him at the school as it gives us the weekend together before we go back to normality. "Everything all right?" he asks, kissing my temple. "You're very quiet."

"I'm nervous," I say. "Marina isn't going to be happy about all this."

"Is Marina happy about anything that doesn't suit her?" he replies, and I chuckle. "I don't know the girl, but between the short time I met her and what you've told me, I would say you could have brought the King of Spain home and she wouldn't be happy."

"That is true. Are you still coming with me?"

"Of course, Beautiful. I told you, I'm here for anything you need."

Marina is in the garden when we arrive. Today is an abnormally warm day in October. She's sitting on a sun lounger reading a book with a wide sun hat pulled down on her head. I walk up beside her, and she lifts her eyes at the sound of my footsteps. "Where have you been?" she says, annoyed. Before I can respond, her eyes enlarge as Max steps into view. Her jaw drops open and she looks from me to him. "What's going on?" she stammers.

"We need to talk to you," I tell her. "Let's go inside."

The three of us are sitting in my living room. Marina resembles something between tomato and beetroot. Her shriek when I told her about the baby had resonated off the walls. My elderly neighbour had rattled on the other side, shouting at us to keep the noise down. Max sat silently beside me, holding my hand, his unspoken support evident but understated.

"So, let me get this right?" Marina snaps. "During your summer fumble, you managed to get knocked up by him." She signals to Max with a finger. "You're forty-five years old, Mum. What the fuck were you thinking?"

"This has happened to women all over the world for thousands of years. I thought my ability to have a child was gone. I was wrong."

"Obviously," she says with a sneer. "And what do you think about all this?" Her attention turns to Max.

"I'll admit it was a shock," he replies, "but I want to make this work, for all of us."

"You're including me in your shotgun family?" she snarls. "How long till you decide she's too old, eh?"

"Marina, I'm sitting right here," I hiss.

"I'm well aware of that mother," she replies.

"Listen," Max snaps and stands. "Your mother and I love each other. We're going to give our relationship the chance it deserves, whether you agree or not. Our baby is an unexpected surprise, but we're all adults here, Marina. I'm sure we can work it out." She hisses audibly through her teeth. "I'm here to stay, so get used to it."

"Fine," she shouts and storms from the room.

Max looks at me, and I give him a sad smile. "Beautiful, I mean it. I'm here to stay. You and our baby are my world from now on. I'm sure given time, Marina will want to be part of our family too."

"I hope so," I whisper. "I hope so."

Chapter Nineteen

Max

"Linda Butterby," the nurse calls, popping her head out of the consulting room door. Linda turns to me and smiles.

"Are you ready?" she asks. I nod; everything I want to say is lodged in my throat and has been since we arrived here at Homerton Maternity Centre for this ultrasound scan twenty minutes ago. The car park had been crammed. Where are people meant to park for fuck's sake? I'd driven around for ten minutes after dropping Linda at the entrance. Finally, I'd squeezed the car into the only available space.

As I walked through the glass sliding doors into the reception area, I'd looked up at the sign to get directions to the maternity unit. This is somewhere I never expected to be anytime soon. I followed the blue signs with white arrows along some ridiculously long corridors, past countless identical waiting areas, until I found her sitting waiting for me. Her nose stuck in a lifestyle magazine. She glanced up as I walked over and sat down.

Now, she's asking me if I'm ready to see the baby we created together. A new human growing within her, that popped into our lives out of the blue. She stands, offering me her hand; I rise and take it. We follow the nurse through the wide white door into the consulting room.

The room is as you would expect any doctor's office to be. There's a wide desk complete with a computer and piles of paperwork. A high single bed sits in the corner draped with white sheets. Various items of medical equipment and supplies are organised meticulously around the room. The nurse gestures for us to take a seat, signalling to two blue plastic chairs on one side of the desk. We both sit, and she does the same opposite us in a large black leather chair. She smiles kindly.

"First of all, congratulations on your good news," she says. "My name is Nurse Simpson, but please call me, Donna. I'll be your community midwife for the duration of your pregnancy." She's a larger woman with curly black hair and a beaming smile. Her focus moves between us as she speaks. "Can I just confirm your names?"

"I'm Linda Butterby," Linda replies. "And this is my partner, Max Gordon."

"And Max, you're the baby's father?" she asks. The question hangs in the air for a moment. I glance at Linda unsure whether she's looking for her or me to respond. I take a breath.

"Yes," I say. "I'm the father."

"Ok, I'm sorry to ask that but I just like to make sure I know who I'm speaking to. Things are not always as straight forward you see. I've been caught out before, so I make no assumptions." We nod at her in unison. "Do you know how far along you are?" she asks Linda.

"Around twelve weeks, I think."

"So baby was conceived at the end of July/beginning of August then."
She says to herself as she scribbles notes on a pad. "And have you had
any issues, pains, sickness?"

"Mornings are difficult," Linda tells her. "I don't seem to be able to
keep anything down until well past lunchtime. And I'm incredibly
tired. It didn't feel like this the first time around with my daughter."

"How old is your daughter?" she inquires, and Linda tenses. Her
cheeks flush as if embarrassed.

"Twenty-three," she mumbles. Donna replies with a small smile encouraging her to continue. "This was..." she trails off and her eyes
move to me. I keep my face blank, not giving away what I'm thinking,
the nervous worry I have eating away at me. Does she want this baby?
"This baby was a surprise," she says.

"A lot of babies are," the nurse advises, "but that makes them even
more special."

***

Linda

My heart rate steadies with her kind word. *Special*. I've been worried about this appointment since we made it last week. Our first
ultrasound scan. Being an older mother there is an increased risk of
complications during my pregnancy. Also, the fact the father is so
much younger than me is causing me to stress. I'd expected raised

eyebrows and tsk's through pursed lips. Disapproving comments and judgemental glances. They hadn't materialised.

Max sits beside me, still holding my hand. He's been quiet since we left my house to come here. Uncertainty emanates from him. It's only been a week since our reunion, our time together wonderful. He's still the loving attentive man I met during the summer. Every day he asks me a few more questions about my life when Marina was small. Did I breastfeed? How did she sleep? Did I want to bottle feed this time or not?

Last night, I'd found him sitting on the sofa, transfixed on his phone screen. As I walked up behind him, I'd leant over and wrapped my arms around his neck, popping my chin on his shoulder. "What are you studying?" I asked. He looked at me then back at his phone.

"The benefits of breastfeeding and how I can support you," he muttered, his eyes never leaving the screen. "It's all so complicated."

"Darling," I whispered, softly in his ear. "You don't need to know everything before our appointment tomorrow. I'm only twelve weeks. We have time." He'd sighed quietly, his shoulders sagging slightly. "Most new parents are just winging it anyway. There's not a test to prepare for."

"But you're not a first-time parent," he said, "and I am. It makes me feel…" He'd trailed off, not finishing his sentence.

"Makes you feel what?" I prompted, slightly unnerved. The last thing I want him to feel is unsure.

"Behind," he replied, glancing at me. "I've no knowledge of babies or how to keep them alive, Linda. My experience is next to nothing. I'm worried I'll let you down." I'd tightened my embrace on him then, willing him to realise how thankful I was for him.

"You're here," I told him. "You didn't run when I turned up and told you about our baby. You've stood by me and wanted to create a family. That's a lot more than some men do. You're going to be an amazing daddy."

Max squeezing my hand alerts me to the midwife still speaking. "Linda, as I'm sure you're aware as pregnant women go, you are in the older age group. This means we just have to be more aware of any changes or symptoms that may arise. I'll talk you through the treatment pathways, and the birthing options available. You don't have to decide now. Please take the information home." She hands me a pile of leaflets. "Discuss it between you, then tell me when you're ready and we can construct your birthing plan."

"Birthing plan?" Max interjects. She turns to him.

"Yes, we create an ideal plan the mother wants. Whether that be a hospital, home, or water birth."

"A water birth?" he repeats back to her, clearly confused. I smile to myself; he really is clueless on all this. But, I suppose, a young man like him would never have to think of these things until he met the woman he wanted to be with. The woman he chose to start a family with. Max hadn't been given that option. I'd fallen pregnant within weeks of meeting him, even though I told him I couldn't.

"Yes," she replies, "the hospital has birthing suites complete with birthing pools, sound systems and relaxation areas. I'll give you a tour after your scan. We're quiet today. I'm sure there will be one free." He gapes at her as if she's speaking a foreign language. Her focus returns to me. "The extreme tiredness and sickness are normal during the initial weeks of pregnancy. If it continues though, please do let me know or if your symptoms start to affect your everyday life."

"Thank you," I mumble, dropping my eyes. "I think my age probably doesn't help."

"Linda," she says, without missing a beat, "there is no shame at being pregnant in your forties. Try to enjoy this amazing time with your partner." My eyes lift to hers. She stands. "Shall we meet your baby?"

***

Max

Donna directs Linda to lie on the single bed. She climbs up, her eyes staying fixed on the ceiling above her. I walk around to her other side. Donna stands next to the ultrasound machine. "Lift your top please," she says. Linda pulls her blue wool jumper up exposing her flat stomach. I still can't believe a baby is in there. My baby. She tells me he or she is no bigger than a strawberry. Donna pulls down Linda's leggings slightly and tucks a blue towel into the waistband. She picks up a squeezy bottle and plops a dollop on her stomach.

"Oh, that's cold," Linda mutters, and I chuckle, then drop a kiss to her lips. I'm holding her hand nearest me, my other hand stroking her hair. She flushes at my public display of affection; she always does. Our eyes focus on each other. "Are you excited?" she whispers.

"That and bloody terrified." She smirks at me.

"Ok," the midwife says, flicking a switch. The black screen next to her springs to life. She picks up the white scanner from its holder and places it directly onto the gel on Linda's belly. She spreads the substance out then begins to move the paddle around, searching her skin. Seconds pass in complete silence. No one speaks. My eyes stay glued to the screen, waiting for something to appear.

"Should there not be a heartbeat?" Linda says, panic evident in her voice. I look to Donna then back at my beautiful woman, lying here exposed on the bed waiting to see our baby.

"Give me a moment," Donna replies, her voice calm. "Sometimes, babies like to hide." She screws her eyes at the screen as she continues to sweep the device over the surface. Suddenly, a whooshing noise fills the air, and a small blob appears. "There's baby," she sings. I stare at the screen, fascinated. She starts to explain what the different parts are and confirms we won't be able to find out the sex for another few weeks. To me, it's barely a shape. "We offer private sixteen-week scans to confirm the sex, or you can wait for your twenty-week check-up. Have you discussed whether you want to know or keep it a surprise?"

"Did you find out with Marina?" I ask Linda. She shakes her head. "Whatever you want, Beautiful. We can find out or leave it, it's completely up to you."

"He's a keeper," Donna says, bumping Linda's shoulder with her free hand. "You're a lucky woman." Linda glances at me then back to Donna, a breath-taking smile appears on her lips.

"I am," she says. "I won the lottery when I met him."

"Everything looks good," Donna confirms, bringing our attention back to her. "I would suggest, being a bit older, that you look at the additional tests we offer, more for your own peace of mind. I can also tell you're past twelve weeks. According to this, baby is thirteen weeks and three days, give or take." Jeez, she must have fallen pregnant pretty much after she told me we didn't need to use protection. I push the thought from my mind; it's pointless thinking about this now. She is pregnant, whether she thought she could be or not.

Donna takes a wad of white cloth and cleans the gel from Linda's stomach, then invites her to stand. Linda readjusts her clothes. She hands her a A5 sized image freshly printed. Our scan photo of our baby. She passes it to me, and I pinch it between my fingers at the corner, not wanting to mark it. I feel her eyes on me, assessing my reaction. She touches the base of my back to get my attention. "Are you all right?" she asks, and I turn to her.

"Yes, Beautiful. You've given me the most wonderful gift." I cup her face with my palm, and she closes her eyes, relaxing against my skin. "I feel so lucky to have found you." Donna clearing her throat breaks the moment.

"Shall we go and see the birthing suites?"

Linda

As we walk back to our car, Max chats animatedly about everything we've seen today. He's excited. Actually, he looks ready to combust. "That's not a hospital," he says. "It's a hotel with doctors." I giggle under my breath.

"Things are certainly different since the last time I was planning a birth."

He opens the passenger door for me then walks around to his side, sliding in. "Beautiful," he says, "I'm going to worship you tonight. Today has been the best day of my life." His eyes are wide and excited. "I'm going to be a daddy."

I smile at him, then say, "You always worship me, Max."

"Well tonight is going to be your usual service on steroids."

"Promises, promises," I whisper. "You have high standards to beat."

"You ain't seen nothing yet," he replies, flashing me a sexy smile. "The next six months I'm going to be waiting on you hand and foot. If I could wrap you both in bubble wrap I would. And always keep you with me." I roll my eyes.

"Pregnant, not breakable," I remind him.

"And completely irreplaceable." He leans across, pecks my lips then turns the key in the ignition of his car. We move forward out of the car park and head for home.

Chapter Twenty

Max

Marina is sitting in the living room when I come downstairs to make Linda's morning coffee. She's holding the image of her future sibling in her hands. I pause at the door, and she glances at me, saying nothing, then returning her attention to the photo. "Morning," I say, sharply. This girl has no fucking manners. She blatantly ignores me. "Morning, Marina," I snap, louder this time "Do you want a coffee?" She shakes her head and grunts but doesn't use any coherent words. I walk over, pinch the photo from her hands and stroll into the kitchen. I can almost hear her growl in annoyance.

After putting the kettle on, I replace the scan on the fridge held securely by a magnet displaying the London skyline. I've spent hours this past week looking at it. I'm not sure it has quite sunk in yet, but bloody hell it makes me happy. The mug rack sits on the counter. I take two blue cups and begin to make a coffee for both of us. Marina appears behind me, standing a little too close, her hands on her hips, occupying my space.

"Are you going to be staying here every night?" she asks, her tone hard.

I shrug. "Possibly, we haven't made any decisions about our living arrangements yet."

"You don't know her," she says, gruffly. I ignore her. "She's not who you think she is."

"What does that mean?"

"Well," she pauses, tapping a single finger on her lips. "She's still in love with my dad. She was with him for years, Max. Since they were kids. She'll never love you the way she loved him."

"I'll take my chances," I tell her and wave her away. Linda's ex-husband destroyed her. I know he's no competition for me.

"There's still time you know," she says, "time to wriggle out of this situation. I know it wasn't your fault. She tricked you." As her words hit my ears, I'm lifting the two cups into the air. They return to the surface quickly, liquid splashing over the sides. I spin to face her, furious at what she's implying.

"What are you suggesting?"

"You know damn fine what I'm proposing. Tell her you don't want it. This whole little charade you're playing is cute and all, but we both know it won't last." She straightens her shoulders as my temper skyrockets. "My mother needs constant praise; you'll get bored. You know you will. Give it a few more years and her tits will be at her toes. Getting pregnant was a good way to trap you, her own personal plaything."

"You really are a spoilt brat," I snarl. "You've no idea how I feel. And your mother wouldn't be so bloody manipulative. Don't judge her by your standards."

"I know men," she hisses, "and you'll fucking let her down. Do us all a favour and end the dream before it begins. At least this way she has options."

"Marina," I say, taking a deep breath. "It's not me who doesn't know your mother. It's you." She blinks at me. "The woman I met and fell in love with is confident and sexy. She loves life and lives in the moment."

"You love her?" she stammers, and I nod. Her face pales.

"I do. Now if you don't mind, I'm going to take her, her coffee." I walk past her through the kitchen door and up the stairs, not looking back. She's furious, and so am I.

"Sorry, Max," Linda says. The coffee I brought her ended up in the toilet bowl. "I should have known it wouldn't stay down. But I so miss my coffee in the morning." She's knelt over the toilet. I pull her dark curls behind her head and secure them with a band.

"Baby Gordon is already in the doghouse, and they've not even arrived yet," I say. She reaches for the handle to flush then sits back on her heels. I crouch down beside her, placing my hand on her stomach speaking to my errant child inside. "If you make mummy's life hell now, Baby G, you'll be grounded until you're ten." Linda sniggers. I run my hand down her back. "Let me run you a bath," I tell her. "It's the weekend. There's no rush to be anywhere."

"That would be lovely," she says. I stand and go to the tub, turning on the taps. Once the water runs hot, I pop the plug into place. There is a large purple bottle of bubble bath sitting on the side. I pour in two generous blobs. The scent of lavender fills the air. I return to Linda and hold out both my hands; she takes them, and I pull her up.

"Jeez," I mutter, "what have you been eating? You'll be birthing a toddler." She swipes at my shoulder but rewards me with a soft smile. The silk dressing gown she's wearing hangs open. I slide it from her shoulders, and it falls to the floor in a puddle of pink roses. Underneath, she only has a pair of green cotton shorts and vest to match. I carefully remove them from her body until she stands in front of me naked. I pass her a cup of mouthwash which she swirls around her mouth, gurgles then deposits in the sink. "Better?" I ask and she nods.

As I glance over, the water level is a few inches from the top of the tub. Bubbles spread across the surface. I quickly turn off the taps then take her hand to support her as she steps in. She stills as her foot hits the water. "Too hot?" I question.

"No, it's delightful." She lowers herself into the water, her breasts disappearing below the surface. She lies back, bubbles surround her like a halo, and she closes her eyes. I go to stand, but she holds my hand tighter. "Stay with me." She whispers, "Or why don't you join me?"

"Not today, Beautiful. You need your rest." I kiss her knuckles as I settle myself against the side of the bath. We sit together silently for a while, relaxed in each other's presence.

"We'll need to enjoy this while we can," she mumbles.

"What?"

"Peace and quiet," she says with a smirk. "In a few months' time the whole of hell will let loose. Full nights of sleep and private time will be a thing of the past."

"No, our baby is going to be a phenomenon. They'll sleep through the night from day one, talk by six months and be potty trained in a week." She snorts and bubbles scoot across the water. "My sperm is top notch. How could they not be?"

"You tell yourself that," she says, "but I can assure you all babies shit... everywhere."

The pub is packed wall to wall on a Saturday night. "Mate!" Jace shouts to me as I approach him at the bar. "Where the fuck have you been for weeks?" He raises his eyebrows. "You missed an incredible Halloween. The talent was on point. You could have had your pick of angels, devils, or slutty secretaries."

"Things have been a bit...," I pause, considering what to tell him. Linda and I have agreed to keep the baby and our relationship between us for the moment. Not that I was happy about it. "Things have been busy between work and some personal stuff."

"Personal stuff? Care to elaborate."

"You know, trying to juggle everything gets on top of you sometimes."

"You've been moping?" he says, raising an eyebrow. "Sitting at home feeling sorry for yourself, ignoring my messages."

"Pretty much," I reply with a chuckle. I hate lying to my friend, but he won't understand. And right now, I don't want his advice. Linda and I need to sort this out between us; we need to be on the same page with it all.

"You really can be tragic, mate," he mutters. "Right, you get the beers, it's definitely your round."

We stand at the bar, nursing a bottle each. There is a live band playing rock music if you can call it that. Beats cause the old-fashioned pictures on the walls to shake. We have to shout to each other over the music. Jace is giving me a blow-by-blow account of the weeks I've missed, every woman he's hit on and his success rate; it's not high, it never is. Unfortunately, he more often than not ends up in the *friend zone*. Jace has a never-ending queue of friends, but little to no romance in his life. There was one girl, Diana, but she disappeared a while ago. He never told me why, and I didn't ask. My friend is liberal with information; if he's not telling me, he doesn't want to.

"Oh, check this out," he says, pointing over my shoulder. I turn to see what he's looking at. A group of eight women, all look to be similar ages to me, totter into the bar in high heels and tight dresses. All are wearing bright-pink feather boas around their necks and flashing headbands. One, presumably the bride, has a veil and her white garter exposed on her leg. "Fuck, imagine getting in the middle of that lot." He rubs his hands together. "That would be a night to remember. What is it about women on hen nights...they're bloody delicious."

"They're also completely inebriated," I tell him, "and most likely all taken."

"Don't be such a spoil sport," he says, waving my comment away and scowling at me. "Let's go over and introduce ourselves. We're both hot single guys after all. Maybe they'll be looking for some entertainment."

"I'm not in the mood." I attempt to diffuse the situation, before I get myself into a predicament. "Can't we just enjoy a quiet drink?"

"No, come on." He turns to the bartender and orders a tray of shots.

"What kind?" the bartender asks.

"Any. Let's make it a Russian roulette. Twenty of your best shots." Once the tray is filled, he picks it up and marches towards the table of women. They all glance up as he approaches. I follow behind, trying to stay out of sight but failing because I'm so much bigger than him. "Good evening, ladies. I believe congratulations are in order." He nods at the bride to be, who grins at him. "I'm Jace and this is my friend, Max. This is a little gift from us." He places the tray on the table in front of them.

"Hi," a petite redhead says, her eyes moving between Jace and I. "So, if you're the barman, Jace." She pauses and a smile plays on her lips. "Does that make you the stripper, Max?" Everyone laughs, except me.

"Oh, I wouldn't mind seeing that," a very drunk blonde says. "Do you have a uniform? A fireman or something. That would be hot."

"He's a teacher," Jace pipes up, "and he's very good with his cane."

"I'd be your naughty schoolgirl any day," purrs the blonde woman. She bites her bottom lip and flutters her eyelashes at me. I need out of here; this is the last thing I need to be dealing with.

Perhaps I should tell my friend my situation. He wouldn't have put me in this position if he'd known. But I promised Linda we would wait and tell people when we're both ready. Marina isn't telling anyone; she's too embarrassed. I want to shout it from the rooftops. Hopefully soon Linda will feel ready to share our news.

"Jace," I say, grabbing my friend's attention. He focuses on me. "I'm going to head off."

"No, you're fucking not," he growls. "Have a drink and sit down. We have ladies to entertain." I glare at him. "Sit and drink." Nine sets of eyes watch me as I turn and leave the bar.

Chapter Twenty-One

Linda

My wardrobe is filled with navy and black fitted dresses; I wear a version of the same thing each day for work. I pull another one from its hanger and slip it on. Nope, that goes in the can't be worn pile too. My bump is starting to show, and we're keeping my pregnancy quiet. I want to keep it hidden. Max wants to tell the world. I'm not ready for their judgement yet. He's agreed to not say anything, but I'm not sure how long it will last. I saw the hurt flit across his face when we talked about it.

"You want to hide us?" he said, confused.

"Not hide, just let people find out as we go. I've been the subject of gossip before. I really don't want to experience that again."

"I wasn't planning on taking an advert out in the newspaper," he muttered, annoyed. Then, he'd left for work without another word. That was yesterday, and we've not really spoken since.

This is the first Saturday morning I've had on my own since we reconciled. He was going out last night with a friend and stayed at his own place. It was closer to the bar. All night I was on edge. The thought of him being out there makes me nervous. He's a good-looking guy; women notice him. But I need to trust him, or this will never work. To keep my mind off it, I'd started emptying my wardrobe at one in the morning. Now, I have ten dresses I can't wear and limited clothing for work this week.

Footsteps in the hallway tell me Marina is awake. She was working last night at the dance club, and I know she has this weekend off. "Marina," I call. I hear the footsteps pause, then my bedroom door opens and she comes into view, still wearing her nightdress. "Morning, sweetheart. I'm surprised you're up so early. Was work all right?" She shrugs. "Are you free today?"

"What for?" she says, giving me a quizzical look then scans the room. "Where's lover boy?"

"Don't call him that," I snap. "He's at his flat."

"Did he need to get directions? I'm surprised he remembers where it is," she says, sarcastically. *Don't rise to it.* I sigh. Maybe this isn't such a good idea, but I need to do something to try to improve our relationship which is gradually getting worse.

"Do you want to come shopping? I need some new clothes that are less clingy." I ignore her earlier jibes. It really isn't worth arguing with her about this. It won't change anything. "Everything I own doesn't hide much."

"Why would you want to hide it?" she grumbles, rolling her eyes. "It's not as if you've been knocked up on holiday by your plaything." She wags her finger at me. "Oh wait, yes you have."

"Marina," I squeak, "do you have to be so cruel?" Tears fill my eyes. The confident expression on her face wavers as my emotions burst to the surface. "I'm doing the best I can. None of this was planned, but here we are. I'm trying to do the right thing, sweetheart. Please meet me halfway."

"Ok," she says, not looking at me. "I'll come with you, but you're buying lunch."

Our journey to the shopping centre is made in relative silence. Marina speaks for the first time when we pull into the car park. "What kind of clothes are you looking for?" she asks.

I smile at her in silent thanks for making an effort to speak. "Anything that won't cling to my growing stomach. I'd like to wait until January before telling my work. That way we're over halfway through the school year. Ideally, I'd like to work right up until I go into labour, but I don't know how realistic that is. Especially the way my body has reacted to this pregnancy."

"Was it not the same with me?" she asks. The look she gives me tells me she's genuinely interested in my answer.

"No, I was hardly sick with you. It makes me wonder if it's a boy this time with the differences."

"Are you going to find out?"

"I'm not sure. Max has said it's up to me, but I think he would like to know. I had a surprise with you, so I may find out this time so I can plan better." I glance at my daughter, a beautiful young woman with her whole life ahead of her. It's a shame her attitude leaves a lot to be desired. "You were dressed in yellow and white for the first six months." She chuckles. "I'm sure that's why you don't like yellow."

"Probably," she agrees. I park in a bay near the entrance and we both climb out. The wind bites. It now feels like we are in early December as temperatures plummet further. We walk into the shopping centre side by side, closer than we've been for weeks.

"What about this?" Marina says, holding up yet another floaty top. I screw my nose up at her. "Mum, you don't want things that cling." She shakes the hanger. "This doesn't. You're going to have to wear stuff you wouldn't normally if you want to hide that." She points at my little bump straining on my jeans. I pull my jacket around me.

"Marina," a familiar voice says, and we turn in unison to face my ex-husband. He looks from his daughter to me. "Linda," he says, curtly.

"Stan," I reply with a nod. His attention returns to his daughter.

"Marina, how are you?" She glares at her father openly. "Please talk to me. You haven't been returning my calls."

"What calls?" I ask, confused. Marina told me he hadn't contacted her.

"I've been calling her every day, but she ignores me. We've not spoken in months."

"Marina, you said…" I trail off when I see her expression. I quickly zip up my jacket to ensure he doesn't notice my secret, not that he would. He barely observed anything when we were together. I doubt it would be any different now.

"Dad, can you not take a hint? I don't want to talk to you. You're still on my shit list."

"What happened between your mother and I is none of your concern," he says, his tone authoritative.

"None of my concern," she shrieks. "You wrecked her. You ripped her heart out, and now she's losing the plot."

"Marina!" I snap. "Not here."

"Embarrassed mum? I wonder why," she says, raising her eyebrows. "If you can't tell the man who cheated on you your secret, whose opinion shouldn't count, then how the hell do you expect to be able to tell everyone else with a straight face."

"What are you talking about, Marina?" her father says, clearly confused.

"Mum's new plaything," she retorts then walks off in the direction of the till carrying the floaty top I don't want.

"What is she talking about?" he asks, focusing on me. "Do you have a new boyfriend or something?" I sigh, considering what to say.

"I'm seeing someone, yes. And she isn't exactly overjoyed about it." He sniggers.

"That I understand. Linda, I know I have no right to ask a favour of you." My eyebrows shoot up in surprise at his words. *You're right, you don't.* "But please encourage her to contact me. I do miss her. I have been trying."

"I'll do what I can, but in all honesty, she's getting more difficult to discuss things with. Every day she gets a little more challenging."

"Anything you can do, I'd appreciate it," he says, then turns and walks away.

I catch up with Marina at the tills. She turns to me, her face like stone. I say nothing. I'll wait for her to calm down. There's no point trying to communicate with her when she's in a mood. When we reach the cashpoint, I add the bundle of floaty tops and skirts I'm holding to Marina's one and lay them on the counter. The assistant scans each one, flashing us a fake smile. "That'll be ninety-five pounds and sixty pence, please," she sings. I rummage in my purse for my card, handing it over. Ouch! I'd could have done without spending that.

Ten minutes later, we're sitting opposite each other in a coffee shop. I'm picking at a chocolate muffin whilst Marina pretends to drink her tea. "Why did you say those things to your father?" She glances up at me then her eyes return to her cup. "You really dropped me in it."

"Dropped you in it?" she says with a sigh. "Why do you care what he thinks?"

"I don't. But I'm only getting my head around all this. I don't appreciate you backing me into a corner like that."

"I'm sorry," she whispers, surprising me. "I'm so angry with him, Mum. He ripped our family apart." I stare at her. "Everything is so different. I don't like it." I reach across the table and place my hand on hers.

"I love you," I tell her. "I want you to have a relationship with your father if you want one. You're an adult now, Marina. I'm not going to tell you what to do. But, what your father did, he did because he didn't love me anymore, not you. He was stupid and selfish, but he's always loved you. Just think about it."

"Can I ask you something?" she says, quietly, and I nod. "This thing you have going with Max, do you really see it working out? He's so..." She doesn't elaborate. I know what words come next – so much younger than you.

"I don't know. We've kind of landed here, and we need to do our best. He's a good man. He says all the right things and he makes me happy. Walking away from him in Spain was one of the hardest things I've ever had to do. Time will tell if it all pans out, I suppose." She doesn't respond, just holds my gaze for a moment then looks away. We finish our drinks and cakes then return to my car and head home.

My phone pings as I dump my shopping bags on my bed.

Hey Beautiful, can I come round tonight? I miss you. M x

Marina told me she's going out with her friends, so we will have the place to ourselves. I need to speak to him about our disagreement yesterday. We didn't fight, but I know there's tension.

Of course, I'll make us some dinner. I'm home. Come over whenever you want. X

He responds immediately saying he'll be with me soon. Darkness is falling outside as late afternoon turns to evening. I wander down to my kitchen and start rummaging in the cupboards for something I can make for dinner. I hadn't really planned to eat, but that won't wash with him. This man could eat a three-course meal and sit down for seconds.

I'm elbows deep in bread dough when he appears at my kitchen door, holding the key I gave him. He's practically been living here. I glance at him, smiling softly. He walks over and wraps his arms around my waist, dropping a kiss on my neck. My body buzzes as he envelops me. "What are you making?"

"Just a quick focaccia to go with the pesto pasta," I tell him, signalling to the pot sitting waiting on the stove with my chin.

"Sounds delicious," he says, squeezing me a bit tighter. "I'm sorry about yesterday. I shouldn't have left without finishing our conversation. It was childish of me." I turn in his arms, holding my hands to the side so I don't mark his clothes with flour. He leans down and kisses me softly.

"It's ok. I know you want to tell people. And we will, soon. I just need some time."

"Anything you need," he replies. He's told me this so many times. I'm so lucky to have him. "I've been thinking..." I raise my eyebrow at him. "There are two weekends before Christmas. Why don't we go away for one? We can leave straight after school on a Friday then come back Sunday."

"Max, I can't really afford –" I start to protest, and he cuts me off with his lips.

"My treat. I want you all to myself, well, both of you. We can go somewhere no one will know us, enjoy some festivities, and walk around hand in hand, not worrying about bumping into anyone we know. We can be together like we were in summer." His eyes plead with me. "Please, let me treat you. Since we got back together, there has been so much to consider and take in." I stop his monologue, not caring about the flour on my hands. I pull him towards me using the collar of his jacket then run my hands through his hair. White speckles glisten on the dark strands. We kiss, deeply. When I release him, I pull back, looking up into his beautiful wide eyes.

"That sounds incredible," I tell him. "Now, I've got you dirty." I bite my lip and his eyes fire. "We best get you cleaned up before dinner. Shower now."

Chapter Twenty-Two

Max

I hit 'confirm booking' on the screen. This week, I've spent every spare minute researching our weekend away. I can't wait to have Linda on her own again, to be able to walk down the street and hold her hand in public. The only place we've been out together is the hospital since we reunited. She'd been nervous about people seeing us together. I'd taken her hand as we walked across the car park, and she dropped it as we entered the building. It stung. This weekend could be just what we need to get back to where we were in Spain.

Jace and I haven't spoken since I walked out of the bar. He sent me a text message the following morning, asking if I was all right and telling me if there was anything I needed to let him know. There was no nasty remark or awkward questions. My friend has taken the hint. I'm not ready to talk, but he's there when I need him.

Linda is standing in the living room window looking out as I pull up in front of her house. She lifts a hand to wave when I climb out of the driver's door. When I'm walking up the path, she disappears from view then the front door swings open. She stands in the hallway wearing a fitted navy dress that finishes just above her knees. The dress gives way to the small bump at her waist. Her breasts sit firm and round in the sweetheart neckline.

After walking up the front steps, I wrap one arm around her waist whilst placing my other over my child. "Hello, my favourite people in the world," I whisper in her ear before placing a kiss on her cheek. Her breathing hitches, and I blow softly on her neck. "You look edible, Beautiful. I can't wait to run away with you this weekend." She chuckles under her breath.

"Where are we going?" she asks.

"I'm not telling you," I reply, firmly. She's been trying to get me to tell her our plans all week. I keep avoiding the questions, wanting to keep it a surprise. "It's almost four o'clock and it's nearly a three-hour drive to get there. Let's go, Beautiful."

"Three hours," she says. "I'll need a pee stop, as your child has decided to keep me running to the bathroom this week."

"My child?" I respond, smirking at her. "Not our child?"

"They're our child when their behaviour is good. All negative qualities, I'm blaming on you."

"Being the perfect woman you are, I take full responsibility for our child's errant behaviour." She pecks my lips. "Where's your suitcase?" She signals to the bottom of the stairs with her eyes. "You get in the car, and I'll get your things."

She wanders over to the stairs and looks up. "Marina, we're leaving now," she shouts. There's no response and her shoulders sag. "Marina," she repeats louder this time. I bristle. She will have heard her. Her lack of respect infuriates me. "Marina!"

"I heard you the first time!" the petulant voice replies. "Goodbye."

Linda glances at me, her cheeks flushed. I walk over to her, pick up the case beside her and lead her out to the car. This is a break we both need.

Broadway is a small village nestled at the foot of the Worcestershire hills. When I'd been looking for somewhere to escape to, I found here. The place is steeped in history and the residents throw themselves into the Christmas spirit. I wanted somewhere quiet but festive. Somewhere we could take walks, eat good food and stay in luxurious surroundings. The honey-coloured Cotswold stone houses mixed with period properties, chestnut tree-lined roads and boutique shops decorated within an inch of their life for the season seemed perfect.

I've spared no expense, wanting to make the weekend special. Our home for two nights is the stunning *Abbots Grange Manor House* which sits in its own rolling fields and boasts five-star luxury. Linda gasps as we arrive in front of the sprawling medieval manor house which is draped in snow. Winter has hit hard this year. Snow has fallen here and not stopped for the past week. Her eyes widen when she sees the helipad in the garden scraped clear. "Max," she stammers, grabbing my hand, "this is incredible. Who stays here?" My heart swells as I see tears fill her eyes.

"I've no idea, but do you want to know the best thing?" I say and she nods enthusiastically.

"It's adults only." Her face breaks into a breath-taking smile. "I thought we should enjoy the last few months of grown-up time whilst we can." She leans towards me and takes my face between her hands. We stare at each other; it's at moments like this I feel completely connected to her. She kisses me, her tongue playing with mine. "Will we go and check in?" She murmurs something incoherent against my lips. "What was that?"

"I love you," she whispers.

"Good, because I'm crazy about you. You can show me how much you love me later," I tell her. Wriggling from her grasp, I slide out of the car then walk around to open her door. I take her hand and she steps out. She pulls her winter jacket around her against the freezing temperatures. After lifting our cases from the boot of the car, we walk up to the old stone building through the dramatic pillars.

We are greeted on entry by a fine boned woman dressed beautifully from head to toe in tweed. She smiles warmly at us. "Good evening. Welcome to Abbots Grange," she says in a quintessentially English voice. "My name is Gloria, and I will be your host for the weekend. I just need to take a few details then I'll show you to your room." She looks to be in her mid-fifties, her chestnut hair pinned into a meticulous bun. We follow her over to a heavy wooden desk where she invites us to sit in deep leather chairs.

"Could I have the name the booking is under?" she asks.

"Gordon," I reply. "Max Gordon." She gives me a knowing smile.

"Oh, yes. Mr Gordon, I remember speaking to you on the phone." Linda glances at me curiously, her interest peaked. She hands me an A4 piece of paper detailing the specifics of my booking. "If you could just sign at the bottom, and I'll need a card on file for any extras." I quickly scribble my name then hand her my credit card. "You're in the Regency Suite." I nod. I know this as we discussed the options on the phone. "That's everything," she trills, standing. "Please follow me."

We follow her through a large sitting area with a high vaulted ceiling, a roaring fire crackles away reflecting against the mahogany wood panelled walls. "Breakfast is served between seven-thirty and ten in the morning," she tells us as we stop outside a tall wooden door. She slips the key into the lock, turns it then pushes it open.

"Ladies first," I say to Linda, gesturing for her to walk into the room with my hand. We step into the suite, and she looks around the space, stunned into silence. It's huge, larger than any hotel room I've been in before. There is a king-sized four-poster bed in the centre of the room made of dark wood. The posts almost touch the ceiling. It is swathed in pillows and throws of red and gold silk. Another fire is alight in the corner, burning away merrily. The room has been decorated ready for the festive season with holly and garlands, it looks as if its straight out of a Christmas catalogue. I glance at Linda beside me as I place our cases on the floor. Her jaw hangs open slightly as she takes it all in. In the corner is a white freestanding roll top bath, which allows the occupant views of the English garden outside. We'll be using that later.

"Is this ok for you both?" Gloria asks. I turn to face her. She's standing just inside the room.

"It's perfect, thank you," I tell her.

"Oh, Max," Linda whispers as she spots the twenty-four red roses sitting on the coffee table in front of the large sofa by the fire. "They're beautiful." She walks over to them, leans down and touches a bud with her finger. The door closing signals Gloria's retreat. I walk up behind her, wrapping my arms around her waist, my hands splayed over her stomach.

"Beautiful flowers for my beautiful woman," I mumble in her ear as she leans back against me. "You're my missing puzzle piece, Beautiful. I adore you, always remember that. I want this weekend to be unforgettable."

"You're too good to me," she says, turning to face me. Her big brown eyes blink up at me then fall away, shy.

"You deserve the best of everything. I want to make you happy." I take her hands in mine. "I've booked dinner here for tonight. I hope that's all right? Tomorrow we can investigate the village, eat in the local bistro, and enjoy the Christmas festivities. There is late night shopping every night. Perhaps we could get a new decoration for the tree? To mark our first Christmas together. The first of many."

"That sounds perfect," she says, smiling up at me. "Let me get freshened up. What time is dinner booked for?"

"Eight-thirty, so we have an hour to prepare. Or..." She gives me a knowing look.

"Down boy," she purrs. "Later you can have your wicked way with me but right now, I'm going for a shower." She turns and struts off in the direction of the bathroom. I watch her luscious behind bounce on top of her slender legs.

The sound of the shower turning on tells me she's already undressed and started her ablutions. I wander over to the bathroom, the door lying wide open. She's under the shower, washing her hair. The liquid bubbles as she massages her scalp. I lean on the doorframe and watch her, my eyes running from her head down the smooth skin of her back, over her backside and down those legs I love to have wound around my waist. She turns slightly to the side, the tell-tale swelling that holds her precious cargo coming into view. I return to the bedroom. If I stand there much longer, I'll be forced to join her. I rearrange myself in my jeans, closing my eyes in an attempt to calm down.

Linda reappears ten minutes later huddled in a massive, fluffy white towel. She's roughly brushing her soaking wet hair. "Come here," I tell her. "You'll rip it out from the root doing that." She glances at me. "Sit down." I signal to the dressing table stool. She follows my instructions and passes me the hairbrush. I gently tease the intertwined strands, starting at one side and working my way around. Her eyes are fixed on me in the mirror. I keep mine trained on my task, but I feel her watching me. Once her hair hangs loose and smooth, I drop a kiss on her shoulder, then lift the towel and move it beneath her arms, securing it across the top of her breasts.

As I stand behind her, I place my hands on her shoulders. We stare at each other in the mirror. My thumbs knead the base of her neck whilst my fingers skim her collar bone. She sighs softly under my touch. "That's delightful," she whispers. "Don't stop."

"I'll never stop," I say. "I'll always want to touch you." Her eyes darken and she releases the towel. It drops around her waist. Her plump pink nipples elongate in front of my eyes. She lifts her fingers to one, pinching the bud between them and rotating it. I harden in my jeans once more as I continue to massage her neck and shoulders. She repeats the process with the second nipple. "We have a dinner reservation," I remind her.

"Do you not want your dessert first?" she says, flashing me a sexy smile and throwing the towel wide open then spreading her legs.

"You'll be the death of me," I tell her.

"But you'll die a happy boy."

"That I will," I growl, releasing my grip and walking around to crouch in front of her. "Lean back and spread them some more." I peek up at her. She's closed her eyes and done as she's told. Starting at her belly button, I trail kisses down over her stomach, pausing at her pubic bone. One of her hands plays with my hair, whilst she balances with the other. My hands wrap around her backside pulling her towards me as my mouth connects with her sex. My tongue plays with the sweet spot, and she groans. "A bit louder, Beautiful. I want the neighbours to hear." She chuckles and I nip at her skin. She pushes against my mouth, wanting me deeper, her juices flowing onto my tongue. "Fuck, you taste good."

"Max," she says, ruffling my hair, "let's go to bed." I stand and lift her with me. She closes her legs around me, and I walk her over to the edge of the bed, laying her down. She's looking up at me as I undress, her knees bent, and legs spread wide. I have an uninterrupted view of her pussy, my happy place.

"Someone's hungry," she says with a smirk. Lifting one foot and running her toes down my rock-hard cock. "Is he needing fed? The restaurant is open and fully stocked."

"Fuck, woman. The way I'm feeling now, you won't be able to walk tomorrow."

"Try me," she challenges. I crawl over her, kneeling between her legs and lining myself up. I nudge at her opening. She moans softly and lifts her legs, crossing them over my backside. She squeezes, encouraging me to slide in.

"Patience, Beautiful," I whisper, edging forward an inch then retreating. She's ready, more than ready. Her pussy is wet and screaming to be fucked. She pushes me harder, so I take her further and withdraw again.

"You're such a tease," she growls as I take a nipple between my teeth, biting down hard. She squeals, and I thrust forward, filling her. She sucks me in smoothly, and we both still, gazes fixed on each other. "Move," she says, her eyes wide with arousal. "Ride me hard. I want everyone in this bloody place to know that my boyfriend is the world's best fuck."

"Your wish is my command." I withdraw and immediately slam her into the mattress. "Legs up," I tell her, hooking them over my shoulders as I move. Hard and fast. She throws her head back and cries out as I feel her pussy clench around me. My hips increase in pace, pushing hard, needing to find my own release. Then it happens, my peak comes, and I shoot up inside her. My whole body convulses as I empty myself within her. After, I lie beside her with my head on her chest. My fingers trail over her stomach then up to her breasts. We don't speak; we don't need to. Our being together is enough.

Chapter Twenty-Three

Linda

We never made it to dinner last night. Gloria knocked on our door at nine o'clock. Max apologized and ordered room service as I hid under the thick duvet. He went to the door in only his boxers, and I watched on as the poor woman's eyes popped from her head when she saw him. Thirty minutes later, two trays of delicious fayre had been delivered, and we sat in soft white bathrobes devouring every morsel.

Today, we are heading into the village after breakfast, and he has a surprise for me this afternoon. It feels so good to be here with him, out in the open, walking along the streets hand in hand. Broadway is quaint and idyllic, filled with gift shops and tearooms. The hotel is only a few minutes' walk away, so we've taken our time and explored the area. Max hasn't let me go; nervous I'll slip on the icy streets.

After two hours of wandering with no clear objective, we stop outside a small coffee shop, Peggie's Tearoom. Max squeezes my hand and says, "Hot drink and a cake?" He signals to the selection of homemade delicacies in the window. I nod, relieved. As much as I've enjoyed our stroll, I'm tired. A seat and some substance sound ideal just now. He places a hand on the base of my back, opening the door with the other, guiding me in. The place is small. Most tables are taken with elderly patrons wearing woolly jumpers chatting animatedly with each other.

We find a pine table for two, the last remaining one. On the matching chairs are cushions similar to ones my Gran used to have, padded with pictures of old houses and gingerbread men. After shrugging out of our coats, we sit down facing each other, and he takes my hands across the table. A man approaches us, smiles kindly, then tells us the daily cakes available. We each order a slice of carrot cake along with a hot chocolate. Within minutes they are sitting in front of us.

I pick up my fork and slice a piece of sponge, then pop it in my mouth. Max watches me intently, lifting is eyebrows. "Does that taste nice?" he asks.

"Delicious," I reply.

"Not as good as your pussy," he whispers. I swipe at his hand.

"Max," I hiss, "you'll give one of these grannies a heart attack with comments like that."

"Everyone has sex, Linda. Even grannies."

"Not an image I want in my head, thank you," I mutter, and he laughs.

"You know for an adventurous woman in the bedroom, you can be a bit of a prude." I scowl at him. "You really do live up to a man's dream woman."

"And what does she look like? Enlighten me."

"Well, she's classy by day. You'd happily take her home to your mother. But," he pauses, a dark smile playing on his lips, "at night, she turns into a sex-mad vixen. Who can't get enough cock." My jaw drops. He just said that, out loud, in the middle of a café filled with what looks like an over-sixties coach trip.

"Max," I squeal.

"Relax, Beautiful. No one is listening. Do you want to know where we're going next? What your surprise is?"

"Ok, tell me. It better not be a backstreet sex club, after that comment." He laughs again and this time, it's the loudest sound in the room. A few ladies glance in our direction. I see their eyes moving between us, assessing the situation. My confidence wavers as I consider what they're thinking. I push the thoughts to the back of my mind.

"A bird show," he says.

"A bird show?" I repeat, confused.

"Yes, not with women. Birds like falcons and eagles. They're flying at three o'clock then I've arranged for us to have a private tour to be able to hold them."

"Hold them?" I squawk. "Hold birds of prey? I don't know if I can..." He beams at me, then stands and walks around the table, crouching down beside me.

"Beautiful," he says, pushing a wayward strand of hair from my face. "You can do anything you set your mind to. You're an incredible woman. Strong and fearless. Sexy and loving. You might not feel amazing every day but believe me, you are." I flush. "And you're all mine." He returns to his seat after kissing me softly on the lips.

We finish our drinks and rise to leave. An elderly lady sitting at the table beside us, holds out a hand as we pass by. "Excuse me," she says. Max walks ahead not noticing the obstruction.

"Yes," I reply, smiling down at her.

"I couldn't help but overhear your conversation. Is that young man your partner?" My heart beats harder, nervous I'm going to get some unwanted opinions on our obvious age difference. I glance up and Max has stopped. He is now standing at the door with a confused expression on his face.

"Yes, he is."

"Well, dear, I wanted to congratulate you. He's a bit younger than you," she says with a smile. "I love to see an older woman in control and those sweet words spilling from his lips told me you have him hook, line and sinker." She chuckles. "A sex-mad vixen. I don't think a woman can get a better compliment." Not knowing what to say, I smile and nod, then scurry from the café.

"What did she want?" Max asks as I catch up with him.

"Don't ask."

Cotswold Falconry Centre is ten minutes' drive away. We return to the hotel to collect our car. We drive through the rolling green countryside before arriving at the centre. Max holds my hand as we walk along the pathways to the exhibition area. A man stands at the centre holding a huge brown bird wearing a hood. Other customers begin to file in, and we sit on huge logs surrounding him. Blankets have been folded on top to ward off the damp.

Over the next hour, he brings out bird after bird that fly and swoop around us. Each one is bigger than the next, it is breath taking to watch. My favourite is a vulture which flies but also seems to skip across the ground. The huge wings cast shadows over the crowd as it passes above us. The show comes to an end, and the people clap and shout messages of thanks.

"Our turn," Max whispers in my ear. He stands, pulling me to my feet. His face has broken into a wide grin. His eyes are alight with excitement making him look even younger. "It's going to be amazing." I smile at him as my nerves rise. Holding birds of prey has certainly not been top or even included on my bucket list. I've avoided it before. I'm normally a coward with anything remotely dangerous or strange. Going out of my comfort zone is a recent experience for me. It started with eight weeks in Spain.

We walk down to the front. Max shakes Brian, the bird trainer's, hand. "Max," he says, "it's nice to meet in person. You were so enthusiastic on the phone."

"I can't wait," he replies. "This is my partner, Linda." Brian nods in my direction in greeting. "Where do we start?"

"You'll each get gloves," Brian says, giving me an encouraging smile. The blood must have drained from my face. "Linda, the birds are all well-handled. You don't need to worry."

"Not something I ever thought I'd be doing," I mutter. Max smirks at me.

"Neither am I," he says, deadpan. I swallow. He's unbelievable today. Sex on the brain. Brian snorts with laughter. "But you know I like to push your boundaries, Beautiful." I feel my cheeks heat, and I scowl at him.

"You're fucking pushing my buttons today," I hiss.

"Pushing your buttons is my favourite hobby," he replies, casually. "All of them."

For the next thirty minutes, we meet each beautiful bird up close. We hold them on thick gloves; it's a surreal experience. A kestrel named Mia is my favourite. She sits on my arm then Brian encourages her to fly, she swoops around then lands back where she started. My arm flexes with the added weight, but my confidence explodes with overcoming my fear. Max watches my every move, smiling each time I pose for a photo with a new companion. Once done, we walk back to the car, discussing each one in detail. The colour, the temperament, and the feel of it on our arm.

"I never thought I could do anything like that," I tell him. "It was amazing being so close to them."

"I told you. You can do anything you set your mind to. It's one of the multitude of reasons I adore you," Max says as we climb into the car and head back to the hotel.

***

Max

Today turned out better than I hoped. We enjoyed unrushed time together and it was perfect. The falconry centre was a risk, but I wanted to do something out of the box, push her boundaries and increase her self-confidence in the process.

She mentioned one evening in Spain that years ago she had visited a similar place with Marina and her ex-husband. At the end of the display, viewers were invited to come and hold the birds. Marina had been desperate to do it, but an adult had to accompany her. Linda was too afraid to go near, and her daughter had missed out. She said since then it was a regret that played on her mind, how she let her own worries lessen her daughter's experience.

She'd been bursting with pride each time a bird was placed on her arm. My heart had swelled as I watched on. This is the woman I love, the woman I met in summer. She's happy and confident, willing to try new things. These past weeks have been wonderful, but I see her nerves and uncertainty. She's waiting for the tower of cards to fall.

I've booked an intimate bistro restaurant in the village for dinner this evening. It comes highly recommended. Linda is standing in front of the full-length mirror. She smooths her soft pink fitted dress over her bump. It's gathered slightly, so if you didn't know our baby was there, you'd probably miss it. Her dark curls are pinned back off her face and cascade in waves down her back. She readjusts the neckline of her dress again and tuts. "I'm sure my boobs have got bigger. Heaven help me in a few months."

"I'm not complaining," I say. She raises an eyebrow at me.

"You won't be saying that when they're rock solid and leaking milk." I laugh, shaking my head. She slips on her high heels, then piles a heavy winter coat on top.

"Ready?" I ask, and she nods, then we head out into the night.

Our meal was delicious. We polished off every last mouthful. I'm sipping at my final drink whilst Linda talks spiritedly about her colleague, Rhian, from work. "She's so free," she says, excitedly. "Every few weeks there's a different boyfriend or place to be." Her eyes light up with enthusiasm.

"And you think that's a good thing?" I ask, ruffled by the comment.

"No, but I think the fact she's not beholden to anyone is a good thing." My eyes run over her face as she looks at me. I'm trying to understand where she's coming from but I'm struggling. "She's her own woman, always has been. You've got to understand, Max, for years I was a shell of who I should be. Always living in my husband's shadow." My ears perk up at the word husband.

"Was Stan not supportive of you?" She gives me a quizzical look.

"In what way?" she asks. We haven't spoken of him much except of his existence and what he did to her. Her life before is none of my business.

"In what you wanted to do in life."

"We were very young when we got together then married. Practically just adults. Back then, what we created was expected. He wasn't unsupportive but the opportunities for me to do more weren't there." She sighs. "We did what we were supposed to do." I go to speak, but she starts talking again. "Marriage was a necessity when I was young.

A woman didn't generally start a family without a ring on her finger and if she did, there were plenty of mutterings to go around."

"You don't think marriage is important now?" I ask, unnerved.

"I wouldn't get married again," she says simply, and my stomach falls. "There's no reason for me to." I blink at her, stunned. She doesn't seem to notice my discomfort.

"U-Um," I stammer, trying to get my thoughts in a logical order. "I didn't realise you felt that way." She shrugs.

"I have everything I want right here at this table, well apart from Marina of course." Her eyes drop to her belly as she places a hand across our child. "I don't think a ring would add anything to what we have." I clear my throat, unable to say anything sensible. A sadness washes over me – this is news to me.

Our conversation moves on to less uncomfortable matters. All the while the diamond ring is burning a hole in my pocket.

Chapter Twenty-Four

Max

Monday morning rolls around as it always does. Linda's school is shut for maintenance works today. I left her under our duvet snoring softly into her pillow. I'm leaning on the kitchen worktop finishing the last of my coffee when Marina wanders in. She's already dressed for her job at the call centre. "Morning," I say. "Day shift today?" She groans and rubs at her eyes.

"I hate Mondays," she grumbles. "And I hate my job more."

"What would you rather be doing?" I ask her, trying to keep the conversation flowing. This is the most civilised one we've had since we met. She shrugs.

"Pole dancing," she says with a smirk. "If I could do what I do on a Saturday night every day, I'd be happy." I still can't imagine Marina swinging around a pole. It's probably best I don't. I doubt her mother would approve. "Other than that, I've never wanted to be anything, but I would like to find a real job that doesn't bore me to tears. And where the customers aren't complete tosspots." I snort into my cup, her humour taking me by surprise.

"I'll swap you my year eleven for your day shift," I tell her. "I'm sure half of them are in training for villain of the year. Last week, they superglued a classmate to his chair." I roll my eyes. "What a fucking mess." She sniggers, then retreats to the living room. Maybe, our relationship is improving. I know that would make Linda happy. I make a mental note to keep the lines of communication open. As much as Marina boils my piss, she's Linda's daughter. I need to make an effort.

My thoughts return to Saturday night and our conversation at the restaurant. Linda well and truly took the wind out my sails with her comments about marriage and her lack of desire to be someone's wife again. Part of me is relieved to find out, but another part is shaken that it may mean we never marry. In hindsight, popping the question without discussing the possibility first was perhaps not my brightest idea. But I wanted to show her in the most sincere way, that what we have, for me, is forever. Thankfully, the ring stayed securely in my pocket. It's now safely stored away, ready if it's required, but only if I engage my brain first.

I place my cup in the dishwasher, grab my coat, and head out the door to work. During my drive, which is much longer than if I stayed at home, it gives me plenty of time to reflect on the weekend and our plans for the future. Not that I have many beyond seeing my baby safely into the world and looking after both them and Linda. We still have so much to figure out, but we'll get there. Both our lives have transformed unrecognisably since we met barely six months ago, but we're here and we're together, that's more than some people are blessed with.

Time will pass, and we'll learn more about each other but right here, right now, this is exactly where I want to be.

***

Linda

"Everything looks great," the sonographer says. "Baby is exactly where they should be." I breathe out a sigh of relief. I didn't tell Max about this appointment. There were extra tests suggested due to my age. He said it was up to me if I went through with them. This was something I needed to do on my own. They all came back clear. I only wanted to speak to Max about these concerns if there were any issues. He's so excited about our baby that I didn't want to dampen his enthusiasm unnecessarily. "Do you want to know the sex?" I pause, considering the question.

After a moment, I reply, "Yes, yes I do."

Christmas day arrives and snow is falling. It dusts everywhere, freezing solid within minutes. It won't last long as it rarely does. The rain comes and creates an ice rink, where it's lethal to walk out your front door. Max and I have the house to ourselves. Marina has yet another boyfriend. How long this one will last no one knows, but he's given her something to focus on other than me and my pregnancy. She's definitely been more upbeat. Perhaps this one could be a positive influence in her life.

I wake from a dreamless sleep to Christmas music blaring through the house and the smell of bacon frying. My stomach growls. I'm relieved that in the past week my morning sickness seems to have subsided somewhat. It's mutated into evening sickness for some reason. I'm not complaining – at least I get to eat my breakfast in peace. No doubt Baby G will change the goal posts again soon.

My bedroom door swings open, and Max bounces into the room. He's only wearing a pair of Christmas boxer shorts, Rudolf's nose covering his junk. A bright red Santa hat is perched on his head. "Morning, Beautiful," he says, sitting down beside me and kissing me softly. "Merry Christmas. I love how you look in the morning."

"Now I know you're fucking lying," I tell him, swiping at his cheek. I catch a glance of myself in the mirror. My hair hangs in rats tails around my face which is pale in the morning light. "You can be such a crawler when you want to be." He chuckles then pops a kiss on the end of my nose.

"Even looking like you've clambered out a bog like you do now," he says, "I'd still fuck you." I roll my eyes at him.

"Not helping," I hiss, sarcastically. "You'll be sleeping in the spare room at this rate. Your Christmas shag will be cancelled." He grins at me then rises, plucking my dressing gown from a chair and handing it to me.

"Come on, get up. Let's get our first Christmas day together started. I want to give you your present."

"Is it a real present? Or are you being a dirty bastard?" I ask him.

"Both," he replies, leaving the room. I watch his tight behind disappear out of the door. I still can't believe he's mine.

As I push myself up from the bed, my feet hit the cosy rug at my feet. I curl my toes into the deep pile before putting on my slippers and shrugging on my dressing gown. The house is warm, but I always feel the cold. Max is like a furnace and wanders around in next to nothing when it's only us here. It makes pleasant viewing for me.

I find him in the kitchen still flipping various pieces of meat in a frying pan. He has plates and glasses laid out ready for us. I watch on as he piles pancakes and bacon onto each plate then drizzles them with maple syrup. My favourite breakfast. It's one of those meals that should taste disgusting, but I find it orgasmic. My dining table has already been set, a scented candle in the centre emitting a fragrance of cinnamon. All the Christmas lights are turned on and the curtains opened to the festive scene outside. It really does feel like Christmas morning.

"You go sit down," Max says, gesturing towards the table. "I'll bring this over."

"You're the best present a girl could ask for," I tell him, and he replies with a smile, a pleased look on his face. I wander over and sit down at the table.

He appears minutes later with a mug of hot chocolate topped with cream and marshmallows. I eye him accusingly. "It's Christmas," he says as a way of explanation. "Calories don't count today. And..." he pauses then smirks, "you're eating for two. Enjoy it while you can." Next, he places a plate piled high with my delicious breakfast in front of me, then he sits down opposite me. We both tuck in.

When we're together, life feels right. For all there is a large age gap between us, it disappears. I won't lie. I still worry about outside opinions, but when I'm with him it all evaporates. He makes me feel like the only woman he wants. I love how he wears his heart on his sleeve. Max is never shy with affection; it's taken a bit of getting used to but I'm getting there.

That day I went to his work and asked him for another chance was the most nerve-wracking day of my life. I thought he would tell me to go. He'd walk away and not look back. But he listened to me and made the decision to give me another chance. Give us another chance. Then, when I dropped the baby bomb, he held me tighter instead of pushing me away. Finding him has improved my life, no end.

After breakfast, we move to the living room and sit curled around one another on the sofa. "Is it time for presents?" he whispers in my ear, and I grin at him. I hope he likes mine. I wanted to do something special for him. He leans down to the side of his chair and picks up a small pink bag, handing it to me. There is a simple white ribbon securing the top.

I release the bow and prise the sides apart. Inside is a small white box, the kind you get from a jeweller. It's too big to be a ring box, which is a relief. I noticed his expression when we spoke of marriage at the restaurant during our weekend away. His face had fell when I told him I didn't want to be married again. Guilt had bubbled in my stomach for the remainder of the evening. It wasn't something we'd discussed. For all we have a baby on the way, our relationship is still very new and unconventional. Marriage is a proposition for another day.

I remove the white box from the bag and open it. Inside is a simple but stunning silver bracelet. A pair of eagle wings engraved into the band. I glance at him, and he's studying my reaction. "Turn it over," he says. I flip the bracelet and on the underside is a second engraving. *You and I can do anything. Together.*

"It's beautiful, Max," I whisper, and he lifts his hand to my cheek, the way he has so many times before. "I love you."

"And I love you more than you can imagine," he replies. "Both of you." He leans down and kisses my belly.

"Ok, time for your present," I say, and my heart rate increases. I hope he loves this and isn't angry about my lack of transparency. I pull the envelope from my dressing gown pocket and hand it to him. He raises an eyebrow in question then removes the various sheets of paper from it.

He sits back on the sofa, scanning each one individually. His brow creased in concentration. "What is all this?" he asks, glancing at me.

"Test results," I reply. "I went for the extra tests, and everything is fine. Our baby is perfect." He looks at me and a breath-taking smile explodes across his face. "I didn't tell you..." He cuts me off with a kiss.

"You don't need to explain," he says. "This is the best present I could wish for."

"There's one more." He stares at me, his eyes searching mine for clues. I pass him the small soft package wrapped in simple red paper. He takes it from me and starts to unwrap his gift. Within moments, the small blue bear comes into view with the word *Daddy* embroidered across its tummy.

"Does this mean what I think it means?" he asks, and I nod.

"We're having a baby boy," I tell him, and tears fill my eyes.

He takes my face between his hands and kisses me, deep and meaningfully. When he pulls back, his eyes are wide and excited. "Thank you," he whispers, softly, leaning his forehead against mine. "I can't wait to meet him."

Chapter Twenty-Five

Linda

"Could you get any closer?" Max says as he pokes his head around our bedroom door. "What are you looking for?"

"Wrinkles," I mumble in response. I'm standing in front of my full-length mirror with my nose almost touching the glass. "Every day, Max," I whine, "another blasted line marks my face every damn day." He walks up behind me, wraps his arms around my ever-growing waist and pops his head on my shoulder. His hands are splayed across my six months pregnant belly, our gazes meeting in the mirror.

"You're beautiful," he whispers. "I love every bump, curve, and crease on your body. Especially these." His hands lift to my breasts, squeezing them softly, then he places a kiss on the side of my neck. I sigh, enjoying the safety of his embrace. He's always full of compliments, but as my body changes with each week that passes, it's getting harder to believe them.

The last time I was pregnant, I was twenty-three and married with youthful skin and years ahead of me. Now as a divorcée of forty-six, who managed to get knocked up by a man twelve years younger than me during an eight-week holiday romance, things have changed somewhat. It terrifies me that I will be sixty when my child is in their teen years. It's even more terrifying that my new partner is young, hot and an absolute charmer. He adores me, I know that, but I can't help wondering if it will last.

"First day back at work after a magical Christmas," he says. "How are you feeling?"

"Nervous," I admit. "Only a handful of people know about this." I signal to my stomach. It's amazing I managed to keep it hidden before the school holidays. I didn't pop like I thought I would. The small bump that appeared in late November was easily hidden by flowing tops. But now, there's no mistaking I'm with child.

"Have you told anyone at work yet?" he prompts, again. I shake my head.

"No, but I've arranged to meet Rhian at eight." I glance at the small clock on my dressing table – that's an hour away. She's the closest thing to a friend I have there. I'm still thankful of our conversation that convinced me to give my relationship with Max a chance.

Our baby kicks directly beneath his hands and his eyes widen. I giggle. "You felt that?" I ask, and he kisses my cheek.

"That was the most amazing feeling in the world," he replies. "I still can't believe my baby is in there."

"Well, he most definitely is. My bladder will confirm it too," I say with a smirk. "Right, I need to get ready." He reluctantly unwraps his arms from around my waist. Walking over to my closet, I pull the double doors open wide. All my work clothes hang in an orderly fashion ranging from black to dark blue, every item is a knee-length fitted dress with a demure neckline. Next to them are the floaty tops and skirts I bought to hide my growing bump. I pick one of each and hold them in front of me. Do I walk in brazen with my condition clear? Or do I hide it? I return the disguise to the wardrobe and hang the black fitted dress on the door handle.

Max stands, leaning against the doorway, watching my every move. He's dressed in a fitted white shirt with smart dark jeans. His bare feet are in stark contrast to the dark wool carpet. His hair is ruffled like he's just rolled out of bed. I glance over my shoulder at him, and he gives me a sexy smile in return. My cheeks heat. "Are you going to stand there all day? Do you not have things to do?" I query.

"Nothing more important than standing here enjoying the view," he says, smoothly.

I pick up a cushion sitting on the armchair next to me and throw it at him. He catches it and grins. "Piss off and let me get ready. You're too much of a distraction standing there, looking like that," I tell him. He winks then turns away and saunters towards the kitchen. I hear the kettle click on and my focus returns to my reflection in the mirror.

My dark curls hang loose around my face and cascade over my shoulders. With a naked face, I look all of my years, so I reach for my make-up bag and start my tedious make-up routine of filling in the cracks and lines. My birthday celebration last week hadn't been a happy one. Once complete, I slip into the simple black dress. It skims my curves finishing just above my knee. The soft wool fabric gives way to the extra bump at my midriff. I notice my breasts sit slightly fuller in the V-shaped neckline than the last time I wore this. Picking up my black court shoes, I carry them through to the kitchen.

Max has finished getting ready and is standing, draining a mug of tea. "Where's Marina?" he asks, "Was she on the night shift?" I nod. She still works in the local call centre, her shifts changing week to week. Her enthusiasm about her new sibling or the fact my boyfriend is closer to her age than mine is non-existent. Since Max started spending more time here, she's continued to distance herself from me. It's something I'm going to have to deal with soon.

"She's in bed," I confirm. "I popped my head in before I came downstairs."

He nods then walks towards me and takes my face in his hands. I stare up into his beautiful green eyes. "I love you, Linda. Remember that. You, me, and our baby haven't done anything wrong. I hope you tell Rhian with pride that you're expecting my child," he says, and my heart aches slightly. After kissing me softly, he grabs his bag and heads out the door, calling over his shoulder, "I'll see you later."

As I drive through the black iron gates of the school, my heart rate increases slightly. It's a frosty winter morning, and I piled my heavy winter jacket on top of my dress before I left the house. Stopping my car in the bay closest to the front door I can, I climb out and make my way precariously across the icy ground. When I finally reach the building and push open the front door, the heat hits me hard and my stomach lurches. *Not now. I can't be sick now.*

Keeping my jacket pulled around me, I walk through the corridors decorated with paintings and pie charts to Rhian's office. Her door sits slightly ajar. Peering inside, I see her moving around organising files and folders. I wriggle out of my jacket and throw it on the waiting area sofa before softly chapping the door. "Come in," she calls, and I push the door open. She looks up and smiles automatically then her jaw drops in a spectacular fashion. "Happy new year, Linda. I see you have plenty to look forward to," she says. "Come and sit down. Let me put the kettle on. You can tell me all about it."

"Hi Rhian," I say in greeting. "Did you enjoy the holidays?"

"No, no, no. You're not skirting around the elephant in the room, Linda Butterby. What on earth happened?" she stammers. "Well, I know what you did but who's the father?" I haven't actually told anyone that Max and I are together. London is a big enough city that we haven't been seen by anyone I know as far as I'm aware. Luckily, my ex-husband and his floozy moved away just before Max started coming around, and I don't know any other neighbours well. They probably assume he's Marina's boyfriend, I think cynically.

As I take my seat opposite her, she pours two steaming cups of coffee and places them on her desk then sits down. Swallowing my nerves, I say, "Do you remember the younger guy I told you about in Spain?" She nods. "Well, he's the father."

"Does he know?" she asks, stunned, and I smile to myself.

"Yes, Max knows. We've been together since October. I went to see him once I knew about the baby."

"Since October," she shrieks, "and you've kept it quiet. I need to keep my eye on you, Linda. Does anyone else know?" She gives me an encouraging smile.

"Only Marina officially," I say, "though I'm sure he'll have been seen by prying eyes around the house. I don't know my neighbours well.

Marina isn't exactly overjoyed with the situation, so I doubt she's shouting it from the rooftops."

She smirks. Her blue eyes dance with excitement, and she runs her fingers through her short blond bob. "I can imagine," she agrees. She sits back on her chair, crossing one long slender leg over the other then takes a sip from her mug. "When are you due?"

"Mid-April," I answer. "It must have happened quite soon after we met." I feel my cheeks heat in embarrassment. Honestly, I should've known better. It was me who suggested we didn't need to use protection. What an idiot.

"Is he supporting you?" she asks, kindly.

"Pardon," I say, surprised by the change of direction.

"Is your new partner supporting you? Is he happy about the baby? I would imagine this was a huge shock for him too. I want to make sure you're all right, Linda." My eyes well up, and a single tear runs down my cheek. She stands abruptly, walks around her desk, and crouches in front of me, placing her hands on my knees. "You can trust me. I'll support you in any way I can. You're not the first woman this happened to; you certainly won't be the last."

"Yes, he's supportive. Rhian, he's everything I need and want. That's what terrifies me." She looks at me quizzically. "He's only thirty-three. How am I going to keep a man like him happy? Once the baby is here and my body changes again..." I trail off, not wanting to disclose all my fears to my boss.

She nods then says, "He's here. That says something. What's your current living situation?"

"He has his own place near his work but is spending most nights with me. We haven't discussed what will happen once the baby arrives."

"Ok, well may I suggest you need to discuss that with him? Meanwhile, I'll complete the necessary paperwork for your maternity leave, and I'll speak with Mrs Hanson about your ongoing role within class. Any issues at all, you come and see me. Do you understand?" She smiles. "Welcome back to work. Congratulations, you're in for an eventful year."

"Thank you," I whisper. We both stand, and she hugs me. I feel like I have a female friend at home for the first time in a long time. A woman on my side. When my husband left, all our friends went with him. The couples we socialised with adopted his new squeeze into the group and left me out to dry. It hurt. A lot.

Chapter Twenty-Six

Max

"Here, get that down your neck," Jace orders as he places my pint of beer on the table. "I still can't believe you're having a kid." I laugh, that's the third time he's said that in ten minutes. "Have you never heard of protection?" he jokes, waggling his eyebrows.

"It wasn't exactly planned," I tell him, again. "Linda thought she couldn't get pregnant. Accidents happen. It's been a happy surprise." He gives me a look which tells me he doesn't believe me. Jace is one of my oldest friends, and I've only told him about Linda and the baby tonight. Four months after we reconciled. Normally, I tell him everything, but this was something I wanted to keep to myself until I got my head around the situation. Time passed and the right moment never came, until he called me out this week.

My phone rang on Thursday evening after the school day. "Friday night sesh?" he barked down the phone before I could even say hello. "No more fucking excuses, mate. I've barely spoken to you in months and when I do, the bullshit you tell me doesn't wash. What the fuck is going on?"

I'd held the phone from my ear as his deep voice reverberated down the line. "Ok," I said. "Yes, I need to see you. There's quite a lot you should know." He tutted into the handset and muttered something about knowing I'd been hiding something. Before he could ask any more questions, I told him, "I'll see you at the normal place tomorrow after work." Then I'd cut the call.

The pub is packed for after-work Friday night drinks, people are crammed into the small space. Most are still dressed in business suits with their ties pulled loose or shirts untucked from their waistbands. Women keep disappearing to the bathroom dressed like secretaries and return fully made up and ready to party. Only a few months ago, I was the same. Often, I would leave for work on a Friday morning and not get home until Saturday.

When I'd returned from Spain last summer, I'd been heartbroken by Linda's rejection. On her last day, we stood on the roof terrace of the hotel, and she told me we had no future. She said that I should try to find a woman closer to my age, whom I could create a family with. Eight weeks later, she turned up outside my work. My initial reaction was to tell her to go, but I bit my tongue and let her speak. She didn't tell me about the baby until I'd taken her in my arms. Part of me wonders if she would have told me at all if I'd rejected her. I've never wanted to ask, not wanting to know the answer.

Jace rattles his fist on the wood in front of me, snapping me from my recollections. "Earth to Max Gordon," he bellows across the table.

"Sorry," I mumble. My old friend sits opposite me wearing a blue checked shirt with one too many buttons undone tucked into denim knee-length shorts. His pot belly hangs over the waistband. Once again, on his feet are his trusty leather sandals. "Are you not freezing?" I ask him. He shakes his head and flashes me a wide toothy grin. "It's bloody January," I mutter. The dark hair on his chest pokes through the gap in his shirt. His beard and moustache are neatly trimmed, but there is not a wisp of hair on his head. The final strands have disappeared over the past year. Only in his mid-thirties, he could be easily mistaken for a decade older.

"How's the venomous daughter handling the news?" he asks, and I roll my eyes. "That bad, huh?"

"Let's just say she isn't over the moon at being made a big sister at twenty-three. Linda didn't tell her about the baby until she'd spoken to me. If we hadn't gotten back together, I'm not sure what she would've done." My heart strains slightly. "I'm not sure if she would have continued with the pregnancy at all."

His eyebrows draw together as he processes what I've just said. "What makes you think that?"

I shrug my shoulders. "I don't know. I'm not convinced that she's happy about the baby. It's only this week she's told her work. She asked me not to tell anyone yet. We've been sneaking around so no one sees us together. She thinks I don't notice, but I do. Perhaps she's embarrassed to be seen with me."

Jace's gaze holds mine. "Max," he says, kindly. "Linda has done all this before." I blink at him, confusion clear on my face. "What I mean is, she's been here before. She's been married, had a child, and lived her life. I'm sure the last thing she expected was to be starting again. Especially after a summer fling with you."

A fling. The word stings. For me, since that first day we spent together, it was always more than a fling. But I'm a hopeless romantic who always ends up without the girl and nursing a broken heart. This time is different though. I've got the girl but I'm not sure if she would have come back to me if the situation was different.

"She's probably scared," he says in an attempt to reassure me. "Have you spoken about going public? What about your families? It's not as if you can keep it a secret forever."

"No one knows. I only really have Aunt Susan to tell, and Linda only has her brother. All our parents have passed on. Friends will find out as we go. Linda has very few left since the breakdown of her marriage and well you know now. I don't have anyone else that I desperately need to tell," I say.

"What about Bex?" he asks. Bex. The girl from my childhood who has rejected me numerous times over the years. The girl who is one of my oldest friends. The girl who broke my heart before I left for Spain last summer by telling me we would never be more than friends.

"We're not speaking," I say. "Again." He gives me a knowing smile. "She doesn't know about Linda or the baby. As I said, she's not speaking to me, it's been months and I doubt it will change anytime soon." Bex and I have played this game for years. I convince myself I have a chance, laying my heart on the line, and she kindly rejects me. Then we don't speak for a while, sometimes it's for weeks or months, but normally she has a crisis, and I swoop in to support her in whatever drama is unfolding in her life.

"How are you feeling about it all?" Jace asks.

"Fuck's sake. What is this? The Spanish Inquisition?" I snap at my friend, and he laughs.

"Mate, I've not seen you since November. You've ignored my calls and avoided my messages. Now, you turn up and tell me the older woman you bonked last summer is pregnant with your kid and you're practically living together," he says, deadpan. "Forgive me for having some concerns. The last time we were here, if I remember correctly, you had a little blonde thing draped around your neck. Does Linda know that your weeks apart were spent in the pub?" I glare at him. It's true. On my return from Spain, I went off the rails. Every weekend was filled with lad's nights attempting to mend my broken heart.

"I didn't sleep with anyone," I hiss. "Linda and I weren't together. I never expected to see her again. She hasn't asked, and I really don't see any benefit in telling her. A few kisses and a taxi ride home when I couldn't go through with it. There's nothing to tell."

"There's not," Jace challenges, raising an eyebrow. "Max, the girl was all over you for two weekends in a row. You went home with her."

"I didn't sleep with her," I repeat. "Linda's already struggling enough with the fact she's pregnant and the difference in our ages. How do you think she would feel finding out I sought comfort in a woman the same age as her daughter?" I place my elbows on the table and put my head in my hands. "I wasn't thinking straight, Jace. I was single and lonely." He nods. "The last thing in the world I want to do is hurt her. I love her. I'm excited to become a father." He gives me a soft smile. "But I know what you're trying to say. These things have a way of biting me on the ass."

He nods. "Mate, I'm just saying perhaps she should know you weren't a monk when you and her split. No one can blame you for satisfying your needs as a single guy."

"Perhaps," I mutter then rise to go to the bar for another drink.

"That's you home, pal," the taxi driver says as he pulls to a stop outside the house. My head swirls as I sit up in the back seat of the car. Screwing my eyes shut, I shake my head to try to clear the alcohol fog. "That'll be £15.80, please."

On reaching into my pocket, I pull out a ball of notes and some loose change. Finally, I find a twenty-pound note and hand it to the driver through the small window in the glass dividing him from his passengers. "No change required," I slur, grabbing for the door handle. The heavy door swings open, and I step out into the freezing night air. There is a thin frost on the ground, and my skin prickles beneath my thin shirt in the icy temperature. The car speeds off as soon as I close the door, the rear tyres spinning as the driver hits the accelerator splattering my jeans with muck. I watch the asshole driving away and flip him the bird.

I turn around and stare at Linda's small semi-detached house that's become my home in recent months. Things are cosy, especially as there are only two bedrooms and three adults living here, one of which openly hates my guts. The outside is simple red brick with white windows and doors. The garden is immaculate being home to perfectly prepared flower beds, ready for planting in spring.

I stumble up the short, paved path and retrieve the key from my jeans pocket with difficulty. Three in the morning shows on my watch. Fuck, I'm a lot later than I planned to be, but after Jace lined up the tequila there was no going back. Time ran away as the drinks flowed. It takes a few attempts to slide my key into the lock, scratching the metal each time I miss. Eventually, it turns, and I push open the door. The sound of voices chattering in the living room surprises me as I enter the hall.

When I walk towards the sound of the conversation, I find Marina and two girls of a similar age sprawled along the sofas, each one holding a glass of wine and speaking at high speed. They are dressed in skimpy vest tops and panties, their make-up and hairstyles from earlier in the night destroyed with their hilarity. All eyes turn to me as I come into the room and pop open on impact.

Marina is a younger version of her mother with long dark curls and big hazel eyes. The other two girls, I've never seen before, both dark-haired but taller than Marina with fewer curves. "Max," Marina purrs, "you're out late tonight. Been anywhere exciting?" They all adjust themselves in their chairs to sit up and rearrange their tops over their breasts. "Do you want a drink?"

"No thanks," I reply. The last thing I need is more alcohol.

"Who is this?" one of the strangers squeaks. "You never said anything about a boyfriend." She looks pointedly at her friend in accusation.

"Oh, Max isn't my boyfriend," Marina says. Her eyes slide from her friend to me and back again. "He's my mother's plaything." The disgust in her voice is obvious, and I glare at her. The other girls' mouths drop open at the revelation.

"You date her mother?" they say in unison.

"I'm Linda's partner," I confirm.

Marina laughs. "What he means is he knocked her up and now he's stuck here pretending to play happy families."

Before I can protest, the creak of the stairs signals Linda's arrival. She appears behind me wearing her pink cotton nightdress with the word *queen* written across the chest. Her dark hair is piled on top of her head, pinned back by the eye mask she's pulled up from her eyes. She looks exhausted but her gaze immediately lands on me and she screws her face up curiously. Then her focus moves to her daughter and her companions. "What's going on?" she asks.

Marina squares her shoulders, shaking her voluminous breasts in the process. I feel the other women watching me as the situation unfolds. "We were just having a few drinks after the pub," Marina says, "then he arrived back." She glares at me then looks back at her mother. "The girls are going to crash here tonight. They couldn't find a taxi. I said it was all right." She looks her mother straight in the eye, challenging her to say otherwise.

"That's fine," Linda says, softly, "just keep the noise down, please." I move towards her and take her hand. She glances up at me from under her lashes and gives me a soft smile. My heart skips a beat. I adore this woman. As we turn for the door to go upstairs, a gasp from one of the girls distracts us and we both whip around to face them again. She stands up and walks towards me, standing directly under my nose.

"Tell me something," she says. Her confidence is high with the obvious alcohol flowing in her veins. "Why would you be with her?"

Taken aback by her directness, I stammer, "Excuse me?"

"You heard me. Marina says you're only thirty-three and well, you're hot. What the fuck are you doing with someone like her," she repeats, signalling to Linda with her hand.

I close my eyes as I try to control my temper. My jaw ticks, and I bring my focus back to the young woman in front of me, then pick up Linda's hand in mine. I raise it to my lips as the three bitches watch on. "This woman," I growl, "makes me happier than anyone ever has. Your opinion means jack shit. Now, fuck off out of this house before I throw you out for disrespecting the woman who owns it. Marina, show your friends out. I don't want them here when we get up."

"This isn't your fucking house," she hisses.

I glare at her. "You're right, it's not. I have a perfectly nice apartment across the city, but I choose to be here with the woman I love. The woman your so-called friends have insulted right in front of you. The woman who puts a bloody roof over your head."

"Max," Linda says, squeezing my hand. "It's all right. Let's just go to bed."

"No, I won't have you belittled in your own home." Marina sticks her chin out defiantly. "Get them out of here, now."

As Linda and I leave the room, I hear giggling behind us. "You're right," one of the idiotic girls whispers, "he's fucking gorgeous. I wouldn't mind him growling on my behalf either."

Chapter
Twenty-Seven

Linda

Max's anger is radiating from him like a furnace. Between the snarky remarks of Marina's friend and the amount of alcohol he's obviously consumed, he's ready to explode. After leaving the living room, we climbed the stairs and I disappeared into the bathroom, needing a moment to myself. The drunken idiot's words hurt, even though I know she only said what a lot of people will think when they find out about us. *What is he doing with her?*

There is a soft chap at the bathroom door. "Linda," he says through the wood, "why are you hiding in the bathroom?"

"I'm not," I mumble. It's a lie. I've been in here for ages rustling the odd packet to make him think I'm conducting my skin routine. My emotions are already on edge because he went out tonight. Not that I wouldn't want him to, but it was one of the few times he'd been out with his friend since we'd gotten back together. I laid in bed watching the clock. He told me he wouldn't be late. A few drinks and a catch-up with his old friend, then he'd be home. The clock laughed at me showing 2.45 a.m. Maybe he's met an old flame, it mocked? Someone more his age? The vision of him surrounded by other women dressed in low-cut dresses fawning over him wouldn't go away. He's a good-looking man; people notice.

The taxi brakes had screeched to a halt outside the house, and I had gotten up to look out the window. I watched him climb out of the back of the car, clearly after having had a skin full of beer. He stumbled up the path to my front door and struggled to fit his key in the lock. My heart sank as I watched him. He's so young and gorgeous. He should be out there enjoying himself, not stuck here with me. My pregnancy has trapped him, literally. I'd caught my reflection in the window as I moved back towards the bed, planning on pretending to be asleep when he arrived in our room. What I saw saddened me further. In the moonlight, there was no hiding what I was. Old.

"Beautiful," he calls again distracting me from my nasty thoughts. The door handle flexes as he tries to open it. "Linda, please let me in." His words slur slightly as he speaks. Downstairs he seemed to sober up instantaneously, but I can hear the inebriation in his voice now. He must have had a good night. I hope he enjoyed his time with his friend. Guilt bubbles that I've kept him away from his normal life. Since our reconciliation, he's only left my side to go to work. We've not discussed our weeks apart since that first day. He asked me if I'd slept with anyone whilst we were away from each other. I hadn't. But something made me not ask him the same question. I suspect I wouldn't like to know the answer, but it plays on my mind.

"I'm ok," I shout back. "I'll be out in a minute." He sighs. A soft thud tells me he's rested his forehead on the bathroom door. I imagine him standing there pissed and at a loss with my strange behaviour. I know I blow hot and cold with him. He gets frustrated but doesn't say anything; his eyes make it clear how he's feeling though – lost.

"Is there a queue?" My daughter's voice cuts through the silence. "Fuck, we need a bigger house."

"Maybe you should move out?" Max suggests, and she laughs.

"You'll be long gone lover boy before I will be."

"What's your problem?" he hisses. "Can you not just be happy for us?"

"Happy for you?" she shrieks. Her words slurring as much as his do. "Max, this is insane. You do know she's going to be sixty when the baby is fourteen. You'll be in your forties. Any sane person can see this isn't going to last. You'll walk away, and my mother will be left with a baby on her hip."

"You don't know me," he retorts. "Don't pigeonhole me with one of your wasters of a boyfriend." I hear our bedroom door slam, then the door handle waggles again.

"Mum," Marina calls, "are you in there? Come on, I need to piss." Steeling myself, I rise from my seat on the toilet then smooth down my nightdress. Taking a tissue from the box on the side, I dab my eyes to hide the tears. My face looks blotchy, but she'll never notice. My daughter is so wrapped up in her own importance, it's astounding. It's my own fault, always giving in to her demands and manoeuvring around her wants. I've created the demon on the other side of the door. I flick the latch and open it. She frowns, then pushes past me and my bump into the bathroom without a word.

Max is already asleep when I crawl into bed. I'm relieved. The last thing I want is my emotions to get the better of me in front of him. He gives me no reason to doubt his feelings. Perhaps it's my haywire hormones causing me all this unrest. He's collapsed on top of the duvet, having managed to undress down to his boxers. The discarded garments lie in a pile at the foot of the bed. His face is buried into his pillow with his arms wrapped around the soft cushion. My focus moves down his arms and back, taking in all his intricate tattoos. He's so different from my ex-husband, never mind being years younger than him.

Stan and I met in our late teens. He had gone straight from school into the bank where his father worked. His parents raised him traditionally with a focus on being married and starting a family. In the beginning, we were love's young dream. He was polite and caring. We went to the cinema and out for meals. Our families met, and it was agreed we were a suitable match. My mother told me he was good for me. Perhaps sparks didn't fly as I expected them to, like they do in the movies, but that's not real life I was told.

At twenty, I was engaged to be married. He asked my father's permission before proposing, and our families rejoiced at the news. I said yes because I didn't have any other option. There was nowhere else I particularly wanted to be. Stan was a good man, and I was lucky to have him. Our wedding was booked for six months later. Before my twenty-first birthday, I became his wife.

His career within the bank blossomed like his father before him. I had a small role in a local clothes shop to keep me busy whilst he was at work. Then, within two years of being married, I fell pregnant. In the sixth month of my pregnancy, I handed in my notice to work and assumed the role of a housewife. We were excited and happy to welcome our new edition. Everything seemed to work out exactly the way it should have.

Fast forward twenty years and our idyllic life didn't quite pan out as we hoped. Yes, we owned our own home and both of us now worked, but life was stale. Once Marina was old enough to walk home from school, I'd gone back to college and retrained in child development which allowed me to work as a classroom assistant. We became more friends than lovers after a few years of our marriage. When it was obvious a second child wasn't going to bless our union, our sex life dried up altogether. In our final decade together, I could probably count on my fingers and toes how many times we'd been intimate.

The day I found him with her had been both devastating and a relief. Stan was becoming more irritated with each day that passed. For all we weren't madly in love with each other, he'd never been mean to me, always treating me with respect. But during the months before my discovery, he was snarky and intense, questioning my whereabouts and constantly querying my motives. "Why do you find it necessary to question me about my day?" he said, one summer morning. "You know where I fucking go every damn day." My jaw had dropped at his language. My ex-husband rarely swore.

"I was just asking what your plans were today?" I stammered.

"Don't bother," he snapped. "It's not as if you're interested."

He had been with her in our bed while I was at work. After being sent home with a headache, I'd turned up unexpectedly during their lovemaking. On arriving, I'd heard the moans from the bottom of the stairs and had crept up quietly, our bedroom door ajar. She was on top of him, bouncing away merrily. I turned around and left, making my way back to our living room to wait for them to finish.

She'd appeared first. Her face fell when she saw me sitting on the sofa watching the stairs. "Stan," she shouted. "Stan." He wandered down behind her, his eyes met mine across the room and his eyebrows drew together, the way they always did when he was considering his options.

"Linda," he said. "You're home early."

"And you're not at work," I responded.

"No," he agreed. "There's no point in me prolonging the inevitable. You obviously know what's happening. I'm not going to treat you like an idiot."

"I think you've already accomplished that," I snapped. "How long has this been going on?" Our neighbour shuffled from foot to foot, nervous about the impending explosion, but she needn't have worried. My confidence was too low and my self-esteem too battered to create a scene.

"Eight months," he told me, and my heart broke. For months he'd been finding solace in someone else. "I'm leaving you. Our marriage is past it, and we need to move on." With that, he turned and went back up our stairs, returning a few minutes later with an overnight bag. "I'll be in touch," he said, leading his floozy from our house. I've always thought he wanted me to find out about his indiscretions. She had no partner then, so why else would they risk being caught in my home?

I glance over at the man who now lies in my bed. If I can't keep a man like Stan happy, how on earth will I be able to hold on to this one. Max has so much life about him. He embraces everything he does with a smile on his face. Being around him is joyous. He only has to look at me and my day gets better.

Unable to sleep, I prop myself up on my pillows and pretend to read. Really, I'm just watching him. This is becoming a common occurrence during the night. I wake up nervous about the future and look at him until I fall asleep once more. He's here, I tell myself over and over, but it does nothing to quash my concerns. A gentle snore escapes his lips, and he wriggles on top of the covers. I place my hand on his shoulder. He's cold.

"Max," I say, softly. "Get under the covers. You're freezing."

Beautiful green eyes flutter open. He looks up at me, treating me to a small smile before pushing himself off the bed then sliding under the duvet beside me. I snuggle down, turning onto my side facing away from him so he can wrap his body around mine. His strong arms come around my waist, his hands protective over my stomach. I feel his growing erection in the base of my back and his lips touch my neck. His fingers lift the hem of my night dress, wriggling it up above my hips so his palms can connect with my bare flesh.

"I love you," he whispers. "I'm proud to call you, my partner." The alcohol fumes waft in my direction with his sweet words. He's still drunk. Then there is silence, and I hear the soft snore of a man with good intentions but very little energy.

Chapter Twenty-Eight

Marina

As I lie in my bed, I hear the creak of the floorboards that signal someone is awake. The small black clock on my bedside cabinet flashes 9.45 a.m. My head is bursting after one too many wines last night. Chelsea and Hayley are a terrible influence on me. I cringe as I remember the altercation with Max both in the living room and outside the bathroom. He'd been furious about the slurs against my Mum, but can't he see how ridiculous this all looks, him being with her?

The girls called a taxi as the sun rose this morning. I'd been tempted to push my luck and have them lying on the living room floor when he appeared. But, after the argument upstairs and knowing my mum heard every word, I decided to send them home. They'd spent the time between Max arriving and them leaving, talking about him and his relationship with my mother. "I can't believe your mum has a better-looking boyfriend than you," Chelsea said with a snigger.

"I don't have a boyfriend," I hissed.

"No, and you've never had one as good-looking as him." My skin prickled in annoyance. "Your mum's getting more action than you."

"Obviously," Hayley chimed in. "She's got a bun in the oven to prove it. That's one way to ensure he hangs around I suppose." They both burst into fits of giggles at their own jokes, and I flushed bright red. This is what I was frightened of, becoming a laughingstock, the woman whose mother ran off to Spain and came back up the duff. None of our family or friends know yet; my uncle will be livid, and thank goodness my grandparents have passed on.

"He won't hang around," I said with more confidence than I have in the statement. "He'll get bored and move on. Leaving her to hold the literal baby." I'd been convinced this would be the case when they'd told me about the pregnancy. But, four months on and he's still here with no signs of leaving. The way he watches her as she moves around the room, jumps to her defence, or holds her hand is infuriating. Every word or gesture is carried out with care and attention towards her. How did she land a man like that, and I end up dating losers. It's so unfair.

I push myself up to sit, and my head spins. Grasping it between my hands, I lower it to my knees. Hell, I feel like shit. My phone buzzes. I glance around but can't see it. It continues to vibrate for a few minutes then stops before restarting again. The sensation rattles the mattress – it's here somewhere. My hands roam around the covers trying to find it. Finally, I locate it inside the duvet cover. How the fuck did it end up in there? Grabbing the edge, I turn the awkward material around until I find the opening, ripping open the buttons and diving inside to find it. The sheet has twisted around it, and it continues to vibrate as

I untangle it. Once released from its bindings, I open the call history. A missed call and a text message from Max.

We need to talk. Meet me in Harley's Café at 11.

I grimace at the screen. Who does the idiot think he is, ordering me around? But I'm curious as to what he wants to discuss. Our relationship has moved from uncomfortable to outright hatred in recent weeks. He monopolises my mum's time, and it's only going to get worse when the baby arrives.

I'll be there at 12.

He better get used to me not dancing to his tune. I want to know what he has to say but I'll be damned if I'm doing it on his schedule. Exasperating prick.

Fine.

Good, he's pissed off. Pissing off Max has become my new favourite hobby in life. I know he doesn't tell her everything I do, like hiding his stuff or moving the car keys. He looks so cute storming around the house in the morning trying to get ready for work with only half the things he needs. Mum normally leaves first; she likes to get in early to set up for the day. That gives me ten minutes to wind him up without being caught in the act. It's the best time of my day.

I pile my curls high on my head and apply another coat of lip gloss. The soft cotton dress I'm wearing hugs my curves and being braless means my nipples poke through the material. After slipping on my knee-high boots, I check myself out in the full-length mirror. I look good. Actually, I look fucking awesome. He's not going to know what's hit him when I arrive.

My mum sits in the living room with her pink fluffy dressing gown wrapped around her. She looks ghastly, her skin pale from being sick and her brown locks scrapped back in a bun. "Morning," I sing as I skip into the room. "Beautiful day, isn't it?"

"Why are you so cheery this morning?" she asks, looking me up and down. "I thought you'd be hugging the toilet bowl."

"That's your department," I say with a smirk. "Is my little brother causing you bother?" She glances at me, surprised. I never mention the baby. Ever.

"Something like that," she mumbles. "Where are you off to? You look nice."

"To meet a friend," I reply, smoothly. "Where's Max?"

"Out," she says with a shrug. Good, he's not told her he's meeting me. That gives me more ammunition if required for later.

Once I've shrugged into my heavy winter coat, I pull the zip up to my nose and shout, "See you later," before heading out the door to see what Mr Lover-Boy wants to talk to me about.

Max sits in a booth at the rear of the café. He's facing the door so he can see me arrive. His dark hair is ruffled and slightly longer than usual, it flops over his forehead. His emerald eyes fix on me as I enter. I do my best to seem unaffected by him but it's a struggle. Living with him, more so. The fact I've developed a crush on my mother's boyfriend isn't ideal.

He rises from his chair as I walk towards him. "Thanks for coming," he says, "and for keeping this between us. I don't want to cause Linda any unnecessary stress." He helps me out of my coat then signals for us to sit down. "What do you want to drink?" he asks.

"Coffee, please." The waiter approaches the table, and he orders for us both.

He clears his throat. "Marina, I never planned for any of this to happen," he says. "But this is where we are. Your mum and I met last summer, and our relationship was completely unexpected." He smiles. "The new edition to our family, even more so."

"Ok," I reply, petulantly, "What has this to do with me?"

"Everything," he says, raising his eyebrows. "Your mum loves you, and it's breaking her heart having all this unrest. She wants us all to get along."

"I'm not sure that's possible, Max," I whisper, breathless. Nerves are rising in my belly. I'm terrified he will work out what the real problem is. Why I'm such a cow with him. If he knew, I wonder what his reaction would be. Part of me wishes I could tell him.

"Why not?" he questions. "We're both adults. I'm sure we can put our differences to the side. For the sake of Linda. It's all become very childish, do you not think?"

"Can you not see how weird you and her are together?" I stammer. His focus never wavers from me. He's strong and domineering when he wants to be, one hundred percent confident in his words.

"In your opinion, it may be," he challenges. "But no offence, it doesn't count for much. I can decide who I want to be in a relationship with on my own."

"The house is too small. It's going to be a nightmare when the baby arrives," I spit, changing the direction of the conversation away from my relationship with him and my mother.

"I've been thinking about that," he says, "and I have a potential solution."

"I'm listening," I say but roll my eyes to feign disinterest. In reality, I'm hanging off his every word.

"My apartment is lying empty. Why don't you move in there?" he suggests. "Short term. It would give us all some space, and you could have your own home for a while." My jaw drops open and he smirks.

"You'd let me stay in your apartment." I'm stunned.

He shrugs. "Sure. I'm never there. If it gets you out of my hair for a while, then it's good for me." He holds my gaze with his. "Whether you agree or not, Marina, I love your mum. I'm determined to make this relationship work. I'd much prefer if we could be friends rather than enemies."

Unable to look at him, my eyes drop to my fingers twisting on my lap. "I'll think about it," I murmur. Our cups of coffee lie on the table in front of us untouched. I hadn't even noticed them arriving. He drains his in one mouthful then stands, dropping a ten-pound note on the table.

"Let me know," he says. I watch him walk away out the door, and my heart sinks. He wants to be rid of me, but his offer is an interesting one. I need time apart from them both to try to get hold of these crazy feelings that are developing. Each time I watch them together, jealousy consumes me. His hands on her skin make me feel sick. I wake in the night, imagining him making love to me. The feelings have become so intense now, he only needs to walk into a room and I flush crimson. Yes, perhaps space is exactly what I need just now, but I hate the fact he suggested it.

That evening, the three of us are sitting at the dinner table tucking into mum's homemade chicken pie. The conversation has been mellow, skirting around topics such as how our days were and plans for the week ahead. I decide to take a little joy in having one up on her, I throw a grenade into the proceedings.

"I really enjoyed our coffee date today, Max," I say, deadpan. He's in the middle of taking a swig of beer and stops with the bottle held to his lips. He focuses on me and glowers openly.

"What?" my mother replies, looking between us. Confusion is clear on her face. Excitement spreads in my chest at her unease.

"He had a proposition for me," I tell her.

"What proposition?" She turns to Max who looks as if he will explode on impact with any hard surface. I pause, waiting to see if he'll take up the story or let me continue with the tale. He takes a deep breath, then places his hand over my mother's beside him.

"I offered Marina my apartment," he explains, "so she could have her own space."

"You asked her to move out?" she says, aghast.

"No, I offered her use of my apartment if she was finding our living conditions here a bit..." He pauses, considering his words.

"Cramped." He rubs his forehead with his free hand. I love making him squirm. "She hadn't told me if she wants to use it yet."

"Do you not think you should have discussed this with me first?" she questions.

"I was trying to do the right thing," he argues. "Things have been strained, and I thought if we all got some space, we could work on getting on a bit better."

She places her knife and fork onto her plate. They stare at each other. It's as if I'm not even here. I hate when that happens. Often, it's like it's only the two of them in a room. They converse silently in tune with each other's thoughts. "Max," she says, her voice firm. "This is Marina's home until she decides otherwise. You had no right to offer her that."

"She's an adult," he snaps. "Well, she looks like one." My mother gives him a dark look, and I stick my tongue out at him when she's turned away from me. He ignores me.

"I'm right here," I interject, and his furious eyes land on me. I find it both terrifying and arousing.

"It's not your place," my mother states. "You're not her parent." He stills at the comment then stands. His chair screeches noisily against the floor tiles.

"No Linda, I'm not. But the baby in your belly is mine, and I'm trying to do the right thing for my child. I'm sorry if you feel I overstepped the mark, but my intentions were good." He runs his hand through his hair and his t-shirt lifts slightly to display his toned abs. Shit, he's hot. "I'm going to head home tonight," he says, and my mother's face falls. "I need some space." He walks out of the room, and I hear him climbing our stairs, appearing back minutes later with a backpack over his shoulder.

My mum stands and walks over to him. He takes both her hands in his, then drops his lips to her ear. I can't hear what he says but she smiles sadly. After a soft kiss on her cheek, he leaves without as much as a look in my direction. My mother returns to the table and drops back into her seat.

"Everything all right?" I ask, and her eyes rise to mine.

"What do you think?" she whispers, her voice strained.

"Mum." She cuts me off with a look.

"Don't. You've got what you wanted. He's left." Her eyes fill with tears. "Why do you have to be so difficult? What have I ever done to you?"

"I only told you what he said," I justify.

"Yes, Marina. Yes, that's all you did." She sighs softly. "I'm tired. I'm going to bed. Can you clear the table and tidy up?"

"It's only eight o'clock," I say.

Without another word, she stands and leaves the kitchen.

Chapter Twenty-Nine

Max

I sit on the red plastic chair with my head in my hands. Fuck. They've left me in this empty room to make me sweat. The only things in here with me are a cheap desk, three more of these bloody uncomfortable seats and a tape recorder. I glance over at the mirror on the side of the room – it will be one-way glass. I wonder if they're watching me now. Finally, the heavy wooden door swings open.

"Mr Gordon," a tall man says as he walks in. I stand, and he gestures for me to sit back down. "I'm sorry it took so long. We had a few loose ends needing to be tied up before we talked to you."

I nod, and reply, "No problem."

He fixes me with deep brown eyes, the same colour as the brown suit he's dressed in. His white shirt is undone, and sweat stains are obvious on the collar. His sandy blond hair is short and styled neatly; it looks as if it never moves. He pushes his suit jacket sleeves up beyond his elbows as he sits down opposite me. His features are large, almost too large for his face. It gives him a distorted look.

"Mr Gordon," he says, "we are just waiting for my colleague then we'll begin."

"Is she all right?" I stammer.

"Let's just wait for my colleague," he replies, and the door swings open once more. A short, bald man wearing a police uniform enters the interview room. He's carrying two paper cups. His eyes dart between them, assessing the contents, ensuring nothing spills over the edge. He shuffles across to us, then places the drinks on the table in front of me.

"Tea or coffee?" he asks. "I brought both. Whatever you don't drink. I'll have."

"Coffee, please," I say, and he slides the relevant cup across to me.

The two men settle themselves in their chairs opposite me. The larger man signals to start the recorder, and the smaller man flicks the switch. "Mr Gordon," the man in the suit begins, "I'm Chief Inspector Davis, and this is my colleague PC Trent. Do you know why you're here?" I nod. "Please speak for the tape."

"Yes."

"Can you confirm you were read your rights at the scene of the incident and have refused legal representation at this point?"

"Yes."

"Thank you," he says. "Mr Gordon, this evening at around 9 p.m. you were driving along Brenthouse Rd. Is that correct?"

"Yes, that's correct."

"Where were you going?"

"To my apartment on Allitsen Rd."

"Where were you coming from?"

"My partner's house. She lives in Hackney." He nods. The other officer is scribbling notes enthusiastically on a notepad. "Is she ok?" I ask again. The two men glance at each other.

"Mr Gordon, unfortunately, the lady died on route to the hospital." My jaw drops, and I stare at him. Terror runs through me. *I killed her. I'm a murderer.*

"She's dead?" I stammer.

"Yes, Mr Gordon. Sadly, the woman you hit died of her injuries."

"Have you been drinking this evening?" My heart sinks. Tonight has deteriorated at a monumental rate.

After the disagreement with Linda over dinner, I needed to get out of that house. The whole atmosphere is like being stuck in quicksand. Every fucking day that bitch Marina gives me a hard time. Her catty comments or awkward actions drive me insane. I'd been biting my tongue for weeks, but the last few days had been the final straw. The way she speaks to her mother infuriates me. The bloody girl doesn't know how to spell respect, never mind how to be respectful.

Linda's disapproval at my suggestion Marina used my apartment stung. It wasn't surprising though; that's why I hadn't spoken to her about it. Her daughter has her so tightly wrapped around her finger, it's impossible to untangle the knot. She spends her days smoothing over the cracks of their failed mother and daughter relationship. Her desperation for them to be close breaks my heart.

When Linda walked over to me in the kitchen, I prayed she would ask me to stay, but she didn't. I whispered that I loved her in her ear and left. Hurt, furious and at a loss, I got behind the wheel of my car. Normally, I never drive after a bottle of beer, but my need to put some distance between that house and I had skewed my thinking.

"Mr Gordon, have you drunk alcohol this evening?" the chief inspector repeats. My hand runs over my face as panic takes hold and I nod, slowly. "For the tape, please."

"Yes," I tell him, "I had two small bottles of beer with my evening meal."

"Thank you for your honesty. As you know, you've already agreed to a breath test. I can confirm your results show you were under the legal limit for alcohol consumption whilst driving. You've been lucky, this time." I blow out a breath I didn't know I was holding.

On driving away from Linda's house, I decided to take the long route home to waste time. The thought of lying in my bed alone wasn't a welcome one. The rain started battering off the roof of the car within ten minutes. Darkness had fallen and the road filled with water quickly. With my headlights on full beam, I crawled along the streets, trying to make my way home. I needed to collapse in my bed, not that I'd been in it recently. The old woman stepped out in front of me from between two parked cars. I hit the brakes, but the distance was too short and the road too wet. She was knocked to the ground, cracking her head off the black tarmac.

Once stopped, I jumped out of the car and ran to her side. Blood poured over the ground, mixing with the still falling rain. Pulling my phone from my pocket, I'd dialled 999. The blue lights seemed to descend on the scene within minutes. I'd knelt beside my victim, holding her hand which was reducing in temperature by the second. Men in green uniforms crouched down to assess her injuries as the police officers led me away. I was piled into the back of a waiting car. My car was left stranded in the middle of the road.

"You're free to go," the officer says, snapping me from the morbid recollection.

"Pardon?"

"As I said, Mr Gordon," he repeats, "you're free to go. A witness at the scene has corroborated your story. We will continue our investigation so please let us know if you plan to leave the area, but at this point in time, we are not looking to press charges." I stare at him blankly. "PC Trent will show you out and return your belongings."

"My car?" I ask.

"It's still parked on Brenthouse Rd. You can call a taxi at reception to go and collect it."

"Thank you," I mumble, unable to form any other words.

Back in the reception area, the jovial-looking PC Trent retrieves my belongings and passes me a business card with a number for a taxi company. Wanting to be as far from this bloody place as possible, I walk out of the sliding doors into the night with sheets of rain still falling from the sky. Standing under the overhang at the entrance, I call the number on the card. Within ten minutes the taxi pulls up. I climb in gratefully.

"Where to?" he asks.

"Brenthouse Road, please." When he realises I'm not interested in speaking, he turns the radio up a few notches. I glance at my phone. Three unopened messages from Linda. After how this night has progressed, I doubt I want to read them. The journey takes a lifetime but eventually, we arrive back at my car. After throwing whatever note I find in my pocket at the driver, I jump out of the back seat and climb into my own vehicle.

I'm sitting in the driver's seat, letting the car heat up before setting off when the taxi pulls up beside me and I lower my window. "You gave me a fifty, mate," he shouts at me. "Do you not want your change?" I shake my head and he smiles. "Thanks, mate," he calls before driving off.

The drive home is painfully slow between the terrible weather and my wandering thoughts. Tonight could have ended very differently if things had not gone my way. I could have been spending the next few years in a jail cell. The thought horrifies me. I can't afford to be so reckless. I've too much to lose.

My apartment is in darkness when I arrive home apart from a single lamp in the living room. I don't remember leaving it on. Perhaps I've left it on a timer, but it seems improbable. I'm never that organised. "Where have you been?" she whispers as I enter, stopping me in my tracks. Linda is sitting on my sofa, her arms wrapped protectively around her swollen belly. We stare at each other for a moment in the dim light. "You didn't reply to my messages." Part of me is happy she's here, another part just wants to crawl into bed and forget today ever happened.

"I had a problem on the way here," I say. "It delayed me. How long have you been here?" She glances at the digital clock blinking on the wall.

"Since midnight." It's now three in the morning. "What could delay you for seven hours?" she asks. The room is deathly silent, her question hanging in the air. "Where have you been, Max?" I can see her jumping to the completely wrong conclusions in front of me, convincing herself I've been with someone else. Her lack of confidence is something I've gotten used to. Her need for encouragement and compliments is a daily requirement. Tonight, I don't have the energy. "Max?" she prompts.

"I was at the police station," I say, and her big brown eyes blink at me in confusion.

"The police station?" she repeats back to me. I sigh, then walk over and fall onto the couch beside her.

"Yes, Linda, the police station. On my way home from your house," I say.

"Our house," she corrects me, and I glance sideways at her before looking back at the floor.

"Your house," I argue, and she sighs softly. "I was driving back here, and someone stepped in front of my car on Brenthouse Rd. She's dead," I explain, bluntly. She gasps, covering her mouth with her hands. "The police aren't filing any charges at the moment. A witness supported my story that the woman walked out without looking."

She takes my hand in hers. "That must have been terrifying," she whispers. "Why didn't you call me?"

"I only just got my stuff back and had to go to retrieve my car. Today hasn't exactly been the most successful day. I didn't want to bother you."

"Bother me?" she says, and her eyebrows draw together. "Max, I love you. What would ever make you think you were a bother to me?" I shrug. "I'm sorry about earlier." I don't respond, unsure what to say. She tenses beside me. "Do you want me to leave?" she asks, and I look up at her. Her eyes are wide, full of concern. "Will I go? Do you not want me here?" Guilt weighs heavy on me. It's been a terrible day for both of us. I'm being an ass making her squirm. It's not her fault someone walked out in front of my car.

"No, Beautiful, stay. I'm sorry it's been a difficult day." I squeeze her hand softly in encouragement. "Let's go to bed." She visibly relaxes with my words. We both stand in unison, and I lead her through to my bedroom. She clings to my hand as if her life depends on it.

Once inside, she wriggles out of her jumper and jeans, standing before me in her black lace bra and panties. She walks towards me as I lift my t-shirt over my head, her arms wrapping around my waist as she lays her head on my chest. Her growing bump presses against me, and I feel the sharp tap of our baby within her. "I love you," she murmurs, placing her lips against my skin. My fingers trail up and down her back. I unhook her bra, and it falls to the floor. Her breasts spring free, and I cup them gently in my hands.

"Bed," I whisper. "I need you tonight."

We climb under the duvet, facing each other. My hands explore her changing body, my erection growing with each touch. She pushes herself up to sit, her dark curls flowing over her shoulders. I lie back on my pillow as she stares down at me. Her hand moves to my face, and she brushes the tips of her fingers against my cheek before they head south, down my neck to my chest. They glide over my skin, causing the blood to rush to the surface in arousal. She leans down and kisses the side of my neck, nipping and sucking as her hand moves lower until she slips her fingers beneath the waistband of my boxers.

My cock is rock solid, desperate for some attention. She wraps her fingers around me, holding firm. I groan at the contact, flexing my hips to encourage her to move. She giggles and bites down hard on my nipple then moves to straddle me across my stomach. "Patience," she scolds.

"Fuck patience," I growl. "Fuck my cock."

"And how does your cock want to be fucked?" she purrs. "Does he want attention from here?" She runs her tongue over her bottom lip. "Or here?" She grinds her pussy against my abs.

"I don't care as long as he's inside a part of you and that part is wet." Her breath catches, and I smirk. *I can talk dirty too, Beautiful.* She shimmies down my body until her pussy is pressed against my length. Only two thin bits of material divide us. I sit up and she rocks backwards. My arms snap around her. "Beautiful," I say, "quit teasing and ride me." She flushes. "Or I'll take matters into my own hands."

"Maybe I want you to," she challenges, and I raise an eyebrow.

"You don't have to ask me twice. Get on all fours," I order, and she moves onto the mattress beside me. I quickly slip off my boxers and when I glance at her, she is on her hands and knees, ready for me. The black lace panties are easily pushed to the side as I kneel behind her. My tip nudges her opening. She whimpers slightly at the intrusion. Holding her hips between my hands, I tighten my grip as I slide in. Once inside, we both still allowing ourselves to enjoy the sensation of being joined. Then, I start to move, slowly at first but increasing in speed with each thrust. "Fuck, you feel good," I growl. She presses back against me, greedily wanting every inch she can inside her. I fuck her hard, both of us needing the release. When it comes, it's beautiful. She goes to pieces beneath me, dropping to her elbows. Her pussy vibrates around me as I ride the wave until I shoot up inside her, emptying myself fully.

Afterwards, we lie together, her head on my chest. Our baby squirms and wriggles within her. At first, I struggled with the concept of sex whilst she is pregnant, but now I love the connection it gives us. There is an honesty in our lovemaking, a rawness. Our need for each other has created a new person who will soon be here with us, and for that, I will always be grateful.

Chapter Thirty

Linda

Max walked away from me for the first-time last night. He's never been the one to leave before; it's always been me. As we stood in my kitchen with my daughter watching on, I'd wanted to drop to my knees and beg him not to go. The thought of being without him terrifies me as much as being with him does. Max Gordon stepped into my life seven months ago and etched himself permanently on my heart, the carving so deep it stings.

Once again, I'm sat up in bed watching him sleep. We haven't spent much time here, in his apartment. Max doesn't want me having to get up any earlier than needed for work, so he insists on staying at my house.

My heart sank when he told me where he'd been last night. The police station. Before he explained what happened, three million dreadful images flashed through my head as suggestions of what could have happened. My gaze ran from the top of his head to his toes ensuring all of him was still there. Physically he looked perfect but when I met his eyes, they were broken and scared. He was completely shaken.

When we made love, he felt like the man who has shared my bed these past months, but during the night he wasn't settled. Normally, he falls asleep and doesn't wake until his alarm sounds the following morning. I woke a few times with him talking to himself, then tossing and turning under the covers. Finally, around six in the morning he'd relaxed into a deep sleep. I'd snuggled down next to him, my head in the crook of his arm. He always makes me feel safe; last night I wanted to give him the same comfort.

The incessant trill of the alarm sounds, and sleepy green eyes blink open. He glances up at me with a sad smile. "Please tell me I imagined everything that happened yesterday," he whispers. "Tell me it was all a bad dream." I reach over and stroke his cheek with my finger.

"I can't do that, darling. But hell, I wish I could." He's lying on his front. He turns away from me and buries his face in his pillow. His huge frame rises and falls as he breathes. When he turns back towards me, his eyes are filled with tears.

"I killed someone, Linda," he says, choked with emotion.

"No, a woman stepped out in front of your car. You had no chance to stop." I slide down under the covers beside him. We stare at each other as the tears make tracks on his skin. "You did nothing wrong. The police told you that. It was a tragic accident."

"Things could have turned out so different. If I'd had another bottle of beer or the rain hadn't been so heavy. Life can change in a blink of an eye; I could have missed everything." He reaches forward beneath the covers and places his palm on my stomach. "I could have missed out on both of you."

"Why don't you call in sick to work? We can spend the day here, together. You've barely slept."

"Do you not have work to go to?" he asks.

"Your son gives me the perfect excuse to stay home. Plus, I just want to make sure you're all right. I could look after you for a change." He blinks at me. "You make me feel safe, Max. Please let me try to do the same for you."

"That sounds perfect, Beautiful. And the perfect remedy for a Monday like today." He rolls onto his back then wipes at his eyes with the duvet. "Sorry, everything hit me at once when I woke up. It was overwhelming." He pushes himself up to sit as I lie on my side staring at him. "I'll phone the school then the police station to make sure I've not misunderstood anything. I want to go to her funeral anyway."

"Are you sure that's wise?"

"It's something I need to do," he replies simply before swinging his legs out of bed and standing. He's still naked from our lovemaking last night. He wanders over to his wardrobe and pulls the doors open, then removes a t-shirt from a hanger and a pair of shorts from a shelf, slipping them on. "I'll go make the calls. You call your work," he says and disappears through the door into the living room.

I pluck my phone from the bedside cabinet and quickly shoot a text off to Rhian advising I won't be in today due to issues at home. She replies within seconds telling me not to worry and that she hopes I'm all right. Max appears back a few minutes later.

"Did you speak to who you needed to?" I ask. He shakes his head.

"The school is fine, but the officer in charge won't be in until later. They are going to get him to call me."

"Ok, what do you want to do until then?" He looks at me, then swallows before dropping his gaze away. "Max..."

"We need to talk about what happened yesterday in the kitchen," he mumbles. "You let me leave without a word to stop me."

"Did you want me to beg?" I snap, suddenly annoyed. His eyes meet mine. He holds my focus, unrelenting.

"No," he says, his tone strong, "but it would have been nice if you'd asked me not to go. Sometimes I'm not even sure..." He trails off. His eyes are pleading with me for an answer to a question he hasn't asked.

"Not sure of what?" I prompt. My heart beats hard in my chest with nerves, each one more forceful than the last. "What do you need to know?" He takes a breath before speaking. I watch as his rib cage expands then contracts.

"I need to know if you're here for me, or if you're only here because of our son." The comment hits me square in the chest. "Would you have come back to me if you weren't pregnant?" He snaps his eyes away from me and walks over to the window, looking out onto the grey streets below.

After being momentarily stunned he even asked the question, I answer honestly, "Yes." I've never seen him as vulnerable. I wonder how long this has been a concern for him. "I'd decided to ask you for another chance before I knew I was pregnant. Finding out was the kick up the backside I needed to find you, to lay my heart on the line and ask you to have me back." I pull myself out of bed and walk over to him, wrapping my arms around his waist and leaning my cheek against his back. The cotton of his t-shirt is soft against my skin, in stark contrast to the firm muscle below. He places his hands over mine. "I love you," I say, fiercely.

"And I love you," he says, turning in my arms to face me. "I've loved you since the moment you took that damn dress off on the beach. When we were in the water together and you wrapped your legs around my waist. I've been crazy about you ever since." He leans down and places a kiss on my lips. "This isn't where I planned to be, but I don't want to be anywhere else."

"Snap," I murmur against his lips. "You're everything I shouldn't want and everything I can't live without." We stand, holding each other for a moment before he speaks.

"I'm sorry," he says, quietly. "I'm sorry for speaking to Marina without talking to you first. She's exasperating, and I was trying to do something to help all of us. Since Christmas, it feels as though her hate radiates from her. Saturday night it became too much, I needed to find a solution. It was all I could come up with."

"Marina is testing, even on a good day," I tell him. "She's always been difficult but since her father left, more so." He nods. "Your idea isn't a bad one, but I don't want her to feel pushed out. Perhaps, we could offer the apartment as an ad hoc place to stay when she wants. When she needs space."

"Do you think she'll go for it?" he asks, and I shrug.

"She'd be crazy not to. What twenty-three-year-old wants to be stuck in a two-bedroom house with a new baby and a lack of bathrooms. I'll speak to her this week. We need our own space too." I glance up at him, it's easy to forget how tall he is when I wear heels. Now, standing in my bare feet beside him, he towers above me. "Her boyfriend dumping her at new year really hasn't helped her mood."

"I think we can safely assume she's high maintenance," he mutters, and I chuckle.

"Yes, I love my daughter, but I wouldn't want to date her." His arms tighten around me, and he kisses my forehead. "You must be exhausted; we didn't get to bed until after three, and you didn't settle until six this morning."

"Beautiful, it's you who needs to be resting. Why don't you go back to bed for a while? I'll go make you a cup of tea." I go to protest, but his phone ringing stops me before a word passes my lips. He releases me and walks over to the chest of drawers he left it on. "It's the police station," he says, lifting the handset to his ear. "Hello." I watch him as he walks from the room.

Exhausted, I go back to the bed and slide under the duvet, still naked. I lie on Max's side when he's not in bed. It's something I do to feel him all around me. Snuggled into his pillow, I doze off, not fully asleep but unaware of time passing. Baby G chooses this moment to come to life and start wriggling in my belly. I put my hands on my stomach and a limb hits my bladder. I groan. I'm too comfy to get up and trail to the bathroom. "Settle down," I mutter. "Let Mummy have a few minutes more rest please."

"Mummy can stay in bed as long as she wants," Max's deep voice replies. I peek out at him over the top of the duvet. He's standing above me, a soft smile on his lips. "They've confirmed that they've no intention of pressing charges. It was an accident. Unless anything else comes to light, I may never hear from them again. The officer suggested perhaps attending the funeral wasn't a good idea." He pauses. "I just felt it was the right thing to do."

"We can go and lay flowers after if you want. They won't have a date yet?"

"No. He told me to keep an eye on the announcements in the local paper." He sighs. "Anyway, you stay in bed, and I'll go get your tea, then I might join you."

Chapter Thirty-One

2 months later...

Max

I stare down into bright green eyes the mirror image of my own. My son lies in my arms swaddled in a baby blue blanket. "Your mummy is incredible," I tell him as I wander around the room. "You put her through hell. I hope it's not a preview of what's to come." He stares up at me, silently. "If you're anything like I was, you're going to be a handful." He smiles. The nurses say its wind, but I prefer to think it's a smile.

Linda is sleeping soundly; they've got her doped up on painkillers. Thirty-six hours of labour took its toll on her. She suffered a fourth-degree perineal tear during the birth and had to be taken to surgery directly after. Jackson was over ten pounds and doesn't fit into any of the newborn babygrows we bought. My boy entered this world looking ready to crawl with a full head of chestnut brown curls. Linda had nurtured our son beautifully. He's strong and healthy. I'm so proud of her and besotted with him already.

The nurse walks into the room and hands me a bottle of milk. We discussed breastfeeding. Linda had been embarrassed to tell me she didn't want to. "I did it with Marina," she said. "It was exhausting. I ended up tied to the house. I wasn't confident enough to feed in public. I'd rather make the decision not to try this time."

"It's your choice," I told her. "As long as our son is fed, what does it matter?"

"All the advice is to breastfeed if you can. I want to do the best for our baby."

"A happy mother is the best thing you can give any child. If you don't want to breastfeed, don't. Anyway, it means I can help with the night feeds from the beginning. We can share the load. Your body, your choice." I'd wrapped my arms around her. "Decision made. No breastfeeding unless you change your mind."

"So, how does it feel being a daddy?" Marina's voice snaps me from my recollection. I glance up as she's closing the door.

"Surreal," I reply. "I can't believe he's actually here." She walks over and stands at my shoulder, staring down at her new brother. It's the closest she's been to me in weeks. Normally she keeps her distance.

"He's quite cute, isn't he?" she says.

"Is that almost a compliment?" I ask her and she rolls her eyes at me. "He is, but I'm biased." Since Marina started staying at my apartment part-time, we've all been getting on better. She comes home a few nights a week but most of her time is spent there. She even thanked me last week for the opportunity. I'd almost fallen off my chair in surprise. Her focus moves to her mother lying asleep on the bed. She walks over and takes her hand.

"Will she be all right?" she says, her voice laced with concern. "You said on the phone she needed surgery." Marina is becoming more bearable to be around. She loves her mum, though she struggles to show it. Her attitude blows hot and cold which is difficult to keep up with, but recently there has been more warm spells.

"She'll be fine. This monster caused some damage on the way out, and she needed some stitches." Her face distorts in disgust. "Seemingly it can happen. Well, so your mum said when I was freaking out," I tell her, remembering Linda speaking to me clearly and slowly, even though she was the one in pain. "She was happy but tired before drifting off. I think she'll wake up soon. Why don't you hang around for a while and wait for her. She'd love to see you." Her gaze holds mine, and her cheeks flush crimson. I've noticed that happens a lot when we talk. It makes me uncomfortable, so I try to ignore it. I don't want to consider what it means.

"Can I hold him?" she asks, then looks away embarrassed.

"Of course." I wander over to her and gently place my son in her arms. "Just support his head. That's what everyone keeps telling me."

"He's so small," she whispers, almost to herself. "I'd be terrified of the responsibility of keeping him alive."

"Trust me, I am," I say, and she grins at me. "But I'm sure your mum will keep me right. Things can't be that different from when you were small."

***

Marina

When I was small...the statement hits me like a freight train. I have a brother, a sibling. It is something I wanted when I was younger. Company, someone to play with. My brother blinks up at me. He really is cute. Just then my mother's voice cuts through the silence. She sounds weary. "Marina, you came," she whispers, and I turn to face her. "I'm so pleased to see you, darling." She holds her hands out to me and Max takes my brother from my arms. I walk over to her and take her hands in mine. "I love you, Marina," she says.

"I'm going to get a coffee," Max interrupts from behind me. He places Jackson in his crib and leaves the room. He's giving me some time with my mum. I appreciate it. I've noticed in the past two months, whenever I visit, he leaves for some of the time. It lets mum and I talk freely without him there; our relationship is improving slowly. As for Max, I try to not be around him or talk to him, my feelings grow stronger with every interaction. It's hard to hate someone who puts everyone else first. He genuinely loves my mum, I see that, though I don't understand why. The differences between them are still too vast for me to accept.

"How are you feeling?" I ask her, and she smiles softly.

"Sore, tired and as if I've pushed a sofa out of my vagina."

"Gadz, did you really have to tell me that?" I whine, screwing up my nose. "There's such a thing as too much information." She giggles, her eyes never moving from my face.

"Give it time. You'll meet someone and be in the same position I'm in. This is one of the most terrifying and painful experiences you can have as a woman, but it is also one of the most fulfilling." She's still holding onto my hands. "Just make sure when it happens for you, you're ready and settled with a partner who adores you." *Chance would be a fine thing; I only seem to attract losers.*

"Is it really as painful as it looks in the movies?" I ask, and she grimaces.

"I'm not sure you want me to answer that. My poor body has been sewn back together so I'm maybe not in the best mindset for too many birthing questions." My eyes run over her face, for all she's tired, she looks genuinely happy. "Put it this way," she adds, "Max will not be getting near me for a while. And when he does, he'll be gloved, and I'll be on every contraception possible." I laugh out loud. "I'm not joking. There's no way I could do labour again. Thank goodness it never progressed to a c-section though. That would have been cruelty on top of the torture I went through."

"I think one baby in your forties is enough," I agree. Her eyes light up, and a grin spreads across her face. "What is it?" I question. "You look like a Cheshire cat."

"I don't think the hospital would let me back again," she says with a chuckle. "I believe every second word out my mouth began with the letter F. And," she pauses, "I'm pretty sure I told Max I'd amputate his cock if he came near me again."

"You did," his deep voice says as he closes the door behind him. My skin prickles. He only needs to speak, and my body reacts. It's completely disconcerting. My reactions to him are out of control. "You gave me a hair-raising description of what you would do using a bread knife. I wouldn't be surprised if the nurses have reported you to the police for surveillance. I'd feel safer if they have."

"I was high on gas and air," she retorts. "I'll feign ignorance. You'll never prove anything." She smiles at him as he walks across the room, dropping my hands. He comes to her side and kisses her forehead. My stomach somersaults at the gesture. I can't help but wish his lips landed on me. Every sweet contact I witness pushes my jealousy up a notch. My face is getting harder to control. I feel it move in displeasure every time.

"You were amazing," he whispers. "Now I know why they say women are stronger than men. I'd have been begging them to cut me open and get him out of there." She laughs out loud then winces.

"Ouch, don't make me laugh. I'm not sure which parts of me are still holding together, but it doesn't feel like many." He kisses her again and mouths *sorry*. "Have you phoned Jace and your aunt?" she prompts, and he nods.

"They want pictures," he tells her. "My Aunt Susan is very excited and was asking when we'd be coming to visit." My mother rolls her eyes. "Yes, I told her to give us a chance to get home, never mind expecting us to book flights, but I did say we might try to visit later in summer like we discussed. There was a cheer when she told the other ladies in the hotel. No doubt they're on their second bottle of bubbles already, celebrating on our behalf."

"I'd love to see them all again. What a summer and a result of it," my mother says, glancing towards the crib. "I certainly changed up my life. Mission accomplished."

I clear my throat and two sets of eyes turn to me, as if remembering my presence. "I'll be getting off then," I say, and my mother's lips thin then she relaxes her expression when she realises. "Bye. Let me know when you're home." I turn away, walking past my sleeping sibling and straight out of the door.

***

Linda

Marina's visit went better than I expected. Well, it happened which is more than I thought would. Her coming to the hospital had never been discussed; the reason was I'd been too frightened to ask her to as I assumed she would say no.

In the final months of my pregnancy, since Max's accident and her starting to use his apartment for breaks away from the house. Things have improved between us. We were talking, and she wasn't being *as* snarky most of the time. Part of her errant behaviour is her personality, I know that, but it's been nice being able to talk to her with my guard down a little. I'm enjoying spending time with my daughter.

Max has also taken on board what I said about needing time with her on my own. He often makes himself scarce when she visits, by either pulling on his running shoes or disappearing to the supermarket. But he appears back before she leaves to make a little conversation. They're both trying, I think. But I'm under no illusion that they'll ever be best friends. It's quite clear they tolerate each other for my sake.

Jackson's cry fills the room. How something so small can create so much noise still confounds me. I push myself up onto my feet and waddle across to lift him out, cuddling him against my chest. Max is sitting in a chair in the corner. He watches me intently as I sit down on the edge of the bed. I take the bottle of milk sitting on the bedside cabinet and settle my son on my arm before popping the teat into his mouth. My son may only be a day old, but this experience of motherhood is already more relaxed than the last.

For all I had a rough labour, knowing I wouldn't have to try breast feeding had been a relief. With Marina, I'd felt obligated to try and it'd been pure hell. My milk didn't appear as it should, and when it did, my nipples cracked painfully from day one. The whole experience had been soul-destroying. I'd soldiered on for months feeling completely useless and alone in my predicament. We'd been short of money, so breastfeeding saved us an unnecessary cost in Stan's eyes. It was part of my job description. This time, that stress had been lifted as soon as I told Max of my concerns. He told me it was completely up to me, and he would support whatever decision I made. I didn't think I could love him more, but in that single moment, he proved me wrong.

"Are you ready to go home, Beautiful?" he says, and I glance at him.

"I can't wait to be back in my own bed," I reply with a smile, "and cuddled up next to you." He slept on the chair last night after refusing to go home. His dark hair is messed up and falls over his forehead. Three days' worth of stubble coats his chin and cheeks. He looks rough in comparison to his usual clean cut look.

"Hopefully the doctor will give you the all clear," he says. Just then the door swings open and my doctor walks in. He's older, probably in his sixties, with wispy white hair and thick rimmed glasses perched on the end of his nose.

"Linda," he says in a sing-song voice, "how are you feeling? And how is little Jackson?"

"I'm good, and Jackson seems to enjoy sleeping. Long may that continue," I reply, and he snorts.

"Doubt it."

"Me too. But yes doctor, we're both well. I'd really love to go home."

"Well, let me take a look at you, and I'll see what I can do," he says. I put Jackson back in his crib then return to lie on the bed. Max stands and comes to my shoulder, taking my hand. He watches the doctor like a hawk as he pulls my gown up exposing my legs and waist. I squeeze his hand, and he glances at me.

"Just bend your knees if you can, Linda," the doctor instructs. "I'll need to take a look at your stitches. Apologies, I know this isn't the most dignified examination, but it needs doing." I bend my knees and open my legs to let him look. I really don't care. I'd even try to do a handstand if it meant I might get home. "Everything looks fine." He moves to my son, peering into his cot then checking him over. "You should both be good to go home. Let me sort you a prescription for some medication then you're free to go." He leaves without another word.

I turn to Max. "Are you ready to take us home?" I say, and he rewards me with a breath-taking smile. "Could you go and get the car seat from the car please? And my bag with the clothes for travelling home?" He releases my hand, kisses my forehead then takes off at a run towards the door. I smile softly to myself at his boyish excitement. I hope it continues when he's elbow deep in nappies and grouchy from sleepless nights.

The next few years will be a challenge for both of us. Neither of us have ended up where we expected to be, our lives have dramatically changed in a matter of months. But as unplanned life events go, this is an enjoyable one and there is no one else I would rather be navigating this with other than Max Gordon.

Max and Linda's story continues in Embracing Us.

Read on for an excerpt.

If you enjoyed Discovering Me, I would appreciate it if you would take the time to leave a rating and review on Amazon, Goodreads or Bookbub. Reviews are so important to authors, it really does help.

Thank you for reading.

Embracing Us

Max

"You're sure it's all right that I go out tonight?" I ask Linda again and she waves me away. "I don't want to go. Please tell me I can't."

"I'm not your mother. I don't control you," she scolds then laughs, causing her breasts to rise and fall. I harden. We've not been intimate since Jackson's birth, but I can tell the time is getting closer. In the past few days, she's been touchier in bed. I'm waiting for the sign from her that we can resume our sexual relationship. However, she tells me I need to wear a condom, which is unwelcome but necessary news. I love the natural feeling I've been spoiled with of being inside her. I'll miss it. There's a packet of condom's waiting patiently in my bedside drawer for the day to arrive.

"Go and socialise with Jace," she replies. "He's been wanting to celebrate with you for weeks. You can't keep avoiding him." I groan. She's right. Jackson just turned eight weeks old today, and Jace has been nipping my head about marking his birth with tequila since the day after he was born. I've run out of excuses, but I hate the thought of being away from my new family.

We are in the kitchen, our son lying in his bouncer watching us preparing the dinner. His bright green eyes move from his mother to me then back to the most important person in his world. I'm chopping vegetables whilst Linda grates cheese. We move around each other, working in unison but separately. We've only known each other a year, but it's as if we've always been together. Things just work between us, most of the time. Since we met, she's felt like part of me. All I've wanted to do is be with her and make her happy.

"I won't be late," I tell her, and she frowns at me.

"Max, go out and enjoy yourself. If you want to stay at Jace's house that's fine. You've not left our side except for going to work or the supermarket. I'm capable of looking after Jackson for one night, and I'm feeling much better." She puts the block of cheese down and turns to face me, then slides her arms around my neck. "No arguments. I don't want to see you until tomorrow. Marina is out as well and staying at the apartment, so I'll have peace and quiet. I plan to read and go to bed early. The last thing I need is you bouncing in the door half-cut, waking me or worse Jackson up."

"Orders understood," I mutter, and she snickers before pecking my lips.

"Good, now, let's get some food into you to soak up the alcohol you'll consume," she says with a smile. "I want you to have a great night with your friend."

***

Linda

I hope my words and expressions convince him to go. Deep down, I'm terrified. Deep down, I want to beg him to stay here, with us. But his friend is important to him, and he deserves to celebrate becoming a father with him. This is a significant night. I want him to walk out of the door confident of my support.

We finish making our meal then sit at the breakfast bar. Our stools are pulled close to each other, our bodies angled in each other's direction. His hand sits on my knee as we eat. Jackson is still settled in his bouncer. Every so often, I see Max glance at his son, ensuring he's safe. My heart swells each time. He's stepped up to the role of being a father incredibly. His eyes tell me he loves him with all his heart.

"Do you know where you're going tonight?" I ask him. He shrugs.

"Somewhere on the Southbank. Jace has an itinerary all planned out." He rolls his eyes. "I'll be legless after a few. I've not had a drink in weeks." He squeezes my knee. "I'd much rather be here with you." We finish, and he leaves to get ready. I clear our plates, and I'm sitting in the living room with Jackson in my arms when he reappears, dressed to go out in the city.

His dark hair sits in its usual rough style. He's wearing a simple white t-shirt and jeans. It's warm out so a jacket won't be needed tonight. The sofa sags beside me as he sits and starts to slip on his trainers. "You're going for a casual look tonight?" I jibe, and he grins at me.

"I've no one to dress up for. Left my mini skirt in the cupboard," he replies, leaning towards me and placing a kiss on my lips.

"You're such a smooth talker," I say. "A skirt doesn't do it for me. Maybe a kilt though."

"You like the idea of a man with no underwear. Interesting. I'm sure that's what the Scots do, go commando. That could be arranged. I'll buy one."

"I like the idea of you commando," I tell him, and he kisses me again, deeper. My body responds with hardening nipples and wetness between my legs. My libido is returning, albeit slowly, but I'm getting there. "You better go. Jace will be waiting for you."

"He can wait," he says, cupping my face in his palm, his eyes boring into mine. "I love you, Beautiful." He glances at his son then drops a kiss on his forehead. "And you little man. You both are my world. I'll see you tomorrow." With that, he stands and walks out into the night.

***

Max

I meet Jace at Waterloo Station, and we walk to the Southbank together. "Why could we not go to the local?" I ask him, again. He'd insisted on coming into the city to celebrate *properly*.

He slaps my shoulder, then barks, "Because this is probably the only time we can honour you spawning a kid. Or is Linda broody all ready?"

"Don't be so bloody vulgar," I scold, and he laughs. "I think the only way I'll get near her is by wearing three layers of condoms." He looks at me and smirks.

"Not getting any action yet then?"

"What the fuck do you think? She was practically ripped in two, her breasts exploded with milk and now, we barely get three hours of consecutive sleep. It's not exactly sensual surroundings. Never mind the fact three of us are squashed into a small double bedroom."

"You're really selling this father thing to me," he replies, raising his eyebrows. "Let's get you a drink. Just don't fall asleep on me tonight. If you do, I'm leaving you where you lie." We walk to a glitzy cocktail bar named *Precious*. From the front it looks tiny but as you walk through the reflective glass door, it opens into a sprawling room. The edges are lined with booths trimmed in purple velvet. A square mirrored bar sits in the centre of the room, lines of multicoloured bottles behind the counter.

On entering, we are approached by a tall woman dressed in a fitted pink corset, black miniskirt, and sky-high heels. She smiles broadly at us. Her deep brown hair is poker straight down her back, her face heavily made up with jarring make up. She purses her bright-red lips then drops her gaze down to my toes and back to my eyes. "Good evening, gentlemen," she purrs. "Welcome to Precious. Would you like a table for just the two of you?"

"A booth please," Jace replies, "and just line up the drinks. We're celebrating. This man here." He grabs my shoulder, harder than necessary. "Has become a father for the first time."

"Congratulations," she says with a fake smile. "This way please." We follow her across the room. She strides in front of us swinging her hips then gestures to a free booth. Jace and I slide in as the woman retreats to the bar. We each pick up a menu off the table.

"A bucket of beer or shots to start?" Jace asks.

"I've hardly had a drink for months. Can we go easy please?"

"Not a fucking chance," he scoffs, signalling to a waitress. She walks over. Jace orders a selection of drinks then turns back to me. "So, tell me, what's it like being a daddy?"

I take a breath. There's so much I want to tell him. "Incredible, terrifying, and completely consuming. I never realised you could love someone so much." My old friend beams at me. "Life before Jackson has faded away. I can't imagine never having him."

"That's brilliant, mate," he says. "And Linda, is she coping with it all?"

"Jeez, I don't know what I'd do without her. She keeps me right. You should have seen me trying to put his nappy on for the first time." I smirk to myself at the memory. "It took me three nappies and five attempts to get it to stay on. Every time I lifted him up, it slid right off." Jace snorts.

"I now have visions of you getting pissed on by your bare-assed son," he replies with a chuckle.

"That has happened," I mutter, remembering the shower of baby piss that coated my t-shirt this morning. "It's an everyday danger." He belly laughs and takes a swig of his beer.

"I'd pay to see that," he says. "I can imagine your face."

"Linda is much better than she was a few weeks ago. The sadness seems to have receded for now, anyway." My voice drops to a whisper, and he frowns at the change of topic. "I was concerned the week after he was born. She was so down and brooding. But she seems to have perked up. She told me it was the crash in her hormones that caused it." Jace's eyes run over my face as I talk. He can be intense when he wants to be.

"Well, if either of you need anything, you know where I am. Uncle Jace is here to teach my nephew the ways of the world," he says then waggles his eyebrows.

"Yeah, I'm not sure if I want my son being trained by you," I tell him, and he scowls at me. "I don't want you using him to pick up women."

He snaps his fingers and shouts, "Damn! That was my first lesson for him. *How to pick up hot women*."

"I think you need a few lessons yourself," I say as he passes me another beer. He ignores my jibe and continues his interrogation.

"And how are you?" he asks. "After the accident and everything. It's been a challenging few months." I let out a breath and my shoulders sag. *The accident.* It's something I don't like to think about too often, but I have demons I know need addressing.

"I'm all right. Jackson and Linda have been keeping me busy. She's been staying home a lot, and isn't keen to go out. Her stitches took a while to heal, and she's only now feeling more herself. I've done more housework and cooking in the past eight weeks than I've ever done." He laughs. "And I'm back to work as well. Paternity leave was a bonus, but I wish it'd been longer. I hate leaving them."

"I'm honoured you graced me with your presence," he replies, snarky.

"When it happens to you, Jace, you'll understand."

"I think there's more chance that *Angelina Jolie* will stride in here and ask me to marry her than me having a kid, mate. It's not in my life plan." He smiles softly. "But I'm delighted to be a surrogate uncle to Jackson."

"He couldn't ask for a better man to be his uncle," I tell him.

"Thanks, mate."

"I called the counsellor," I say, before I can change my mind. "To talk about the accident and what happened." His face twists at the change of direction of our conversation, but I need to speak to someone about this, and Jace is the only person I feel I can. He sits silently, leaving space for me to talk. I need to fill the void. "I've been having nightmares. Rerunning that night in my head."

"Ok, getting help sounds like the sensible thing to do. A lot has changed in a year. It's a lot to process."

"Tell me about it," I agree, "but I wouldn't change where I am now."

We clink our beer bottles together.

Suddenly, a gaggle of young women appear at the door. Jace and I glance over. There must be ten of them at least, all dressed in skin-tight dresses with killer heels. "Oh yes," Jace roars, "the talent has arrived." I laugh and shake my head before looking back at the group. My heart sinks as Marina's eyes meet mine. Standing next to her is a familiar blonde woman, I know better than I want to admit.

Embracing Us is available for preorder now, grab your copy here:

https://books2read.com/embracingus

About Author

VR Tennent writes contemporary fiction for women filled with love, heartbreak, and spice. She never promises a happy ending, but guarantees a rollercoaster of emotion. Her flawed characters will navigate their journeys through life, often making controversial decisions in the process. Be prepared to laugh, cry, and scream in frustration as you read.

In January 2022, she decided to put pen to paper and write a book after joining the writer's group of her favourite author. Five months later she was offered a publishing contract on that very book.

Sign up for my newsletter at www.vrtennent.com

Find me on social media

Facebook: https://m.facebook.com/vrtennentauthor/

Instagram: https://www.instagram.com/vrtennentauthor/

TikTok: https://www.tiktok.com/@vrtennentromanceauthor

Goodreads: https://www.goodreads.com/author/show/22716361.
V_R_Tennent

Bookbub: https://www.bookbub.com/authors/vr-tennent

Also By VR Tennent